THE
FAKE
MOTHER

D1565253

BOOKS BY JENNA KERNAN

The Adoption

The Ex-Wives

THE ROTH FAMILY LIES

The Nurse

The Patient's Daughter

AGENT NADINE FINCH

A Killer's Daughter

The Hunted Girls

THE
FAKE
MOTHER

JENNA KERNAN

bookouture

Published by Bookouture in 2025

An imprint of Storyfire Ltd.
Carmelite House
50 Victoria Embankment
London EC4Y 0DZ

www.bookouture.com

The authorised representative in the EEA is Hachette Ireland
8 Castlecourt Centre
Dublin 15 D15 XTP3
Ireland
(email: info@hbgi.ie)

Copyright © Jenna Kernan, 2025

Jenna Kernan has asserted her right to be identified
as the author of this work.

All rights reserved. No part of this publication may be reproduced, stored in any
retrieval system, or transmitted, in any form or by any means, electronic,
mechanical, photocopying, recording or otherwise, without the prior written
permission of the publishers.

ISBN: 978-1-83618-247-4
eBook ISBN: 978-1-83618-246-7

This book is a work of fiction. Names, characters, businesses, organizations,
places and events other than those clearly in the public domain, are either the
product of the author's imagination or are used fictitiously. Any resemblance to
actual persons, living or dead, events or locales is entirely coincidental.

For Jim, always
This year his help allowed me time to make my deadlines and write through the cleanup and repairs following Hurricane Debby, Hurricane Helene and Hurricane Milton.

PROLOGUE

The woman misses the flashing yellow light as she sails through the intersection. Something streaks before the pickup. Too late, she registers motion and braces. They smash into something. The impact flings her forward.

Metal on metal shrieks in a deafening wail.

Inside the truck, the airbags explode, blinding her as she moves her foot to the brake too late. The pickup fishtails. Next comes another bang. The guardrail?

And then... stillness. Deathly silence as the seconds tick to minutes.

The white powdery dust from the airbags chokes her, and her ears buzz from the impact of the airbag slamming her in the face.

The man climbs from the truck first, stumbling out of sight. She follows, calling his name.

The smell of burning rubber fills her nostrils.

Above her, the yellow caution light flashes on and off and on and off, mocking her.

They hit... what? She doesn't know. She never saw it.

"A deer," the woman whispers. "Please let it be a deer."

She stumbles to the railing, ears ringing, legs wobbling and clothing soaked in blood. The world is silent except for the metallic buzz that comes from inside her head. There's a break in the guardrail before her truck.

No deer could rip such a gap in a metal rail. Could it?

Her passenger uses the hood to steady himself as he continues two steps more, then sinks to the ground.

She limps forward.

The damage on the grill and bumper is minor and she considers driving home before someone happens by.

Then she sees it and pulls up short.

Oh, no.

At the shoulder's edge, between her and the broken guardrail, a body sprawls on the grass.

Not a deer.

Her skin goes cold and her teeth clatter. She shakes her head, refusing to accept what she sees.

Before her sprawls the inert form of a small woman, dressed in cutoff blue jeans and a white tank top. For several beats of her pounding heart, she watches for movement, for breath, for some sign of life, but finds none.

Her gaze flicks from the body to the man now lying on the ground before their pickup.

Finally, she gazes past the twisted guardrail and down the embankment into darkness.

Seconds tick as her vision adjusts.

Below the road, the hillside slopes to a fence line and pasture.

As she stands motionless, the insects resume their buzzing. Fireflies wink on and off above the tall grass. Tiny leather-winged bats dip and dart over the pasture above the place where the late model sedan lies, smoking, upended, and twisted in the netting of barbed wire fencing.

She wonders if she's dreaming. Nothing seems real and her

movements are clumsy and slow as she turns to squat beside the body. Checking for a pulse, she finds none.

Still her brain screams denials, and she forces herself not to run. Not to fall to pieces. Not to panic. It feels like someone is kneeling on her chest.

Shaking now, weeping and choking on blood and tears, she drops to her knees beside the bloody heap. A person. Just moments ago, this was a person. And moments ago, she had not taken a human life.

Her words are meant for the victim but also for herself.

"I'm sorry. I'm so sorry."

But the regret is quickly pushed away by fear.

She's killed someone. The gravity of what she has done sweeps away the haze as she claws in her pocket for her phone. She needs to report the accident.

The death.

The woman lifts her phone and then... hesitates.

Her mind races as she kneels between the man and the body. The fear is pushing at her. Trying to warn her.

How can it be so quiet when the whole world has tilted off its axis? Implications lift their heads, poisonous snakes in the grass, threatening her.

Her phone screen glows. With one push she can summon help. For the victim? She is already past all help.

And they'll ask her what happened. Of course they will.

She glances from the body on the shoulder to the man lying before the pickup's grill and makes her decision.

She'll lie. It's her best hope. Only hope. Because she will not go down for this. Not now. No way. With a single tap she connects the call. They answer on the second ring.

"911. What's your emergency?"

ONE

BAILEY—NOW

Schoharie County, New York—late April

All Bailey Asher ever wanted was a family of her own. A husband. A few kids. A place to raise them. Basically, everything the woman seated before her already had. And Bailey would do anything to get it. Even if it meant lying.

"I'd like to offer you the job as my personal assistant," said Eliza Watts.

Yes. *That* Eliza Watts. The mommy mega-influencer, organic farming phenom with five million followers and counting.

Some of those followers were outside the gates right now, cellphones at the ready to catch a glimpse of their idol. Meanwhile, Bailey had been directed to the lesser known, more covert back entrance which also had a locked gate, security box, and entrance code.

Overwhelmed, Bailey couldn't even speak. Hadn't she dreamed of this day for years? Through welling tears, she managed to nod.

Eliza Watts chuckled. "Is that a yes?"

She choked out a single word. "Yes!"

"Well, that's fine." She extended her hand. "Congratulations."

Bailey accepted the offered hand and found Eliza's warm, strong, and callused.

This was a woman accustomed to outdoor work on her three-acre organic farm. Her sun-kissed skin, dewy fresh face, and smattering of freckles across her pretty upturned nose were enough to make her the quintessential organic farming, uber-mommy blogging, social media influencer. But she was also lovely, with big blue eyes, perfect teeth, and an engaging smile. Bailey thought Eliza was the aspirational model for all those overworked, overtired, pasty, flabby mommies living in drab suburban homes and wishing their kids would stop playing video games and chugging energy drinks.

They were standing now, both smiling, and Bailey wondered if she would ever feel comfortable in this woman's presence.

Likely not. To most, she was a goddess of positivity, while Bailey was just like many of the people drawn by Eliza's intense gravitational pull.

Not to mention, she wasn't as qualified as she'd let her new boss believe.

But everyone exaggerated on resumes. Didn't they?

"Wonderful," said Eliza. "You said you're available immediately. Is that still the case?"

"Yes. Right now, if you like."

"Well, not so fast, though I appreciate your enthusiasm."

She'd sounded too eager. Eliza was giving her a critical once-over. Had she come across as a crazy, obsessive fan?

Bailey held her smile, but inside she was trembling. Had she blown it? Was Eliza about to press pause? If Bailey spoke, would she just make things worse?

"We need to go over some ground rules and you'll have to

sign some confidentiality agreements. Also, I'll need your personal information to add you to the payroll."

"Oh, yes. Of course."

This made Bailey wonder how many folks were currently working on this farm that outwardly appeared to be handled only by Eliza, her husband Kaiden, and their engaging, adorable three kids, Aubree, Mason, and Harper.

She just managed to check herself before saying she would sign anything Eliza Watts put in front of her to get this job.

What would a less desperate person say?

"Could you give me time to look over the agreements?"

Her boss's smile was back, and Bailey drew a long breath in relief.

"Of course. Run it past your attorney. I'd encourage you to."

"I sure will."

Bailey didn't have an attorney, and she was living out of her truck.

"Great."

Keep an open posture, she admonished herself. *Keep eye contact but don't stare. Hold your smile.*

She hated her smile, because of the overbite. Most people didn't notice her but when they did, they mentioned one of three things: her height (above average), her weight (too skinny), or her thick wavy hair that took on a reddish shine in the sun.

Bailey forced herself not to clasp her arms before her. But just to be standing here so close to Eliza Watts gave her the chills.

Today, Eliza wore her honey-blond hair loose over her shoulders. This woman was memorable and everything she touched went viral. So it was natural for Bailey to feel overwhelmed. Wasn't it?

And this office! The windows filled the space with brightness, offering views of the flower fields. The setting was never featured on the blog or in streaming videos. But it certainly was camera-ready.

The perfect woman in her perfect workspace.

On the wooden desk sat a closed laptop, fresh tulips, and a misshapen ceramic pencil container which held an assortment of pens. The drippy paint job alone marked it as a child's project. Minimal, cheerful, functional—completely on-brand. Not a loose paper in sight. Even the wire waste basket was empty. And her wooden desk chair appeared to have survived from the 1930s. The loveseat under the window held a multi-colored quilt that Bailey knew Eliza had made with Aubree as a school project.

But then Bailey realized there was only one desk.

"Do you share this office with your husband?"

Eliza's smile remained in place, but her gaze grew intent. Baily felt sure she'd said something wrong. Wasn't she supposed to know all the members of this farm?

"Kaiden's not much for office work. That's why we need an assistant. Mostly he's occupied outside. Or in the house."

"Of course."

Bailey knew that Eliza thought the world of her husband, and it would be hard not to. He was such a charming, happy-go-lucky guy.

He effortlessly made fatherhood look fun. Bailey had watched his videos repeatedly. She enjoyed the moments he made his kids laugh.

She was disappointed not to catch even a glimpse of him today. Bailey suspected she was not the only fan to have a crush on him. He was blond, with dimples, worked like an ox on the farm, and loved his kids and wife. Who wouldn't envy all Eliza and Kaiden had together?

"Would that be all right?" asked Eliza, and Bailey recognized she'd missed something.

She focused on her future employer.

"I'm not sure," she hedged.

"Well, it's a condition. I'd need you on site if you are accepting the position."

"Yes, I see."

"You're expected to live on the property. After hours, you'd be off duty but must remain onsite, in case I need you. So, to be clear, unless you are running errands for me, you are here on the farm six days and nights a week. You'd have Sunday off, of course."

Eliza expected her assistant to leave the property only once a week. That meant after she finished work, she could not drive out to grab some fast food. It was a crazy condition. Wasn't it?

Bailey wondered how long most of Eliza's assistants lasted under such an unreasonable schedule. Was this the reason the position had been vacant? Had the last assistant felt trapped on this farm? She didn't care because Eliza was talking about Bailey living right here with them. It was better than she could have imagined, and Bailey suppressed the urge to bounce.

"I'm sure that would work."

"Oh, great." There was that stunning smile again. Bailey blinked at the brilliance of this woman.

Images of waking in one of the Watts family's sunny bedrooms fluttered through her mind like a perfect yellow butterfly. She pictured creeping downstairs to the welcoming kitchen for a cup of coffee made from that elaborate brewing machine she'd seen Eliza use dozens of times. Then Bailey would be working at the pine table when Eliza and the kids appeared.

Bailey had listed work experience on two farms in the Adirondacks and Thousand Islands regions. And the agriculture degree from SUNY Cobleskill gave her education cred. Clearly all that effort at getting the work history and education right in her resume had been worth it because she had beaten out the other finalists and here she was with Eliza offering her the job!

Or had she been chosen because she had shown enough knowledge of the business to sound informed, but not so much to appear obsessed? Eliza didn't need to know that Bailey had studied everything up to and including knowing which drawers held the silverware.

She was a member of The Coop, Eliza's fan group—they were officially the Coop Group, but if you mentioned The Coop, everyone knew you meant Eliza Watts.

"Let me get the paperwork. You can look it over and if you want to move forward, we'll arrange to meet again."

Eliza turned to her filing cabinets and withdrew several forms from various folders, all color-coordinated and labeled. The woman was uber-organized.

Bailey couldn't resist a quick glance toward the house, visible to the left of the picking fields. She was nearly desperate to get inside and meet the kids.

She knew every corner from the social media posts. But now she realized the home was much bigger than it appeared online. An entire wing extended behind the main house. The front looked familiar, the inviting wrap-around porch festooned with lush hanging ferns and dotted with gathering places including a hanging porch swing, hemp rugs, and baskets woven from grapevines. She liked the outdoor living areas best. They came through so clearly in the reels: the golden light, birdsong, and peepers. She loved the peepers. They reminded her of her grandmother's home after her parents dropped her off for the summer, and she was safe from the violence for five weeks. Her childhood was shit. Nothing special there. Lots of kids dealt with worse.

She stared at the house, knowing somewhere beyond that blue front door were the kids. This was really happening. She needed to pinch herself.

"Here you go." Eliza passed the documents, now sheathed in a sage-colored, branded folder which Bailey decided she was keeping. "Give those a look and we can circle back. Shall we see where you'd be staying?"

Bailey tucked the paperwork into her canvas tote. She'd chosen to wear dress jeans, loafers, a white blouse, and a navy blazer. No jewelry. Farmhands knew the injuries that occurred when combining rings, bracelets, or necklaces with animals, kids, and farm equipment.

Would they see Morris? Their donkey was a much-loved character with his own merch. She'd passed several fans waiting for the store beyond the main gate to open wearing branded headbands with long fuzzy gray ears.

"Here we go," said Eliza. She drew on a gorgeous colorful hand-knit sweater over her gauzy linen dress, then plopped a straw hat on her head. Beside her, Bailey felt drab as a brown sparrow.

Eliza led them across the main yard. Bailey trailed slightly, in deference and to allow herself a good long look at the house.

April in Upstate New York was still cool, but the lack of rain was as unusual as the bright blue sky.

From behind them, the family's pet donkey brayed a greeting. Bailey smiled. As a child, she'd never been allowed pets but her grandmother had dogs and many cats and she'd loved them all.

"That's Morris," said Eliza and chuckled. "He's our watch dog and cuddle bug. We'll introduce you to him and the goats next time." She glanced at Bailey. "I can't remember what you told me. Did you grow up around farm animals?"

"We had horses and a pony for a while," said Bailey.

"What was the pony's name?" asked Eliza.

There was no pony. Never had been.

"Sugar."

Eliza nodded as they continued walking, side-by-side. Her

stride was confident. Her chin up. The brim of her straw hat shaded her face. That skin was not to be believed. Bailey tamped down her jealousy. If she started being envious of all Eliza had, she'd never get her work done.

But instead of walking directly to the house, Eliza cut along the side. Perhaps Bailey would have her own private entrance. Anxiety built. She hoped she wouldn't be in the back part of the home, the part she'd never even seen on any of the posts.

A long poly greenhouse with a plastic covering and arched struts sat beyond the backyard that included a familiar tire swing and treehouse. Bailey had never seen that building in any post.

Where were they going?

Her heart sank as she realized she might not even have access to the Watts' home.

This was terrible. But what could she do?

She forced down her disappointment as they continued down the hill.

"Your place is past the Ultra Van."

Each step away from the house was a step too far. They passed the motorhome, a classic turquoise 1966 Corvair with a smile painted between the round headlights. The vehicle had a vintage interior, with a wooden bar for a dashboard and wall-to-wall carpeting. Bailey had seen the inside, including the macramé curtains, in one of Eliza's fall camping trip videos.

Delight sparkled through her at the possibility this upscale camper would be hers but Eliza marched right past, following a trail in the tall grass. Bailey fell in behind her.

"Schoharie Creek is just past your place. It's actually a river. Comes from the Catskills and drains into the Mohawk and it's wide here and deep enough to paddle. No motorized or sail boats allowed, so it's nice and quiet. Do you canoe or kayak?"

"Love to," she said, having never even sat in a kayak, let alone navigated one.

At the tree line, Bailey spotted a small rectangular structure and her steps faltered.

Despite telling Eliza she was a farm girl, she did not fancy staying alone at the edge of an unknown forest in what looked like a storage shed with a single window.

"It's a pop-up building!" Eliza's tone of elation was familiar to Bailey from her posts.

But Bailey's mood soured as she stared at the ugly little rabbit-hutch that more resembled a shipping container than a house. Luckily, Eliza's attention was on the new quarters.

"We installed a 12-amp solar electrical system, a septic tank, and you have water from our spring." She pointed at the four blue plastic barrels on the roof. "You'll have to keep an eye on the levels. You also have a hot water heater and propane stove."

Bailey just managed to wipe the scowl off her face as Eliza turned her attention from the hideous little toadstool of a house to her new assistant.

"Something wrong?" asked Eliza.

Bailey said exactly what was on her mind.

"I thought I'd be staying in your house, as your assistant, I mean." Clumsy, she decided. Eliza had her head cocked as she stared in silence.

Finally, after what seemed like hours, she said, "No one but my kids and I live in the main house. But if this arrangement isn't what you envisioned, we can call a halt."

Eliza had a list of viable candidates as long as her arm, itching to take Bailey's place.

"No, no. I just thought..." What? That the job included joining this family?

As if Eliza would let a virtual stranger near her kids.

And showing her disappointment while revealing her desires was careless. She'd need to be much more cautious and earn some trust before making even the smallest demands. Eliza didn't know her and had no reason to allow her near her kids. But she'd get there.

"You're wise," said Bailey. "Keeping strangers at a distance."

Eliza's warm smile returned, and her shoulders dropped an inch. "I'm so glad you understand. And I'm optimistic that you won't be a stranger for very long. So, just to clarify. One day off a week. Remain on site at all other times and you'll live here and work in the first barn from the small outer office outside of mine."

Bailey recalled glimpsing a tiny desk and filing cabinet just outside Eliza's office.

"And this place should be fine for a new graduate right out of college." Eliza grinned as if she had Bailey's real motives all figured out. "A resume builder. Right?"

Bailey did not correct her. Correcting supervisors was never wise. And despite what her resume said, she'd never been to college because she'd dropped out of high school to run away from her abusive parents. She rubbed her cheek at the memory of that last stinging slap.

"Have a look. I'm sure it's better equipped than your dorm room."

It wasn't. Inside squatted a small table with one plastic chair and a twin bed draped with a cheap comforter. The kitchen sat between the door and the window and included a compact sink, refrigerator, and a two-burner stove with a small cupboard above. There wasn't even a closet. Bailey walked to the only inside door and found a tiny bathroom with a toilet and narrow shower stall with a plastic curtain. There was no sink here. She glanced back at the one in the kitchenette and sighed. She'd had worse.

Back outside, Bailey shook off the claustrophobia.

"So. What do you think of your very own tiny home?" asked

Eliza, using the same appealing enthusiasm that had made her an internet phenom.

"Oh, it's great!"

Her future boss grinned, offering a generous, perfect smile. "I'm so glad you like it. And I won't invade your space. This will be your little sanctuary. Private. You know?"

Bailey forced a smile. "How wonderful."

"Shall we head back?" Eliza didn't wait for a reply but started walking away.

Bailey paused, narrowing her eyes on the structure that reminded her of a single jail cell.

And she's spent enough nights in one of those for a lifetime.

TWO

On her first day of work, Bailey slowed at the metal barrier and punched in her new code.

The display reported: *entrance logged.*

The gate rolled back on rubber tires and Bailey was in, breaching the outer wall of Eliza Watts' feudal fiefdom.

She needed to be perfect. This all might slip away if Eliza saw the gaps in her new assistant's skillset or if she or her kids took a dislike to Bailey. Bailey couldn't be caught in a lie.

"Stop it. Just be what she needs, and you'll be fine."

The gate glided closed and Bailey's breathing accelerated.

"You are not locked in," she told herself. "They're all just locked out."

Eliza's popularity came at a cost. Privacy needed to be protected. She knew it. But still her body was on full alert. She didn't like locks, gates, or security cameras.

This back gate looked nothing like the welcoming front entrance. There, fans lined up for Eliza's store, The Country

Coop, where members could get their yearly badge, available only onsite, and a ten percent discount on purchases. The store included signed merch, not available online, and life-sized cutouts of Eliza, her with her family, and a single of her husband. Bailey bet Kaiden's cutout was a top seller.

Eliza also held monthly gatherings at her store. Bailey had been among the attendees of various functions exclusive to the Coop Group and the all-female Coop Chicks on more than one occasion, though Eliza had never noticed her.

The large store sat beside the main entrance, which seemed designed for selfies and more resembled a theme park entrance, with colorful cartoon characters of Morris, the chickens, and the goats, of course. Past that, and tucked from sight, was the secure front gate and accompanying wall. The back entrance also had both gate and wall. How far did the barrier stretch? Around the entire three acres?

Bailey rolled slowly down the private road.

She parked her white pickup where she'd been told, before the barn that served for sorting vegetables and merchandise storage. In the office, she found a note directing her to the greenhouse.

On the way, she glanced at the house and saw a teenager gripping one of the porch's upright beams and staring out at her.

Bailey knew her instantly from her online presence.

The wavey tousled hair, tapered from chin to shoulder blades, the slender form, the crop top and jean shorts, which were age-appropriate for a fourteen-year-old, showed nothing but miles of slender legs.

Aubree Watts had curly auburn hair, different in every way from the wispy golden blond of her siblings and mom.

Bailey lifted a hand in greeting. The girl raised her hand as if to wave, but then thumbed her nose at her. Taken aback, Bailey's step faltered but she continued past the second barn to the greenhouses.

There were two. The poly hoop tunnel she'd seen on the first visit and this greenhouse that looked like it had dropped out of a formal English garden. The brick and glass building was adorned with pots of flowers and hanging ferns. She glanced about, expecting to see a white rabbit peering at a pocket watch.

Bailey recalled when the family had built the now well-established greenhouse.

The grape vines and the flower fields thrived. The hidden solar panels supported plant growth in frigid winters and unpredictable springs.

This tiny greenhouse could never have held all the plants she saw transplanted to the vegetable gardens. Why had that never occurred to her?

Smoke and mirrors, she realized. Like a Hollywood movie set.

How much else was illusion?

On the side of the hoop-house, she found Eliza working with her gardener, a solidly built, middle-aged woman dressed in green campus boots, a faded T-shirt, and a soiled green and yellow John Deere hat over short cropped hair. She looked fully capable of throwing an entire hay bale unassisted.

By contrast, Eliza wore sandals, a denim skirt with white lace trim, a gauzy blouse, and her broad straw hat. In the basket looped over her arm lay a collection of freshly cut white nasturtiums. Bailey thought she looked like a cover model for a magazine about healthy living.

"Here she is!" Eliza cast her a bright, welcoming smile and then motioned to her companion. "Bailey, this is my indispensable head gardener, and my first assistant, Victoria Nichols. But she prefers—"

"Tory," barked the woman, cutting off Eliza's introductions.

She tugged off a worn leather work glove to extend a hand lightly dusted with soil.

Bailey tried not to wince as Tory squeezed so tight Bailey's knuckles cracked.

Eliza's gardener had ruddy cheeks and a ready smile.

"Welcome aboard." She grinned as she released Bailey's hand and spoke to Eliza. "You're right, she is young."

"I'm twenty-two." Luck and good genes made this claim pass unquestioned.

"First real job out of college," said Eliza.

"That's nice. Let me guess. Business degree."

"Agriculture. SUNY Cobleskill. Concentration in business."

"Even better," said Tory.

"She'll be handling posting for the vlog and subscriptions, merchandise, fan interactions, and so on."

"Running The Coop?" asked Tory.

"Online portion," said Eliza. "Maud still has the store."

Tory replaced her work glove and pressed a hand to the top of her hat, leaving dirt behind on the crown.

"All Greek to me."

Eliza's laugh was contagious. "Tory doesn't own a computer or a cellphone."

"Or a television. Don't need 'em. I got an answering machine and a subscription to the papers," she said proudly.

"A gem is what she is. She can make anything grow. Just look at my cutting fields."

"Not so hard. All plants need the same things: light, water, good soil, and time." She motioned to the tiny plants spaced evenly down the raised row of soil.

"Don't let her fool you. These fields were more rock than soil when we started."

Much of the cutting fields showed only the promise of blooms, but the nasturtiums were up and thriving. These would be for sale at this week's farmers' market. The tulips were coming along. As for the tiny broad-leafed plants, Bailey had no idea what those were. They grew out rather than up and long stringers reached over the dark rich soil.

"There's a difference between dirt and soil, you know," said Tory.

Bailey didn't know. But she did know how to edit and post a vlog. And chances were good that she'd meet Eliza's children today because they'd likely be in the video, or she hoped so. With luck, she'd soon be doing more than editing. Filming, for instance.

Tory wished her well and then returned her attention to the pitchfork and forking dry hay into a cart.

"Tory's laying straw between the rows of strawberries. Keeps the weeds down."

Bailey feigned interest, nodding.

"Tory, can you get the ATV for us?" asked Eliza.

Tory strode away and Bailey followed Eliza back to the office.

Inside, Eliza placed the fresh flowers in a tin pitcher on her desk. A perfect fit, Bailey realized. The room had a citrusy scent of grapefruit and lemons. Clean and fresh and completely on-brand.

Once seated, her new boss asked for the required paper-work. As Eliza checked every page, Bailey took the moment to take another look at the interior of Eliza's office. But other than the orderly appearance, there was little to discover about her new boss, except that she preferred earth tones for paint and fresh flowers.

"This all seems in order," said Eliza, glancing up with that appealing smile. "Welcome aboard, Bailey." She tucked away the pages. "Why don't you go settle into your cabin and I'll see you after lunch for orientation. Say one o'clock?"

Eliza pushed a key attached to a keychain that Bailey recognized was sold on the Watts Farm website's merchandise page.

It showed a chick with an eggshell upon its head and read, "I'm a Coop Chick!"

"Oh, nearly forgot," said Eliza. "The gate registers all entries. And your code will work only during daylight hours, so on Sunday, be sure you are on site before dusk."

That was another odd condition. Not only was she trapped here six days a week, but her day off was limited to daylight hours only. Bailey didn't like losing her freedom to come and go, but still felt that being here was worth the sacrifices.

What happened after dark that Eliza felt she needed to have everyone on site? Who did she think would try sneaking off after dark? Bailey's mind immediately went to Aubree, her teenage daughter.

Had Bailey ever sneaked out of the house at fourteen? Not until fifteen, she recalled. And not always after dark.

Her mind flashed a perfect image of the day she'd feigned illness to miss the all-day marathon that was the Sunday service in their church. One of the congregation had spotted her outside the corner market drinking an orange soda.

Her dad had thrown her bedroom door open so hard the knob had broken through the sheetrock wall. He had his belt off before she could scramble away.

"I'll beat the devil from you."

The lashing hadn't shown through her white tights and pinafore that Monday. But sitting had been torture.

But Eliza was a good parent, there for her kids in a real and genuine way. She was the kind of mom all kids wanted, the kind of friend all women wanted. And she was wise to keep her children home and safe because there were dangers out in the world. That, they both understood.

Her boss gave her a long look, scanning from her head to her feet. Then she grimaced.

"My fans will never see you, so you don't need to dress like an office drone here."

"Oh, all right."

"You should wear a T-shirt and jeans. Coveralls, sweatshirt. You know, as you did on the other farms."

"Oh, great. I wasn't sure."

"But no more sneakers. Steel-toed work boots. I'm sure you have a pair."

Meanwhile she'd seen Eliza wearing sandals with straps that crisscrossed up her tanned calves.

"I do." She didn't, but she would get some on her first day off.

Dismissed, Bailey left the office and found Tory on an ATV with an attached cart beside her pickup.

"I can take my truck," said Bailey, wanting some privacy as she moved in.

"No outside vehicles past the parking area."

Another weirdly specific rule.

Why couldn't she take her truck if the ATV was fine? Was this all about control?

Tory waited for Bailey to open the tailgate and peered in, her expression concerned.

"Don't let her see that candy and junk food. No processed foods in her place." Tory poked into a bag. "Is that Styrofoam?"

Her shocked alarm made Bailey stiffen. You'd think she'd found a human head in her truck bed.

"No Styrofoam." Tory aimed a finger at an empty fast food drink cup. "Hide that. She sees it and you're done."

"Done?"

"Fired. Instantly. She hates it. Calls it the plagues of man."

Bailey crushed the cup and stuffed it into her pocket. The remaining dregs of coffee soaked through the denim and left a damp spot on her jeans.

"Anything else?"

"Plenty. Plastic bags. Plastic bottles. Plastic garbage bags, produce bags. Half the food in here alone will get you fired."

"What am I supposed to buy?"

"Flour, salt, oats, beans, lentils, fruits and vegetables, meat. You know? Food. Canned goods are okay."

This was crazy. Wasn't it?

Tory lifted the duffle bags into the cart. "You better hurry. Oh, and lose the blazer. Chickens don't need impressing."

"She told me that one. And steel-toed boots."

"You have a pair?"

Bailey flushed. She should have them. Any farmhand would. "I forgot them back at home."

"I have an extra pair in the truck. What size are you?"

The boots she offered were only a bit too big and Bailey accepted them gratefully.

"Put 'em back in the equipment barn when you got yours again." Tory left her to finish loading.

Bailey drove to the rectangular capsule that Eliza called a cabin. Inside, she tossed her bags on the bed and stowed the food on the table.

Something scratched at the door. Opening it, she found a gray, short-haired tomcat seated on her cinder step, his tail wrapped neatly about his feet. He wore no collar, his coat was patchy, eyes watery, and a chunk of one ear was missing.

"You don't live here," she said, beginning to close the door. But the cat darted inside. "I don't have time for you."

But the cat rubbed against her legs.

"I have to leave," she told him, but still opened a can of Spam and set it outside on the step. The feline interloper wasted no time, leaping back out and eating in ravenous gulps.

Bailey leaned to stroke the skinny creature. He let her pet him while he gobbled down the meal.

"You a stray?" She could feel his ribs. "You're skin and bones. I'm calling you Bones. But you don't live here."

Bailey left him with his meal, locking the door. She'd just

parked the ATV when Eliza appeared, swaying along as peaceful as a breeze.

"Hey, there you are. You ready for the tour?"

Eliza walked her past the house and Bailey tried to memorize every detail.

"You've already seen the greenhouses and two barns. The part you didn't see in the first barn, that's the one with my office, is used for packing and shipping the products we sell, plus storage of merchandise. The jams, honey, and candles, for instance. The second barn holds most of our equipment.

"On this far side we have the animal enclosure for the goats and donkey. Currently the mobile coop is on this side, too."

They reached the whitewashed fencing of the paddock and paused.

Eliza pointed at the two small outbuildings, identifying them. "Milking shed and goat shelter. The other is the donkey's shelter. Down the hill, we have the orchards, grapevines, berry bushes, two vegetable fields, and a cutting field for fresh flowers."

"Don't you have sugar bush?" Bailey asked, referring to a grove of sugar maples for making syrup.

"Yes, a small one. To the right of the orchard."

Her boss paused to lean on the sturdy plank fence of the paddock.

"Morris, our mule, has two goats for company." She pointed at the goats, now trotting toward them. "That's Thistle with the two kids, Popcorn, that's the white one, and Speckles with the spots."

Bailey looked at the white nanny with one white and one pinto baby, thinking the names on-point.

"And this is Thistle's mom, Bonnet. She's the Schwartzel with the brown kid. I don't keep the males."

Of course, Bailey knew what would happen to the little

nameless goat, what happened to most unwanted male goats. He'd be butchered.

"Schwartzel, that's mostly white with a dark head."

Eliza paused and her expression brightened. "That's right. Thistle is a first-time mother. The twins took a lot out of her." Eliza studied the goat in question then shook her head. "I'm worried because she still doesn't seem quite right. We lost a goat last summer, had to have her put down."

Bailey remembered. The kids were inconsolable.

"I'm sorry."

"Buried her myself down at the tree line at the river."

Bailey knew most farmers buried their dead livestock. It was a less costly, legal means of disposal.

"The first real death the kids had to face." Eliza's expression turned grim at the memory, then she seemed to force away her melancholy as she watched the twins cavort with tiny sideways leaps. "They were just shattered. I know it's part of life, but I hope we don't lose any more stock for a while."

She pointed at another outbuilding.

"The milking shed is right here. I handle the evenings. Aubree milks in the morning. Bonnet's baby is eating grass now, so her bag is usually full. And Thistle..." She shook her head. "How does she look to you?"

Bailey had never been this close to a goat.

"A little thin, I think." Assertive, but not overly confident.

Eliza nodded in agreement and then continued between house and pasture.

"It's lovely here," said Bailey.

"Yes. We're very lucky." She cast Bailey a dazzling smile. The woman was stunning.

Eliza continued between Morris's pasture and the house, giving Bailey a better look at the small, forest-green shelter with a run-in so Morris could get out of the weather.

The donkey appeared from his shed and trotted toward

them making a racket. The nanny goats fell in behind in a game of "Follow the Leader".

"Maybe we'd better say hello." Eliza drew out her phone and pressed the record function, talking to the camera as if she was speaking to a dear friend. "Hello there! What a beautiful day. I had to stop what I'm doing because Morris is demanding my attention. And as you know, Morris is the star of his own story. So, he deserves star treatment."

At this moment Morris began braying, as if this were a practiced routine.

Eliza switched the view to the donkey.

"Don't you, Morris?" she said, in that voice she used on baby animals and her beloved donkey.

Morris extended his head over the top rail of the wooden fence and accepted both a scratch under the chin and around his long ears. Then Morris began to nudge Eliza's side.

"All right, my friend. I have something for you." Eliza reached in her skirt pocket and drew out a carrot that included the green lacy, wilted top. "It's one from last season, but he won't mind." Then she spoke to Morris. "Here you are, sweetheart."

Morris took the carrot and crunched.

"I don't know who likes my carrots more, Morris or Harper. I'll check in later, but I didn't want you to miss Morris's snack time."

Eliza stopped the video and worked her phone, adding text, hashtags, and posting before Morris finished chewing.

"May I pet him?" asked Bailey.

"Sure." Eliza spoke to the animal. "Morris, this is Bailey. She'll be with us. Part of the farm."

Morris's ears were pointing straight forward. Bailey had the feeling he understood.

She offered her hand, and the donkey sniffed and then lowered his head, allowing Bailey to scratch his cheeks.

"Give him this," said Eliza, offering a small red apple.

Morris took it out of Bailey's open hand.

Eliza nodded. "Nice to see you know how to feed a donkey and keep all your digits. Oh, that's right, you had a pony. Sugar. Right?"

"Right."

Bailey smiled. It was getting easier and easier to lie.

What would her boss do if she discovered Bailey's actual work history? Likely faint dead away.

THREE

Bailey arrived at the office on day two in borrowed boots, a royal-purple T-shirt, cotton athletic socks, and faded jeans. She might not be qualified, but now she looked the part.

The orientation was daunting. Many of her jobs were outside her wheelhouse for obvious reasons. If she had Wi-Fi she'd find some how-to videos. But the signal didn't reach her cabin.

"Would it be possible for me to come into the office at night, to get started?" she asked.

Eliza's silence stretched for several moments.

"I appreciate your enthusiasm, but you should be able to finish your workload in normal hours."

"Just until I'm more familiar with everything." Bailey realized too late that needing extra time pointed squarely at her incompetence. A woman as confident and successful as Eliza wouldn't respond well to groveling or an incompetent assistant.

It also occurred to her that Eliza might check her search history, see instructional videos, and reconsider her choice in personal assistant.

"Well, we can't see the office lights from the house, so it

shouldn't disturb the kids' bedtimes. But you need rest, too. So, let's set a limit of ten at night. No work after that. Will that do?"

"Yes." She said that too fast and too eagerly.

"Maud handles the store and main gate during business hours. She'll text you when deliveries are incoming. When anyone stops at the rear gate, I get a text alert. During work hours, you'll get a text also. I want you to handle the entry. The list of people who don't need to show ID are on that clipboard." She pointed to one of several on the wall beside Bailey's new work area.

"And if they're not on the list?"

"They present their ID to the camera. You snap a photo and file it. Also ask them what their business is here. Then you send me a text before they are admitted. No exceptions. Got it?"

Sounded simple enough. "Yes. I do."

"Great. Give me your phone."

Bailey handed it over. Eliza downloaded an app and headed into the settings. "For a while we'll both get alerts. Then, if that's working well, it will be just to you."

"Of course. I can handle that."

Eliza gave her a "we'll see" look, completely lacking in confidence.

"I've got to meet with Tory and check on the kids' school-work. I'm not sure I'll be back—unless you need me?"

"Oh, I'll be fine." Bailey needed time alone to panic and possibly scream and then get her ass up to speed.

Eliza left and Bailey watched tutorials on the spreadsheet program and looked up the terms that were unfamiliar. At this rate she wouldn't be here long enough to get close to the family.

She needed Eliza to entrust her with more than gate entry, social media posting, and members' support. Otherwise, why was she even here?

* * *

By dinnertime, her business vocabulary had improved. But there were still gaps.

She decided to pop over to her cabin, as Tory called it. To Bailey it was more an oversized shipping container or under-sized prefab.

Unfortunately, she ran right into Eliza at the fence line.

"Wow, working past five. I think I picked a good one," Eliza said to an unfamiliar man. He looked about fifty, barrel-chested, with a full beard and closely trimmed sable brown hair; he wore a neat powder-blue polo shirt with a logo featuring a padlock.

Bailey noted that he was allowed to drive his truck past the barn, because it was parked beside the fence.

"Bailey, this is Richard Garrow. He's my go-to for security challenges. Isn't that right?"

He offered a smile and nod, but did not extend his hand.

Bailey's brow knit. "What kind of challenges?"

"Folk sneaking onto the property." Eliza waved both hands as if disgusted. "Have to protect ourselves from unstable fans and creeps."

"I've got you covered," he said. His voice had a pleasant baritone and revealed a downstate accent. Perhaps Westchester or one of the boroughs.

"Check in at the house before you go," said Eliza to Richard. "Will you?"

"Absolutely."

So, he could drive through the fields, park where he liked, and he was allowed in the house.

Bailey concealed her annoyance as Eliza walked away, leaving Richard typing on his laptop. Clearly, he had the farm's Wi-Fi password.

"What kind of security does she have beyond the gate and perimeter fencing?" asked Bailey.

Richard's gaze swept her, giving her the once-over.

"What's your position here?"

"I'm Eliza's personal assistant." Bailey lifted her chin in a show of both arrogance and defiance that she hoped would not come back to bite her in the butt. "And I handle visitors' admittance at the rear gate."

Was Richard going to mention her question to her boss?

"Well, I'll leave it to Eliza to give you the details. Shall I?"

"Sure," said Bailey. "You have a good evening."

Bailey scurried away, feeling the prickle of his gaze. A glance back showed him staring.

"That went well," she muttered to herself.

Dinner was a tuna fish sandwich and a contraband bag of chips. She ate a handful of cookies on the way back to the barn office and found Richard Garrow had gone.

Probably up at the house having a slice of homemade strawberry-rhubarb pie.

Bailey recalled watching Eliza make a berry pie in a recent video. The opening used footage of Eliza's kids picking three generous cups of fruit for baking last summer. The new footage included Eliza explaining how last season's frozen berries could still make a wonderful pie.

"The risk of frost is gone and we have our strawberries in the ground. We'll go visit them tomorrow. Shall we?"

It seemed she was talking directly to Bailey. This was the Eliza her five million followers adored. Organic style. Healthy. Glowing. Warm and welcoming.

Then at the kitchen table, little Mason's school work involved learning fractions using flour, sugar, shortening, and water. The pie crust was perfect, thanks to chilling the dough and Eliza's skill with a rolling pin. The lattice crust top could have won a blue ribbon at any county fair.

Who was filming? It wasn't her assistant, Bailey knew.

Bailey had less access to the family than Morris. And she lived further away.

That needed to change.

Back in the office, she figured out which jobs for tomorrow she still did not feel competent to undertake and focused on those. Her alarm beeped at 10pm and she left the barn, as instructed.

The walk back in the dark was a different experience. The fog had rolled in from the river, giving the hayfield an eerie atmosphere. She shivered as droplets of water beaded on her hair and clothing.

The ground-floor lights of the main house glowed with a hazy corona. The upper windows were all dark. Those were likely the children's bedrooms.

She knew each room so well, they might have been hers. Mason's was bright primary colors and his bed looked like a smaller version of a horse stall. A mural of ducks, chicks, and pigs filled one wall. Another held his chalkboard. Mason, the artist, had a talent for drawing and his creations were often featured.

Harper's room was mint green because Eliza had not known if she was a boy or girl. The trail of hand-painted butter-flies had been a project for Aubree, Mason, and Eliza during her final months of pregnancy. The playhouse allowed for many videos of little Harper's dress-up games. Princesses and fairies were the current favorites, though the animal costumes were never neglected for long.

Aubree's room perfectly suited a girl becoming a woman. Her canopy bed and the tiny LED lights made an ethereal vision. And the desk, chair, and lamp were a must for such a studious child. Her knowledge of nature was impressive; she knew the names of nearly every type of tree and plant on the property.

Bailey had spent many hours obsessively scrolling the Watts' feed, all the while wishing her childhood had been like theirs.

She tried to sneak a peek at any of the three familiar rooms, but it was impossible.

What time was bedtime for a fourteen-year-old?

Morris did not let her passing go unnoticed. He brayed loudly and she walked over to the wooden fence.

The goats with their babies appeared from behind the enclosure, hoping to get fed. Only Thistle came at a walk. Bailey offered them each a hank of green grass.

The donkey trotted over, nostrils flaring, and caught her scent. The braying stopped and he tossed his head, then nosed her pockets for a snack.

"Oh, I forgot. Hold on a second."

She drew out a cookie, twisted it into two pieces, and offered them. Morris sucked them up and chewed, then tossed his head in appreciation.

"Good, right? Better than organic carrots? That's real processed sugar, my friend." She scratched around the base of his ears and then waved goodnight. He followed as far as his enclosure allowed.

Now she had the long walk through the damp grass.

The tree line loomed, dark and ominous. Fog billowed. Her place had vanished. Why hadn't she left a light on?

Her phone flashlight only made the fog seem thicker and whiter. So she switched it off and continued.

Something moved in the trees, parallel to her position. Some deep instinctual part of her brought her to a dead stop. She held her breath, listening, straining to see past the fog and the darkness.

The sound came again, the rustle of the dead leaves left from last fall and then the snap of a twig.

She recalled Eliza mentioning trespassing fans and creeps. She glanced about the empty field.

Bailey's grandmother's place was on a hillside much like this. She knew the nocturnal animals that roamed the woods. Deer were large, raccoons common. The occasional porcupine, skunk, or fox. All sounded larger than they were when you were alone in the dark.

She tried to tell herself it was nothing.

But the hairs prickled on her arms and a buzz of electric energy sizzled through her. She crouched, torn between the urge to run and the urge to fall flat in the tall grass.

Bailey could no longer hear past the pounding drum of her heart and the pulsing rush of her blood.

Like a deer leaping from cover, she took off at a run. Rushing blind, she charged forward, the wet grass lashing her thighs.

Where was her tiny house? She'd gone too far, hadn't she? Missed it in the dark.

But returning the way she had come was too terrifying to consider.

There.

A large structure loomed, the square corners and straight lines revealing it was not a form found in nature.

The hut. Her hut. Oh, please let it be her hut.

Bailey veered to the left and halted, grappling in her pocket for the key. As she found it, it slipped through her fingers.

She crouched again, feeling with both hands, afraid that using her phone flashlight would reveal her position.

There was another sound now. Closer. The whisper of grass brushing against nylon pants, the kind hunters used to keep their legs dry.

Where was the key?

Something glinted to her right. The metallic glimmer revealed the keyring.

Bailey scooped up the ring, stood, and rammed the key into the lock. She gave a twist and push, simultaneously rotating the knob and hustling inside. Then she slammed the door closed and engaged the flimsy lock.

She stood there, heart slamming inside her chest, panting

and wheezing, eyes pinched closed with all her weight against the door.

After a few moments, she opened her eyes. Still drawing breath in and out like a bellows, she thought she should check that the door was locked and wrapped her fingers tentatively around the handle only to feel the knob turn in her hand.

FOUR

Someone was outside, turning the handle. Trying to get in.

And all that stood between her and that person was a cheap lock and composite door.

Bailey slipped her hand in her front pocket, gripping the four-inch multitool. It was the cheapest one at the box store. She held the thing in her palm searching the options for something useful to protect herself with. The tools—scissors, screwdriver, a bottle opener, pliers and a sawblade—were of no use for self-defense.

"Stupid thing," she muttered, and opened the three-inch blade. Raising her voice, she called, "You come through that door, I will shoot you where you stand."

The knob stopped moving.

Bailey waited, knife ready. What happened to Eliza's great security? To no one getting past the gate without her knowing?

But what if they came from the woods or the river? Would she know?

That security specialist, Garrow, had been doing something at the fence line. Bailey hoped whatever he did allowed Eliza to be aware that someone was here, in the dark, right outside her little hut.

She reached for the window blind, then hesitated, stopped by the possibility of seeing someone peering in her window. She waited in the dark, open multitool gripped tight in her sweating hand.

This stupid little knife was her only defense. That was a problem she planned to rectify. An axe, shovel, even a sickle made an excellent weapon. And they could all be found on a farm.

At the very least, she'd find a stout piece of oak for a walking stick. Something with a nice knobby, gnarled burl at the top. And she'd never walk back here alone without it.

The sweat on her forehead turned cold. She lifted her cellphone and hesitated.

If she broke Eliza's rule about coming to the house or contacting her after lights-out, would the woman fire her? She didn't know but was more afraid of that possibility than of whoever was lurking at her door.

Decision made, Bailey lay the open blade on the table just inches from her bed.

As Bailey's eyes adjusted to the dark, she made out the faint glow of light beyond her window.

Was he still there? Waiting just outside?

She didn't hear anything.

A dash to the big house occurred to her and her throat squeezed tight. No. She wasn't going back out.

"This is ridiculous." She stood, lifted her chin, and flicked on the light in the center of the room and the one in the bathroom. Feeling a little embarrassed, she looked under the bed.

She heated soup and ate while reviewing videos she had downloaded to her laptop from Eliza's blog.

Eventually, even the terror of a possible intruder lost out to exhaustion. She washed up and hit the hay, surprised to sleep more soundly than she had for a good long while.

In the morning, Bailey woke to her alarm and the pre-dawn gray of a new day. Her first move was to check the window and door lock again. Finding them secure, she enjoyed a contraband pastry.

She showered and dressed for work in one of her solid-colored T-shirts and the darker of the two new pairs of jeans she'd purchased after landing this job. Then she gripped the multi-tool knife and stepped out of her rabbit hutch to face the day.

There was no one about. Birdsong filled the air, and the breeze was crisp and cool.

Then she saw it. The trampled grass under her single window. Someone *had* stood there. She checked the stalks. Whoever it was had left before the dew.

She held the awkward handle of the multitool at her side and followed the obvious trail. Her intruder had circled once and then headed toward the main house.

Her skin crawled, and she retreated inside. Then she grabbed her hoodie and backpack, which included a lunch for her and a cookie for Morris. When she stepped out again, she held the weapon open at her side.

Bailey's head seemed on a swivel as she hurried to the backyard of the Watts' home. A light was on downstairs. She resisted the urge to approach the back door. Imagine what it would look like, her creeping onto the back porch wielding a tiny knife.

Once at Morris's paddock, she expelled a long breath. Morris trotted over to her, expectantly, but did not bray a warning this time.

Progress.

She handed over the toll and scratched along his broad cheeks. He munched the cookie as she rounded the house.

There she found Eliza and Harper crossing the yard, hand-in-hand, carrying an egg basket. Eliza's simple cotton dress showed slender tanned legs and wellies stenciled with flowers. And Harper wore an adorable pink pinafore dress and a straw hat ringed with fresh flowers. They walked right toward a camera set up on a very minimal tripod.

Seeing mother and child together stirred a longing inside Bailey, and made her heart ache.

As she watched, Eliza said something to Harper and then waited. Then she stopped.

This time Bailey did hear Eliza.

"That's when you say it, Harper. Do it again."

Bailey cocked her head. She'd never heard Eliza use that sharp critical tone of voice with her children in her videos.

Bailey didn't know exactly why she did it, but she backed up until she stood mostly out of sight behind the broad arching branches of the hydrangea bush at the corner of the porch.

Harper said something.

"It's too late now. You say it when I stop, right here. Understand? Do it again."

The pair retreated to the entrance of the sorting barn and then returned toward the camera, smiling and hands clasped.

Bailey's brow wrinkled and she squeezed the straps of her backpack as the pair approached Harper's mark.

How many times had the pair tried? Harper was only five and her impromptu comments and little errors in speech were so endearing.

Were they scripted?

Eliza stopped. Harper said something that Bailey could not hear, causing her mother to give a very convincing laugh. Then she scooped her daughter up in her arms and headed toward the house, and the camera.

It was not until the two disappeared into the house and Bailey summoned the courage to walk across the yard that she saw a second camera on the porch.

Bailey hurried toward the barn and her desk, but Eliza stepped onto the porch, retrieving the first camera.

"Good morning," she called.

Bailey turned. Should she tell her now or wait?

Now.

"Good morning. Eliza, something happened last night."

Eliza's brow wrinkled and the smile vanished.

"You changed your mind about the job?"

"Oh, no. Nothing like that." Bailey told her what had happened on her walk to the cabin.

Eliza's scowl deepened. Was she angry at her? Did she even believe her?

Another possibility struck. What if she thought it too dangerous for her assistant to stay so far from the farmhouse? What if she let her into their home? Hope squeezed her chest.

"You saw tracks, of a person?"

"I saw the grass bent in a circle around the place."

"Show me."

FIVE

Last night, Bailey had really missed the rifle she had used in the army. Unfortunately, Eliza had a strict ban on firearms. But there were other ways to defend herself.

As they walked across the backyard, Bailey wondered again what means of protection Eliza had, other than her perimeter gate and the cameras her security guy mentioned.

Cameras were great for recording who did what. But in the moment, they were useless. Who cared what the guy looked like if she were murdered in her bed?

At the cabin, Bailey showed Eliza the trampled grass.

"But you said you circled the cabin this morning," she said.

"Yes, following the path someone made last night."

"Could have been a coyote or a porcupine."

"Porcupines can't turn door handles."

Eliza cast her a sharp look, staring for several long seconds.

"You certain? Not your imagination playing tricks?"

"I felt it move under my hand. Then I watched it move. Someone, a person, was out there and they tried to get in."

"Why didn't you text me?" Eliza's mouth had gone hard.

"It was after ten."

She blasted away a breath. "Bailey, my family might have been in danger. If there is a trespasser, I need to know, whatever time it is."

"I'm sorry."

She gave her a long hard stare. Bailey broke eye contact.

"I didn't want to break the rules."

"Listen, Bailey. I know you're young, but you have to use your head. *Think*."

"Sorry," she muttered, looking at her boots, her ears hot.

"All right."

Was she forgiven? Bailey glanced up. Eliza's attention had shifted to the cabin. "I'll call Richard. What time was this?"

Bailey repeated the information, then they headed back to the house, ignoring Morris, who trotted hopefully beside them.

"Anyone gets near the house, any time of day, Morris lets us know. But you're tucked back there. For your own privacy and for ours. Might be we need to move you closer to the barn. But it will be a lot noisier. With the filming and the farm chores."

"Whatever you think is best."

Moving her closer would be appreciated but Bailey wanted to be inside their house.

Their uncomfortable silence was broken by the birdsong.

Something whizzed past them, making Bailey squeal. A familiar, rail-thin tabby zipped past the barn.

"Damn cat!" Eliza tracked the feline's progress as it vanished into the tall grass. "I think that's the tomcat that knocked up Ginger."

Ginger was Aubree's beloved feline companion who followed them into the fields and filled the reels with so much personality; her posts were always popular.

Bailey had never heard Eliza swear or raise her voice. She loved animals. All animals, so Eliza's obvious venom toward the stray confused Bailey. And from the posts, the entire family were eagerly awaiting the arrival of a litter of kittens.

Naming contests. Fundraisers for local shelters. There were unlimited ways to monetize such an event.

"Not one of yours?" asked Bailey.

"No. People drop off unwanted pets constantly. They think a farm has unlimited ability to care for the animals they no longer want."

Bailey recalled all the "spay and neuter" videos Eliza and her kids did.

"We get between four to six a month. Both cats and dogs."

Bailey didn't try to hide her surprise.

"What do you do with them?" she asked.

"What their owners should have done. Drop them at the pound. It's the humane thing instead of leaving domestic animals to fend for themselves. They can't. They just starve and get sick. It's infuriating."

"A no-kill shelter?"

Eliza stared at her, head tilted as if this question annoyed her, or perhaps she thought that Bailey was just too naïve for this world.

"None in this area, unfortunately."

And that was something they never mentioned in their posts. Taking strays to a kill shelter.

"How's their placement record?" asked Bailey.

"No idea." Eliza stared at the place Bones had vanished. "Most of them are easy to catch. But not that bugger. He's too damn smart."

Bailey smiled at the gray cat's ability to outwit Eliza. Admirable, she thought.

Eliza left her at the house and Bailey headed to the office.

Her boss checked in midmorning and almost caught her gnawing on a sugar-filled breakfast pastry, which Bailey quickly dropped into her open bag.

"All right. Richard has been out to your place. We now have cameras installed at the wood line and behind the cabin. If anyone comes near there, we should get an alert and a recording."

"That's good. Is it still okay for me to take walks on the property?"

"Of course! Goodness. You're not a prisoner here. Feel free to wander. Check out the woods. Schoharie Creek. Stay on the straw between the rows if you're walking in the gardens."

"I will. We did the same up in the Thousand Islands."

"I've got a few reels to post. If it happens again, text me," she said.

"Has this happened before?"

Eliza nodded. "Unfortunately. A few hunters ignoring the posted signs. But also fans. Because of our popularity, some of the Coop Group feel they know us and they're welcome to just show up. They're not. Maud stops most of them at the main gate but some still slip by. We press charges. Always."

* * *

Bailey filled the morning working on the Watts email inbox, which mostly included requests for appearances by Eliza on other sites, guest posts, and endorsements. After that, she recorded the engagement numbers of each post on each social media provider. The video streaming surpassed anything else.

Eliza had posted the three-minute reel of Harper gathering eggs, then requesting pancakes with honey. What followed was a fast-motion montage of making the pancakes: Harper setting the silverware, Mason pouring the goat milk, and Aubree serving her siblings fresh pancakes dripping with honey. The post had twelve hundred views after only twenty minutes. The footage did not show Harper muffing her lines. No, here the family was perfect in their sunny kitchen as they enjoyed their healthy, farm-fresh breakfast.

The other videos included time with Morris. Aubree

milking Bonnet while Thistle's twins tried to overturn the bucket, and Aubree's ginger cat demanding a squirt of milk. The cat opened her mouth and later licked away the drips from her fur. Bailey noted the brown male kid was missing.

Aubree appeared in the next reel, looking clean as morning sunshine as she collected daffodils for farmers' markets.

The teen's grace and beauty made her the perfect promoter for their cutting fields. The way she moved reminded Bailey of a dancer.

Bailey flipped back to an older post of Eliza reading to Mason and Harper, cuddling with both under a log cabin quilt. Aubree, filming, reported to her mother that the pair had dropped to sleep. Eliza tucked in Harper and carried Mason back to his bed. Aubree and her mom whispered as they crept away, and the final shot was two bowls of ice cream.

Bailey longed to sit at that table.

The video ended with a reminder to buy the crockery on their website.

The plug spoiled the moment, but a check of sales showed that after the video was posted, they'd moved fifty-two sets of four hand-crafted ice cream bowls at seventy-nine dollars a pop.

"Unbelievable."

At lunch, Bailey took a walk to the grow-barn but found no useful weapons. But the wood pile yielded a straight piece of hardwood with a knobby top the size of a navel orange. Perfect. She used a borrowed saw to cut the correct length, then stripped away the branches and bark with an axe to create a walking stick. This made a useful tool for clearing the path of snakes and spiderwebs. Eliza could not object.

It also made a handy weapon; at close range this stout club of hardwood could be more effective than either a handgun or knife.

The next time, whoever it was would not find her defenseless.

SIX

Bailey was so focused on her work that she did not hear the new arrival until the door behind her clicked shut.

She straightened at her desk and turned, spotting Aubree casting her an assessing stare.

"Oh, hi. I didn't hear you come in." Bailey pasted a serene smile and a bovine expression of calm on her face. Meanwhile, her heart rate had soared like a fighter jet on takeoff, and it was all she could do not to leap to her feet with the surge of blood.

She was here. Right in front of her! Bailey could not believe her eyes.

"Aubree, right?" Did she sound casual or had the teen picked up on the unstable warble in her voice?

The girl tilted her head, judging Bailey from the opposite side of the chicken-coop of an office. She lifted one arm and rested a fist against her slim hip as her eyes narrowed. Whatever the test, Bailey knew she was failing. She swallowed back dread. She wanted—no, *needed*—them to be friends.

"What are you, a member of my fan club?" Aubree's voice was full of scorn. But the girl wasn't far wrong.

So she *had* noted Bailey's nerves.

Was her face pink? She felt hot.

"Oh, no. It's part of my job to post the videos. So naturally..." Bailey's words fell off.

Aubree moved with such speed, Bailey had time only to grip the arms of her office chair before the girl had snatched up her backpack.

"Whatcha got in here?"

Aubree unzipped the bag and began rifling through the inner compartment as Bailey stood, trying to decide what to do. Aubree came up with both a Ziploc baggie of chocolate sandwich cookies and an unopened pack of sour chewy candy.

"Aha!" Her face was animated in an expression of triumph.

Bailey went on defense too late. Should she address the invasion of privacy, the theft, or that Aubree's mother had forbidden half the contents of that bag?

"Listen, Aubree—I didn't really... I'm not sure you should..." Before she could finish, Aubree opened the freshness seal of the baggie and folded cross-legged onto the carpet that covered much of the wide plank floor to enjoy her ill-gotten gains.

Aubree's teeth turned from a lustrous white to a distressing black as chocolate cookie paste filled the gaps between her pearly whites. Now she was smiling and the sight made Bailey's stomach clench.

"I don't think you should be eating those." The objection came too late, as Aubree poured out the remnants of the cookie fragments trapped in the corners into her open mouth.

Aubree leveled her dark brown eyes on Bailey. Her tongue flicked out to retrieve the crumbs sticking to her full lips. Then she sucked her fingertips, her eyelids drifting closed as if to savor the last pop of sugar on her tongue.

Bailey crept closer, but whether to be nearer to the teen or to retrieve her bag, she was uncertain. Snatching it back seemed ill advised. As she deliberated, Aubree's eyes snapped open.

"Your mother doesn't want you eating that junk." The admonition fell flat as hypocrisy coated her words like powdered sugar on a hot donut.

"How about I don't tell my mother that you brought the twin demons of refined sugar and artificial preservatives onto her property, and you don't tell her I ate them—deal?" Aubree's sculpted eyebrows lifted as she waited for Bailey to make her next move.

The confidence in the girl's expression was rattling.

"Well, I guess that would be all right, but..."

Aubree lifted the clear packet of gummy candy. "And I'm keeping these."

The teen shoved the candy into her pocket. No great loss. Bailey had more. Sugar really was a powerful drug.

With her contraband concealed, Aubree stood and returned the bag.

"Don't you want the rest of my lunch?" Bailey quirked a brow and waited.

Aubree made a face. "Ha ha. I hope you survive longer than the last one."

The teen let that missile land and explode through Bailey. Survive was an interesting word choice. Was that intentional?

Since some unknown person had been at her door last night, the wish held an additional bite.

Had it been Aubree?

Bailey squelched the worried expression too late. The girl saw it, judging from the quirk of her mouth.

Bailey didn't like Aubree's knowing smirk. Of course, she could not resist taking the bait that was dangled before her.

"What happened to the last one?"

"Fired." Aubree held for a dramatic pause.

The possibilities darted through her mind like tadpoles in a drying pool.

Aubree's mouth was pinched tight, forcing Bailey to ask, "Why?"

"Because she reported Mom for neglect."

Bailey could not suppress the audible gasp.

"She what?"

"Something wrong with your hearing?" asked Aubree.

"No, I just..." She couldn't believe it. Eliza was the perfect... well, everything. And she had it all: loving family, great husband, beautiful home, and meaningful work. Oh, and good health and beauty. Plus, all her kids were attractive, smart, and photogenic as all hell.

"Just can't believe anyone would be stupid enough?" asked Aubree. "Well, she was. They came out here."

"Who?"

"Someone from the county. Child services or something."

"Child protective services?"

"Yup." The smile remained, perhaps wider than a moment before. Did she enjoy seeing her mother put in such a precarious position? "Not the first time, either."

Aubree dropped the empty plastic bag into the compartment. Bailey shoved the backpack under her desk.

"To be fired or to call child protective services?" Bailey nearly choked on that possibility.

"She calls it laid off. It was last fall. It's usually fall. Mom thought it might've been the school district because she wasn't picking up the textbooks that they wanted her to use. She calls them propaganda. Never uses them."

"She has alternate educational resources. I know she makes some of her own."

They were incredibly popular. In fact, more than a few homeschooling moms bought the materials for their children's education.

This time Aubree snorted. "Alternative," she scoffed. "Yeah."

Bailey didn't know which was more shocking, Aubree's shakedown or her revelation that Eliza's perfect world might not be so perfect after all.

"Anyway, Mom found out it was her. She admitted it, so..." Aubree drew her thumb across her throat. "Canned."

Never would she have guessed. The social media brand was so strong. Perfect, really. But was that a façade? If it was, would that change things? Her reason for moving mountains to be here now?

Bailey reached for that glimmer of hope.

Aubree folded her arms across her narrow chest and waited.

Bailey studied her for a long moment. This was not the innocent, joyful, and charismatic little girl that was on display in her mother's video blog or social media posts. This young miss seemed years older and much wiser. Her attitude bordered on ascorbic.

Was Eliza parading her kids out like beauty pageant contestants in a talent show?

Bailey hated herself but she asked, "Did anything come from child protective services being called out here?"

The girl pushed off the desk and crossed out of the office, striding into her mother's inner sanctum to stare out the window at the cutting garden. She spoke, facing away from Bailey, and her tone was no longer quite so sarcastic or overconfident.

"Not really. Same two women came, both times."

She faced Bailey.

"Interviewed each of us separately. I guess Mason and Harper remembered their lines because the caseworkers filled out their little forms, called Mom exemplary, wedged themselves into that shitty car, and drove away."

"Well, that's good. Isn't it?" Bailey waited for confirmation or some other detail that would help her understand this timebomb of a teenager. Aubree just stared with a look that reminded Bailey of the ones who had witnessed real action. It was that long-distance stare, out of focus, and turned inward.

Bailey had watched every post since the site launched. But she hadn't seen one about a visit from social services. That little nugget had been edited out.

What other misfortunes had been buffed away from their lives?

"You want to get inside the house, right?" asked Aubree.

Sensing a trap, Bailey remained silent. She did not like the direction of this question. There were too many potential pitfalls ahead.

"I presume that after a reasonable trial, when I have proven myself trustworthy, this would be the normal order of things."

"You presume? Trustworthy? Reasonable? I wouldn't make any presumptions if I were you. And you get in that house a lot faster if I make it happen."

"Why would I want to get into the house?"

Aubree's smirk was back. Most of the cookie paste had disappeared from between her teeth.

"You're curious. They all are. Just can't wait to sit at the breakfast table and bask in our radiance." That last part she delivered with theatrical enthusiasm.

The obviousness of Bailey's ambition gave her pause. No wonder Eliza was cautious. At least one assistant had stabbed her in the back and more than one had been a fan girl.

"I'm not here to join your perfect family. This is a job I can leverage into working on reality TV or something bigger."

Aubree's brows lifted and she sucked on her thumbnail, then removed it to ask, "What's that?"

"What?" asked Bailey.

"Reality TV?"

"It's... Aubree, do you guys watch television?"

"We don't."

Bailey blinked in astonishment. "I see."

"So you do want to keep this job."

"Of course."

The teen smiled, finding her footing again.

"Tell you what," said Aubree. "You keep the snacks coming and I'll see what I can do."

SEVEN

On Friday morning, Bailey peered at her computer, watching a how-to video with the volume barely audible.

"You know she logs your keystrokes."

The intrusion made Bailey jump right out of her seat. Before she landed, she recognized Aubree's voice.

Annoyance at her sneaking up on her yet again was replaced with a flash of panic as Aubree's words registered.

"What?"

"She can check your search history. She does mine."

"I thought you weren't allowed to use computers or cellphones."

"Cellphones, no. Social media, no. Streaming videos, only under supervision. But I'm allowed online sometimes. That's how I know she checks it."

Bailey thought back to what in her search history would be a problem. She'd already considered this as a possibility, so there was nothing truly damning.

"She doesn't have time to check everything you do. But she'll spot check it." Aubree sat on the edge of Bailey's desk. "You're welcome."

"Thank you," Bailey offered belatedly.

Aubree pushed off the desk and walked to her mother's bookshelf, the titles arranged by color.

"These don't leave a trail," she said and drew out a book, returned to Bailey, and dropped the volume on the desk.

The title was a reference book for beginners in beekeeping.

"Thanks again."

"You can thank me with food." She extended her hand. "You're off tomorrow. I want you to buy me peanut butter cookies, the ones shaped like a peanut, and a Mexican Coke. It's made with real sugar."

How a girl with only supervised access to the internet knew this fact about Coke, Bailey did not know. But she promised to fill the order, and for now gave her a chocolate bar and a small bag of spiced taco chips.

"What's your mom doing?"

"Making mozzarella from goat milk for a pasta dish. With the edits it will look like she made it all, the cheese, pasta, sauce, and cutlets in one go, but really Ada does it."

Ada Schmirkus was on the approved list of entries and had her own gate code. But Bailey didn't know her job responsibilities.

"Is Ada your cook?" asked Bailey.

"Our chef."

Aubree wolfed down the chips and then passed back the empty bag. She did the same with the candy bar, then dusted her hands off and headed out without a word of thanks.

Bailey returned to the computer and attempted to wipe her search history, belatedly wondering if that would trigger some alert.

Well, fortune was said to favor the brave.

It seemed Aubree slipped away when her mother was preoccupied.

Aubree wasn't as ascorbic today. Cynical, yes. And still so

different than her online personality. Bailey was struggling to reconcile the two.

* * *

At midday Eliza and the kids were out in the fields. Bailey watched from the window as Kaiden finally appeared. She held her breath as he charged out to meet his kids. Eliza filmed the reunion as Kaiden swung Harper and then Mason high in the air. Aubree hung back until the little ones charged off and then accepted a hug.

What lucky kids to have such a kind, supportive dad.

She was too far to hear their shouts and squeals, but she'd see the reels from Eliza's vantage point after they were posted.

Bailey watched the family transplanting seedlings. The sunshine, laughter, and fresh air were a tempting lure, and Bailey made a trip out to deliver messages and heard Tory offering tips on maximizing strawberry yield.

Later that afternoon, Bailey watched Eliza suggesting cutting runners off the plant as she repeated, nearly verbatim, what Tory had told her to do and why. Were all her helpful farming tips from her off-camera professionals?

Since Tory did not use social media, she might never know. It wasn't illegal. But it was misleading.

Eliza called Bailey to the sorting barn in the late afternoon. She found her boss alone with her desktop before a delivery of boxes.

"Can you log these?" she asked Bailey.

"Of course."

Eliza smiled and stepped away from the long table.

"Kaiden and I will be inspecting the honeybees next week. I wonder if you'd like to do some of the filming?"

Bees? She recalled the book Aubree had offered on beekeeping. That girl knew this was coming.

"Have you worked with them before?"

"A bit. Studied them in school."

"I can give you a suit before we smoke them. I need someone to get in there and show the bees while Kaiden and I are working."

It was a chance to meet her husband.

"I'd love to help."

Really, she didn't know anything about bees, suits, or what it meant to smoke a bee, but she would read up on it before the end of the day.

Thank you, Aubree.

"How did filming go today?" asked Bailey.

Eliza waved her hand. "Oh, fine. Did you see Kaiden's truck?"

"No. It's not in the lot."

"Must have left already. He's working a construction job over in Troy. Long drive, so he camps up there."

"Really? I didn't know."

"It's a closely held secret that our farm isn't quite profitable yet. But I'm hoping this year will change that."

Everyone had secrets.

Bailey wondered why Eliza had opened a store, hired an assistant, a gardener, a chef, a store manager, and subcontracted with a security person if she wasn't in the black.

Or was she lying?

Was her husband absent for some other reason?

"Oh. Nearly forgot. Tory is away this weekend on family business."

"I see..." But she didn't know why Eliza thought to mention it.

"And unfortunately, Tory can't work the market stand with Maud tomorrow, so I'd like you to cover that."

Bailey didn't want to but said, "I'd love that."

"Great. You'll be assisting her at our booth."

She knew of Maud Sergeant, as she appeared on merch videos plugging fan specials and ran the events in the store.

"Of course."

The kids appeared, trailed by Ginger, Aubree's pregnant yellow cat. All three were dressed in sage-green branded coveralls, straw hats and wellies. They looked adorable, but their mom was treating them like props and migrant workers.

They headed out to the fields together and Eliza filmed her kids picking spinach. Once they had collected enough to sell on Saturday, she called a halt.

Aubree carried the crop to the sorting barn and taught Bailey how to use the washing plant.

Eliza appeared as they finished up.

"I'll see you tomorrow at six," said her boss.

"Six?"

"That's what time we load the van. Set up at six-thirty and the market opens at seven."

"Oh, wow. Okay then. See you tomorrow."

"I've got to start supper. You be all right closing?"

"Of course."

Bailey spent the next hour reading about beekeeping. The suits were protective clothing that kept the bees from reaching the wearer's skin if stung. But a sting roused the other bees to attack, so the best practice was to sedate the bees with smoke which made them docile, so it was easier to inspect the hives.

At five, Bailey headed home, pausing to give Morris a grape-flavored fruit rollup before taking the trail to her front door.

The stray cat waited, meowing at the sight of her. She offered a can of tuna, which Bones finished as she stroked his back.

"You aren't so hard to catch," she said.

Finished, the cat meandered under the cabin and out of sight.

Dinner was another lonely affair. The aroma of beef and

barley soup lingered as she prepped for bed. The shower pressure was crap, and the water lukewarm. She curled under the puffy comforter that still smelled like plastic and sighed.

Next week, she'd finally meet Kaiden. That possibility was so exciting she could barely close her eyes.

And that was when she heard something rattling her window.

Bailey rose and collected the stout walking stick she had shaped but not sanded.

The rattle came again. She waited. Should she raise the blind or text Eliza?

Her heat ebbed away in the chilly room and her feet went cold on the vinyl floor. She strained for the next sound but heard only silence.

She rested the staff beside the window frame and retrieved her phone.

Then Bailey snapped up the window covering to find a face at the window, staring back at her.

EIGHT

Bailey screamed and stumbled backwards as her brain belatedly assembled the pieces into a recognizable whole.

She knew that face.

"Aubree?" she said, then choked.

Bailey's nostrils flared and her heart thrashed against her ribs. The hand she clamped tight to her sternum did not slow the frantic pounding.

The terror flipped to anger and then annoyance. "Are you trying to give me a heart attack?"

The girl grinned. "You're too young for that."

But older than they all believed.

"You letting me in? Or what?"

Bailey didn't want to, unless it was to kick her right on the hind end.

What time was it? After Aubree's bedtime. That much was certain, which was why she was here. Off to bed and out the window. Bailey had once done the same.

Bailey released the lock then blocked the door.

They faced off. Finally, Bailey stepped aside, and Aubree bounded in, shivering.

"You're early for a shakedown. I don't go shopping until Sunday and I don't get paid until next week."

"Got any donuts?"

"I'm out. I hadn't expected to be buying for two."

That jibe missed, causing Aubree to grin, her eyes twinkling. She wasn't regretful or embarrassed. Rather, she appeared to enjoy wreaking havoc.

But turnabout is fair play, and whether the girl knew it or not, she was outmatched here.

After Aubree finished extorting Bailey for a midnight snack of vanilla cookies, she lingered by the door.

Bailey held on to her annoyance because she feared that without it her eagerness to get close to Aubree would drive the teenager away. But she was really here. That little spark of hope flared too brightly and she squashed it. Fawning and flattery would not work on this child. Bailey was certain.

Best that Aubree not guess how important it was to gain her trust.

"You need something else?"

Aubree nodded, her attention sweeping through Bailey's little box of a room. Her cautious, intent expression made Bailey nervous.

The girl closed and locked the door.

"Who do you think is out there?"

"My mother. Tonight she was sitting on the front porch just staring into the dark."

Was she thinking back on past mistakes?

"Sometimes she checks in on us after lights out."

"Well, she can't see you in here." Bailey tried for a reassuring smile.

"Can if she has a web camera in here."

Eliza claimed she would not invade her privacy in that way, but Bailey wasn't so sure. She needed to figure out how to sweep the room to see if it was clean.

In the meantime, she glanced around for likely places to put such technology.

"You're going to be in town tomorrow," said the teen.

"Yes. Helping out at the farmers' market until noon."

"Hmm. What a surprise."

"What do you mean?"

"She does this. Gives her assistant extra assignments. Soon she'll have you working in the fields with us. And she steals your day off."

She reached into her back pocket and then extended a scrap of paper.

"Here's my shopping list."

Bailey glanced at the list of junk food in childish print that included several misspellings.

"What do I get in return?"

Aubree lifted her chin, appearing to deliberate. "What do you want?"

She wanted to meet Harper, Mason, and Kaiden. But she kept that aspiration to herself.

"I want a closer connection to the Watts brand."

Aubree groaned, eyes rolling upward. "I knew it. You *are* a fan girl. A Coop Chick. Right?"

"No." Her terse denial did not convince Aubree, judging from her quirked brow. Bailey forged on. "I want out of that shoebox of an office. To help with filming onsite."

Aubree tilted her head and gave Bailey a pitying look. "In our house, you mean. With the family. They aren't little angels, you know?" She clasped her hands before her, taking on a wistful tone. "Oh, to sit in that country kitchen. Bathe in their charm. Touch the magic."

The teen was so spot-on Bailey wondered what else had been written on her face. She hoped that Aubree's mom was not so intuitive.

"Something like that," she admitted.

The satisfied smile annoyed Bailey like a sliver under her skin.

The girl drew a long breath. "Okay. I'll do what I can."

"Great."

"But you'll be disappointed. We aren't what you see online."

"What do you mean?"

"Well..." Aubree stared at the ceiling, tapping her fingers together as she thought. "For instance, Monday is food day. Sometimes Friday, too."

"You mean like grocery shopping?"

"No, that's not what I mean. It's... well, it's hard to explain. You should just see. She starts at four."

"In the morning?"

Aubree nodded. "You should see what you're getting into before you ask to do filming and shit."

"How am I going to do that?" Bailey had been told in no uncertain terms that she was not to come near the house unless invited.

"Kitchen is on the back left side of the house. Our dining table is in front of that window. I'll open the curtain. All you have to do is stand on the milk crate under that window."

"If your mom catches me, I'm fired."

"That's true. But you want into the inner circle. Right?"

Bailey pursed her lips but nodded.

"So, take the risk and you get to see what's real and what's not. Or you can stay in this birdcage for another month and maybe she'll invite you to the front room."

Would it really take so long to gain Eliza's trust? Trust was hard won and so easily broken.

"I'm trying to help. Come and see on Monday morning. After that, if you still want in, I'll see what I can do."

After dangling that tempting piece of bait before her,

Aubree sailed out of the rabbit hutch and into the night. Bailey followed as far as the cinderblock steps.

"Want me to walk you back?"

"No way," she called over her shoulder.

Bailey watched the teen pop a cookie in her mouth and vanish in the mist that rolled off the creek.

Something moved at her feet.

There on the cinderblock sat the gray tomcat. He stared up at her with yellow eyes and then strolled into the house.

"You don't live here," she said to the stray. But then she opened her final can of tuna. The cat jumped on the counter and tried to get to the can. She lifted him and set the cat and his food on the floor.

As he gobbled down his meal, she dedicated herself to killing the insects that had followed her inside before putting out the cat.

After brushing her teeth, she worried Bones wasn't warm enough outside. Then she wondered if Aubree had made it back safely and if the girl might be correct about her mother's spying or just pulling Bailey's leg.

Was she really doing this?

Absolutely.

NINE

On the first Saturday in May, Bailey rose before dawn to find fog had settled into the valley. The mist deadened sound and made everything seem threatening. She lost the trail twice, wandering into tall grass before finally reaching the Watts' backyard and then the loading area. Bailey drove the Watts' van to the farm stand in Tory's place, hunched over the wheel and praying the deer were still asleep.

The woman at the gate handed her a map and rattled off her booth number. She drove on a rutted track across a vacant field already alive with vendors erecting tents and setting up their stands.

She made a complete circle and was heading around again when a woman stepped out before her trundling van with hands raised.

"You Bailey?" she asked.

Bailey had seen her at Coop Chick events at the store and waited to see if Maud recognized her.

She did not appear to and Bailey blew out a breath in relief. "Yes. Maud?"

The woman nodded. She looked to be in her late forties.

Her hair was an unnatural color that was neither red nor maroon, but something in between. She had pink apple cheeks, twin braids and wore a sage-colored branded apron over her white blouse and jeans. Her feet were clad in clean wellies and a wide-brimmed hat covered her head. She was pretty in a "farmer takes a wife" kind of way and chatty as a coven of middle school girls hopped up on energy drinks.

Bailey had opted for jeans and a flowered blouse. Maud offered her an apron with the Watts branding.

Maud was among the first employees who had started working for the Watts Farm shortly after Eliza bought the property nearly eight years ago. She'd transitioned into operating the store.

Maud unrolled a fabric banner. "Hold this."

Together they hung the signage with Bailey looping the hooks over the upper rod.

"Wish I could do that," said Maud, hands on her hips.

The crown of Maud's straw hat did not reach Bailey's chin. She was so pint-sized, Bailey wondered if she lived in a burrow, like a hobbit.

With signage complete, Maud checked her mobile phone then tapped out a message.

"Just texted Eliza and Tory that we're set up."

"We're not," said Bailey. "Wait. Did you say Tory?"

"Yeah."

"You texted her?"

Maud nodded.

"She doesn't have a cellphone."

"What?" Maud laughed. "Where did you get that?"

"Eliza said so. Tory did, too, I think."

"Well, she sure does. I've seen it. It's old but it's a smartphone."

"She follows Eliza's posts?"

"Doesn't everyone?"

Tory lied to Eliza about having a phone. But why?

Bailey placed the fresh flowers and salad greens as Maud directed. Produce was sparce, but because of the Watts' greenhouse, they had a variety of lettuce, microgreens, and radishes along with honey, maple syrup, and preserves.

"Do you have kids?" asked Maud.

Bailey's stomach muscles contracted, and her teeth locked. She took a moment to pull air into her lungs.

"No. You?"

"Single. I raise pigs and goats. Those goats in her pasture came from my stock."

Bailey helped display the honey, candles, and jam, and noticed that there was more product than she'd delivered.

She frowned at the shelving as the first customers sauntered between the row of tents carrying baskets, totes, and wheeling shopping carts.

"Gates are open," said Maud.

Maud was a natural salesperson, chatting with shoppers perusing their wares. While she worked the customers, Bailey compared the products she'd brought with the extra stock.

The differences were very subtle. The candle labels were a near match. And the honey jars, the ones she'd brought had one less bee on the back label. And she knew that Eliza did not sell T-shirts made in Bangladesh. As the morning progressed, Maud sold dozens of the knockoffs.

Eliza's store manager made sales, pocketed the cash, and carefully recorded credit card sales. All told, Bailey estimated that Maud pocketed between eight hundred and twelve hundred dollars. Ten thousand dollars a year.

Very lucrative.

Was Tory in on this or was she just less observant?

Bailey said nothing about noticing the theft. It was an ace in the hole. A way to divert attention if things went sideways or she needed to deliver a scapegoat.

When she got back to the farm, she was greeted by Eliza.

"How did it go?"

"Interesting. You sold a ton."

"Great."

Bailey went back to work, wishing the day away because in two days she'd get a glimpse into Eliza's real life. What did Aubree want Bailey to see?

TEN

Bailey's curiosity buoyed her along through the darkness on Monday morning. She ignored the chill that sent a shiver up her spine.

The downstairs of the Watts' home was ablaze with lights. More than expected.

She approached with care, reaching the window, easily distinguished by the overturned milk crate that had not been there when she had walked past on Saturday afternoon. Aubree had placed the crate, opened the curtain, and cracked open the window.

She stepped onto the platform. She had a clear view of the kitchen table, a rustic creation perfectly suited for a country home. A huge bouquet of lilacs draped from a white pitcher. Though a terrible cut flower, Bailey imagined they would last long enough for filming. The table was set with lavender hand-woven placemats and cotton napkins. The napkin rings woven from last year's wheat made a beautiful tableau.

On the wall beyond the table the following three words were stenciled, each word in its own unique font: *Faith, Family, Farming.*

A silver reflector and light stands were stationed to provide the maximum amount of warm light.

Between two of the light stands, a framed, yellowing sign read: *Panem et Circenses.*

Was that Latin?

Eliza appeared in a loose-fitting cotton dress the color of freshly churned butter and covered with a bibbed apron. The flower pattern picked up both the yellow of her dress and the purple from the bouquet. Bailey's boss favored loose boho fashion and never wore anything tight fitting. Casual comfort, she called it, and it sold her image and her products.

She was speaking to the camera, set on a tripod as she whisked some batter in a crockery bowl.

Just past the camera's view, an older woman hunched over the center island in the kitchen, mashing fresh blueberries before adding them to a large saucepan on the stove.

Now Eliza paused the shooting and adjusted the camera to face the corner that held the large six-burner stove and worktable under the window on the opposite corner from where Bailey watched.

"I've got it set on fast motion. No sound."

The older woman nodded but kept her attention on food preparation.

"We'll do the canning. Then make the fresh whipped cream."

"You want blintzes today?" asked the woman.

"Pancakes. French toast with the bread we made and a power bowl for Aubree. Then we'll make the cinnamon rolls. Is the dough ready?" asked Eliza.

"Proofing in the oven. Just cook the sausage and scramble a few eggs," said the woman, who seemed to be the chef. "I'll do the rest."

One after another, plates of food were prepped and set out on the counter.

Aubree appeared and Bailey glanced at her clock. She'd been standing on this crate for nearly an hour. She shifted, flexing her stiff knees with a wince.

Eliza sent her daughter to rouse the younger kids.

"Put them in the first outfit."

"How many today?" asked Aubree.

"Seven. All breakfast. We'll do dinner after we shoot the scenes moving the mobile coop."

Aubree left and appeared a few moments later leading Mason by the hand. The boy was still rubbing one eye with a fist and looked to have been tugged from a warm bed. Harper straddled Aubree's opposite hip, her thumb in her mouth and her face flushed.

"Here are my babies," said Eliza as Aubree handed Harper to her mother, on camera. "Good morning, sleepy head," she said to Mason. "Do you want some breakfast?"

Mason nodded and yawned.

"Wash your hands," she said.

After Eliza filmed them washing, she seated Harper on her booster seat, not three feet from where Bailey stood.

Aubree glanced up at the window, then moved from side to side, before spotting Bailey. The lights inside and the darkness outside must be creating something of a mirror. The teen offered the slightest inclination of her head. Then she pulled out Mason's chair and he scrambled up onto the seat.

The two younger children looked rumpled and angelic with light glowing off their blond hair as Eliza served them pancakes covered with blueberry syrup, left over after the canning Eliza did an hour earlier.

Bailey's mouth watered at the sight of the breakfast, made over two hours ago, and certainly cold. The two little ones made a fine mess of their plates, as Eliza narrated the wholesome ingredients and reminded the camera that pancake mix and syrup were both for sale on their online store. Before the two had finished, their plates were whisked away.

What was going on?

Aubree's hair was a riot of curls, including one right in the center of her forehead. She looked like a teen model, selling the wholesome life.

Aubree and Eliza shared a charming interaction that ended in both bursting into laughter. But before Aubree had more than a mouthful, the plates were cleared. All four left to return in new outfits.

Had the dialog been as scripted as their meals?

This process repeated as the children were served breakfast after breakfast. The little ones snatched bites before the next plate was paired with a different outfit.

As the daylight began to concern Bailey, Kaiden walked into the house.

He wore worn, tight jeans, but not too tight. A clean white T-shirt and work boots.

Had he come from outdoors? She knew he had not passed this side of the house.

It was time to go. But Kaiden was here.

She lingered. *Just a few minutes more.*

He tugged off his leather gloves as he called out. "What smells so good?"

Kaiden kissed Eliza on the cheek as she ladled out oatmeal and sprinkled it with brown sugar, nuts, and fresh fruit.

Bailey had trouble concentrating because Kayden was more handsome in real life than on the video blog.

He smiled, chatted with his children and his wife, cracking bad dad-jokes and talking about the chores he'd finished up.

The man was so charismatic, she forgot she was standing on the milk crate in plain view. But Aubree did not. She blocked the window with her body and waved her hand behind her back, signaling Bailey to get lost.

She descended from the milk crate. Something touched her ankle. She jumped, just stifling a scream with her hand against her mouth. At her feet stood Aubree's very pregnant yellow cat.

"Ginger?" she whispered, bending to pet the cat.

Aubree was right. Things here were not what they seemed.

Bailey stroked the yellow cat and asked, "If Eliza made all this food today, what are her kids eating the rest of the week?"

ELEVEN

Eliza appeared at the office wearing a flowing, burnt-orange flowered dress, cinched high on her narrow waist, and a wide-brimmed, chocolate-brown felt hat. Her cowboy boots were brown and stitched with pink roses and her bracelets and the long necklace both featured natural turquoise beads, and silk tassels. On her fingers were silver rings set with chunky turquoise nuggets. The splashes of turquoise made her eyes look especially blue. The scooped neckline gave a glimpse of flawless skin spattered with freckles.

"I need you to do some filming."

Bailey could not get out of her seat fast enough. Especially if this was her chance to meet Kaiden.

"Aubree suggested it—if you man the camera, we can get all of us in the frame."

"Did she?" It seemed the snacks were paying off.

"It's just some action sequences that I'll cut together later. But we're all moving, so its best if the camera moves along."

Outside, Eliza turned over her phone, explaining the shots she wanted.

They rounded the barn, to the woodshed and chopping

block, and there he was. Kaiden wore a trucker's cap, a blue checked shirt, open, tight, faded jeans, and boots. The fabric clung to his muscular arms and shoulders as he swung an axe in a smooth arc, splitting the block of firewood. The pieces flew in opposite directions, clunking against the ones already fallen.

Eliza paused and Bailey drew up short. Suddenly she couldn't think. When presented with all that male muscle, she feared her rising estrogen levels might just cause temporary blindness.

"Kaiden, this is Bailey, my new assistant." Eliza motioned toward Bailey, who managed a grimace. "And Bailey, this is my husband."

Had she put a proprietary emphasis on that last word? The change in tone was enough to wipe the stupid grin off Bailey's face.

Kaiden used one hand to sink the axe into the huge, upturned stump that served as a chopping block, then removed one glove and offered his hand to Bailey.

He pressed his damp skin to her cool palm. The zing of attraction stabbed through her chest and a chill shivered over her skin. Her heart didn't seem to know if it should stop or beat faster.

The rough texture of the calluses on his hand grazed her skin as he drew back.

"Nice to meet you, Bailey," he said. His smile seemed genuine, and he looked completely unaffected by the touch that had made her scalp tingle.

"You as well."

"You the videographer?" he asked.

"You wha... oh, yes. That's me."

"Super-dooper." He removed his cap and used his forearm to mop his brow. "Hot one today, isn't it?"

His eyes were so blue. Bluer than either of his younger kids. Though the little ones shared his blond hair, his had lighter highlights, the kind that came from good genes and lots of sunlight.

"Bailey, you'll follow me and keep it on us while Kaiden splits four logs. Just four. Then he'll stop and when I move, follow me up to the house."

"Got it."

She lifted the cellphone and trailed Eliza to the porch, where she collected a sweating glass of a cloudy drink topped with ice. The garnishes included a sprig of fresh mint and a slice of lemon, cut in a perfect disc and then fitted on the rim of the glass.

"Ready?" Eliza asked.

Bailey lifted the phone and pressed record. Then she nodded.

Eliza beamed as she stepped from the porch.

"I thought Kaiden might like to try the new lemonade we made this morning. Lemons aren't in season, and we can't grow them here, but there is nothing more refreshing on a hot day."

They were midway across the yard and Bailey struggled to walk parallel with Eliza, not trip, *and* keep the camera trained on her boss.

"It's a hot one today. Unseasonably so for May. But it won't be come fall. That woodshed needs to be full. Doing a little a day does the job. You remember all those brush piles we made last fall? Well, that wood is now good and dry and ready for chopping. Drop a like if you appreciate honest hard work."

The sound of chopping reached them.

"There he is." Eliza pointed and Bailey panned to Kaiden wielding the axe with smooth efficiency. Then she zoomed in on the magnificent view of a fit, handsome man in motion.

"I'll bet he's worked up a thirst."

Bailey panned out and returned the view to Eliza, following behind as she brought Kaiden a drink.

He paused, sank the axe in the chopping block, and accepted the glass. Then he thanked his wife and gave her a kiss. But the best part, the very best part, was watching his Adam's apple bob as the liquid slid down his throat and dripped down his chin.

Eliza used her bandanna from her side pocket to dab away the fluid that spilled down his tanned neck and chest.

This resulted in Kaiden trapping her against him for another kiss before he returned the glass and resumed chopping.

Eliza faced the camera and grinned.

"That's all the thanks I need." She headed back toward the porch but stopped halfway up the gentle slope, held that position, and then motioned to her throat.

Bailey stopped filming.

While Eliza reviewed the recording, Bailey reviewed Kaiden.

Then, at Eliza's request, she filmed the couple moving the mobile chicken coop, planting seedlings, riding the tractor together. Bailey began to wonder where the kids were all this time.

She didn't think it was her place to ask that question, so she asked a related one.

"Should we get some footage of the kids and their dad?"

Kaiden cast Eliza a knowing look and she frowned.

"They don't have to report out here until four. I wanted all of us in the orchard at golden hour."

"What's that?"

"It's not really an hour but the time before the sun sets when the light turns warm. Golden."

That was why her kids were often haloed with a gilded crown and looked so darn blond.

Bailey had seen questions from followers on what color hair dye Eliza used. She didn't, of course. Some people just led a charmed life. If Eliza had a single worry in the world, it was not obvious.

Perhaps it was just the fear that one day she wouldn't make every mother jealous of her idyllic lifestyle, perfect kids, and gorgeous husband.

But Bailey would bet that the lemonade was made by that woman in the kitchen, who might now be watching Eliza's children.

At the appointed time, Eliza headed to the house to change and pick up the kids.

That left Bailey alone and tongue-tied with Kaiden. He stooped to pet Ginger, who wound around one leg. Tanned fingers glided through yellow fur.

"What do you think of the place?" he asked, straightening, lifting Ginger to his chest.

"The farm? Oh, it's wonderful. I'm so glad to be out in the sunshine today."

"Eliza can be tough. She has to be. And she's slow to warm up to people. Took me forever to get her to let me in."

Hard to believe. She had the feeling that Kaiden's life was even more perfect than Eliza's.

"So you planning on staying?" he asked.

"Yes, for a while."

"Eliza says you're smart. Got degrees up the wazoo."

"Not so many. I have an associate's degree and a bachelor's." The lie came effortlessly.

"So pretty *and* smart?"

The way he said it made her blush. She could not think of a reply.

"You *are* pretty. No reason to be embarrassed."

"Thank you." She broke eye contact, her cheeks flaming hot at the flirtation. She was flattered but also wary.

His and Eliza's mutual affection seemed so genuine. But the

tenderness seemed to cease when the filming stopped. Just how much of Eliza's world was an illusion?

Why would a guy married to a woman as flawless as Eliza be flirting with her assistant?

Bailey's mind flashed her a series of male celebrities and politicians, all of whom had cheated with the help. It happened —a lot. She cautioned herself to avoid that landmine.

"You and your wife have a huge following. You're doing so well."

He waved a dismissive hand. "She's doing well. I'm just lucky to tag along."

He stroked the cat, who purred. Bailey gathered her self-control.

"You finished with your construction job?"

He cast her a mischievous smile. She ignored the little tug at her stomach.

"Which one?" he asked.

"The ones that take you away from the farm?"

"Is that what she told you?" He laughed. "That I'm away on construction jobs?"

TWELVE

Bailey now saw Eliza's explanation for what it was. A lie.

But what was true? Were they having marital troubles? Did Kaiden even live here?

"She said the farm isn't making a profit yet."

He laughed again. "Not... Well, that's a whopper. I don't know what she pulls down from all those endorsements, but it's more than she pays..." He hesitated, glancing toward the house. "Oh, damn! I hate the bees."

He set Ginger carefully on the ground.

Bailey turned toward the house, where Eliza appeared dressed in a beekeeper's suit, open and draped from her waist. She carried a smoker in one hand and a second suit in the other.

"She'll want a few long shots. Stay back until she uses the smoker."

"Got it."

Eliza directed them to the edge of the flower fields where stacks of wooden hives sat in the shade of the apple orchard.

During the next hour, Bailey filmed in golden light.

Once dismissed, she realized it was nearly time to quit. She trudged up the hill and found Aubree waiting for her on the front porch. The teen motioned her to the south end of the veranda, shadowing Bailey to the rail.

"She's got a security camera mounted to the post beside the front steps." Aubree pointed. "Picks up anything in the yard or on the stairs."

Bailey stared back at the outdoor camera fixed to the upright column. The one she walked by each morning and evening.

"You don't want her to know we are talking," Bailey guessed.

"Avoids problems. So, you catch most of that food circus this morning?"

"Yes. What was that?"

The teen perched on the rail in a place that gave her a fine view of anyone approaching from the yard. Bailey, on the ground, craned her neck up at the girl.

"She films most of the food sequences for the week on one day. Breakfast, lunch, and dinner. Ada makes everything. We come to the table. Act delighted. Eat cold food. Then change our clothing and do it again."

"Why?"

"Saves time. Allows for more content production."

"But she still has to cook for you each day."

That made Aubree laugh out loud.

"She doesn't?"

"Mom just reheats whatever they made on Monday and Friday cooking days. The bread never lasts. We're usually still eating whatever is left on Thursday and Sunday. The only reason I like cooking day is it means fresh food," said Aubree and set her mouth in a thin, grim line.

Bailey stammered. "I—I had no idea."

"You thought this was Oz. Right? And we're the perfect farming family? Well, we're not. Not even close. I swear if she could AI all of us, she'd do it."

"How do you know about AI?"

"Heard mom talking with her web designers. Artificial intelligence. Right?"

"That's right," said Bailey. "Do you three use computers for your homeschooling?"

Aubree shrugged. "Not often. The schoolwork is self-guided mostly. I think you can picture how that is going. I mean, I've got Harper to learn her colors, shapes, and ABCs. And Mason can add and subtract single digits. But he should be doing a lot more."

Bailey's shock leaked into her voice. "*You're* teaching them?"

"Yeah." Aubree's gaze darted to the yard. "She's coming. You better go."

The teen pointed to the side yard. But Bailey had so many more questions.

Eliza called for Aubree. The sound caused Bailey to scurry out of sight. But their voices were clear enough.

"Did you see my assistant?" Eliza's footsteps sounded on the wooden planks.

"Heading home."

There was a pause. Then Eliza's voice. "Wow, it's after five. Nearly supper time."

"What are we having?"

"Blueberry pancakes, navy bean soup, roasted carrots, and breakfast sausages."

Bailey pressed close to the outer wall.

"What about Dad?" asked Aubree.

"Oh, he won't be joining us."

* * *

Bailey spent that evening thinking hard on what had brought her here.

Eliza was a fraud. But that didn't mean she wasn't successful, happy, and leading a charmed existence. If anything, it made her success even more unjust.

Everything Bailey learned only made her more committed to gaining a spot in the inner circle.

She mulled over the day as she washed her dishes and then used the same sink to brush her teeth.

The hours of work in the sun exhausted her, and Bailey dropped off to sleep in seconds.

In the morning, the alarm jarred her awake extra early, because she wanted to see if Kaiden's vehicle was parked on the property before she started work.

Bailey walked through the field, with the pink eastern glow promising a lovely sunrise.

Kaiden's red truck was no longer parked near the barn. Either he had left before dawn, or he had not spent the night.

Her surveillance halted as she caught movement and ducked out of sight behind the huge maple that dominated the rear of the property. There, she watched someone appear from the shadows of the barn.

A man crept across the yard. Taller than Kaiden, thinner than her security man. A stranger. And his stealth marked him as an intruder.

Bailey crouched as her instincts told her to halt, hide, and be silent.

He ducked behind the mobile chicken coop.

Bailey knew that Aubree collected the eggs early, then milked the nanny goats, but did not know what time. Bailey drew out her phone to call Eliza as another possibility struck.

Was Aubree meeting a boy? But this was no gangly teen.

More likely this was the person who tried to open her door that first night.

Bailey phoned Eliza, but her call went straight to voicemail.

Swearing, she tapped out a text, hit *send* and waited, staring at the screen.

And waited.

Maybe Eliza was calling the police. Bailey heard something.

She caught a glimpse of Aubree, milking pail and egg basket in hand as she neared the coop.

When she spotted the man, Aubree screamed.

THIRTEEN

The intruder grabbed both Aubree's arms and dragged her from Bailey's view.

Time was up.

The crash of a tin bucket brought Bailey to a run.

She darted across the yard toward the coop, her walking stick gripped tight in both hands. She heard him clearly now, his voice high and unnatural.

"Aubree, it's okay. Just come with me."

Aubree's reply was muffled. Was he covering her mouth with his hands?

Bailey reached the coop and flattened against the side closest to the pair.

"You need to come with me, please." The man's voice took on a pleading tone as if he expected her to just cooperate. "You've been signaling me online. I came. I'm here for you."

He thought he knew her. That she was sending him secret messages. How many fans out there were this disturbed and dangerous?

Bailey peered around the corner. The intruder stood beside

the hens' enclosure, arms spread wide, blocking Aubree's escape.

The teen threw the egg basket at him. He ducked and the basket rolled, causing the chickens inside their nesting boxes to beat their wings and squawk.

He straightened, attention fixed on the teen.

Bailey raised the club and dashed behind Aubree's attacker. She struck him hard across the back of the head. Both hands lifted to the spot Bailey landed her blow.

"Ouch!" He turned.

Aubree shot away but then spotted Bailey and hesitated, breaking stride.

"Go," she shouted to Aubree. "Get your mom."

The man drew a knife, holding it in one outstretched hand as Aubree ran screaming toward the house.

Bailey stared at the knife. It was long and tapered, like a hunting knife. She aimed her staff like a bayonet and retreated.

He was taller than she'd first imagined, and older. From his receding hairline, she guessed mid-thirties. Bailey backed toward the corner of the coop, keeping the staff ready and her focus on the hand that held the knife.

"I'm not here for you."

She narrowed her eyes. "What are you here for then?"

"I just wanted to meet her."

"You're not here to meet her. This is not how an adult man meets a teenage girl. An *underage* child."

He winced.

Bailey took off at a run toward the house, not hanging around to confront a demented, armed man who'd just lost his chance.

Aubree, on the porch, was still screaming for her mother. Bailey glanced back, fearing pursuit, but their attacker dashed between the rows of newly planted strawberries.

What was he doing? There was nothing down there but the river.

The river! Much easier than traveling overland. No gate code. No barriers.

Eliza burst from the house.

"Where?" she said, breathless.

Bailey pointed at the retreating form, already nearly invisible in the bluish predawn light.

"I think he's going to the river."

Eliza lifted her phone and placed a call as Bailey reached the porch.

"Are you calling the police?"

In answer, Eliza lifted a finger, indicating Bailey should hold on or shut up.

A little, frightened voice came from just inside the screen door. "Mommy?"

Bailey glanced at the entrance and found Mason at the door with hands pressed to the screen. Aubree stood behind him holding Harper on her hip.

In the glow of the porch light, she could see the tears on Aubree's cheeks and the pallor of her complexion.

Harper banged on the screen, insistent. "Mommy!"

The girl's small, frightened voice made Bailey's heart clench, raising maternal instincts she thought dead and buried.

Eliza spoke on the phone. "Get here as soon as you can."

She ended the call and Harper wriggled out of Aubree's grasp, bursting through the door, followed by her brother. Their mother squatted to meet them, enfolding each in a one-armed hug.

"It's all right, lambkins. You're all right." Eliza glanced at Aubree trembling on the porch.

"Is he gone?" she whispered.

Eliza nodded and motioned to Aubree. Harper and Mason

clung to their mom like baby opossums, and their big sister joined them.

Bailey stood, wanting to join the communal hug, knowing she could not. She had no family and was not yet a part of this one.

"Who is he, Mama?" asked Mason.

"We're going to find out." The determination of this declaration gave Bailey a shiver. Eliza had a dangerous glint in her eye, familiar to anyone who had ever had a child frightened or harmed.

She wanted her daughter's attacker to burn in hell.

They were emotions Bailey knew well.

Bailey felt herself being watched and turned to find Harper studying her, her Cupid bow lips parted, blue eyes wide and bright. Her fine, blond, fly-away hair glowed in brilliant strands about her head, creating a halo. At five, she was a heavy load for her fine-boned mother, who still held her easily.

And beside Aubree stood Mason, his attention also fixed on her.

Bailey's heart gave a little shudder, and she snatched a breath past her constricting throat.

Here they were. Finally. All three of Eliza's children were standing before her on the porch as she'd long imagined.

It had taken an attacker for Bailey to breach the Watts' castle.

Bailey smiled and lifted a hand, wiggling her fingers at Harper, who shyly ducked her face into her mother's shoulder. But she was peeking again a moment later.

Eliza finally realized her kids were focused on the stranger standing on the wide front porch between the steps and the hanging fern.

She made a sound in her throat that Bailey couldn't interpret. Perhaps resignation or annoyance. It wasn't a happy sound. Eliza motioned to Bailey.

"Harper, Mason, Aubree. I want you to meet someone."

She pulled the two little ones around to face Bailey.

"This is my new assistant, Bailey."

Eliza released Mason's hand and motioned to her eldest child.

"This is Aubree, our scholar."

The misspellings in Aubree's grocery list said otherwise, Bailey thought.

Aubree stepped forward and offered her hand and a slight curtsey as though they'd never met.

"I'm pleased to meet you, Miss Bailey."

Bailey gaped. She didn't recognize this perfect angel of a teenager. It wasn't the hellion she'd been dealing with since arrival.

"Mason?" Eliza ushered the boy forward.

He hesitated, glanced back at his mother, then set his jaw and marched toward Bailey, hand outstretched.

His shake was athletic, as if he was working the old-style slot machines in a casino.

"How do you do?" he asked. Then he released her and charged back to his mother, making Eliza laugh.

"Mason is our artist." Bailey had seen the boy's drawings online and they were marvelous. "He is also my helper with the animals and brings Morris and our goats their breakfast and dinner every day."

"You have an important job," said Bailey and watched the boy lift his chin and straighten his shoulders as his ebbing fear changed to pride.

"You're next, lambkin." Eliza put Harper down, clasped one hand, and walked her forward.

Harper curtseyed and then offered her hand.

"I am Harper. I'm how-do-you-do?" She grimaced, clearly aware that she'd muddled that.

"Try again," said Eliza, scowling now.

"I'm... um, pleased to..."

She glanced at her mother for help, but it was Aubree who offered assistance.

"...meet you. My name is—"

Harper cut her off. "I'm pleased to meet you. I'm Harper. I'm five and I don't like carrots."

Eliza shook the girl's hand, which slipped away like a fish from the net an instant after they made contact.

"Well, perhaps Aubree can bring us all a pitcher of milk and those cinnamon buns to enjoy out here while we wait for Richard."

"Hurrah!" said Mason.

Aubree turned and disappeared into the house.

Had Eliza called her security tech instead of the police?

Bailey didn't ask. All she knew was whoever attacked Aubree, she owed him her thanks. His arrival brought her one of her deepest wishes—meeting the Watts children.

Things were happening just as she'd hoped.

Next step, get inside their house. But gaining trust took time. She needed to be patient.

"Harper, Mason, go help your sister. Harper, you can carry the silverware."

The two dashed off and the screen door slapped against the frame behind them.

Eliza checked her phone for messages and swatted at her ankles, hopping from one foot to the other. Bailey waved away a bug whining about her ear.

"The mosquitoes are bad this morning. Aren't they?" Bailey said, hoping Eliza would invite her in for breakfast. She was desperate to see the inside of the house.

Meeting the kids, seeing where they lived, and gaining Eliza's trust. That was everything to her.

Who wouldn't want to be in the inner circle of this family?

And once there, she could—
"Why were you here so early?"

FOURTEEN

A zip of apprehension shot through Bailey's middle.

Eliza had lowered her phone, her head cocked as she stared at Bailey.

"What?"

"You don't start work until eight. But you were here when Aubree was gathering eggs. That means you were here before six."

Bailey weighed her options. The truth was not one of them. But there were a variety of lies that could account for her pre-dawn recon.

"You said I was free to wander the farm."

Eliza's eyes narrowed, not buying this.

"And... I was hoping to get a photo of the sunrise."

Eliza's expression twisted.

"Why? Are you posting photos from my property on social media?"

"No. That would violate our agreement."

"It would."

"As I told you, I don't have any online presence."

"Yes, you told me. But it's impossible to know if that's true.

So if I see one photo from this farm on any website, you're fired."

Bailey absorbed the threat, blinking.

"I have to protect my family, and just one of those photos, without the geographical data removed, will lead people like that"—she pointed toward the chicken coop—"right to my kids. You have no idea the nuts drawn here. And there's more like that one. Some want to date my underage daughter, or worse. Others believe Mason or Harper are their own kids. Can you imagine? Like I stole them."

"I had no idea."

"Having so many followers comes with risks. I'm trying to manage them. I don't need you undermining my efforts."

"All I did was walk from my cabin to the barn and I heard Aubree scream. I don't know what you expected me to do."

"I expect you to honor our privacy and not be sneaking around the yard like a thief."

Bailey's pulse raced as she stifled a retort. She had just saved Eliza's kid. And *this* was her thanks?

Deescalate, she thought, forcing herself to take a deep breath.

"Yes. I understand. I won't come near the house before or after work. But if I hadn't come today..." She let that image bloom in Eliza's mind.

"I'll look after my kids. That's not your job."

That's what she thought, because Bailey planned to add this to her responsibilities, and soon.

"Yes. Of course. I understand."

Aubree arrived carrying a blue enamel pitcher, flecked with white.

"Change of plans. Bailey isn't joining us. Set up in the family room."

Bailey blinked at this sudden uninvite. And at the words *family room*. She'd never seen a family room on any post; she knew the kids ate in the kitchen and dinners were always in the dining room. Or were they?

She recalled watching the parade of outfits and meals on "food day" as Aubree called it.

Aubree's smile dropped, but she said, "Yes, ma'am."

Eliza shooed Bailey away.

"I'll see you later. Richard will want to speak to you."

"Of course. I'm here to help."

Eliza gave her a long hard stare and then followed Aubree into their home. The screen door slapped shut behind her.

"I'll get past that door. You just wait and see," said Bailey to no one.

* * *

In the office, and with Eliza watching her like a cat at the birdfeeder, Bailey told Richard everything except why she was up so early.

After she had satisfied all his questions, she asked one of her own.

"Does Kaiden know about the attack?" Bailey asked because she felt Aubree's father should be made aware of this situation.

"Not sure," said Richard.

Eliza walked across her office, motioned Richard inside, and closed the two French doors separating Eliza's workspace from Bailey's.

Clearly, Bailey had done something wrong, but she was now certain that Kaiden did not live here on the farm.

There were several possible reasons. The most obvious was marital problems. A divorce. Separation. But Kaiden appeared on the weekend and was there for filming on Monday.

Another mystery.

Bailey worked quietly in her office, not daring to approach

the closed doors. Richard left the office after thirty minutes. Eliza emerged midmorning and asked Bailey to join her on a perimeter walk with Richard.

They found him in the parking area working on his tablet.

"Ready?" he asked.

Bailey followed behind the pair as they passed the chicken coop and set off through the planted fields. Along the way, her security guy laid out the options for boosting farm security. Bailey took notes and tried hard not to gag at the cost. If Eliza Watts could afford any of these, it was clear that her explanation for Kaiden's absence was nonsense.

When Richard left, Eliza headed to the house for lunch. Bailey hustled back to the office and tried to open the filing cabinets beneath the picture window. But they were locked.

Eliza's ultra organization and her habit of not leaving any documents on her desk was becoming a roadblock.

How was Bailey supposed to learn all their secrets if she couldn't get in the front door or into Eliza's laptop or files?

She needed to figure out a way to break into the cabinets or to steal the keys.

In the late afternoon, Bailey was allowed access to the porch once more to film Eliza and Aubree crank the handle to stir the paddles through the thickening ice cream in the stainless-steel can. As the surrounding ice melted, Harper and Mason added more layers of rock salt and ice chips to the wooden tub in which it sat. Each of them took turns spinning the crank to send the paddles turning. When the camera stopped rolling, Eliza moved the mix to an electric version. When it was time to film the kids enjoying the profits of their labor, the ice cream was back in the old-fashioned mill, and they all dipped in with wooden spatulas and spoons.

Utterly charming.

Completely fake.

Bailey wondered what else around here was a lie.

FIFTEEN

Eliza could sell anything. Bailey believed it. Her boss dripped with charisma and her engaging banter and welcoming smile simply dazzled.

By the following Saturday Bailey was getting used to the promotional videos, and filming the family outdoors was one of her regular jobs. As she reached the end of her second week, she had not gotten into the house but was allowed on their perimeter.

She videoed Eliza, dressed in a gauzy blouse and flowing embroidered skirt, pushing her kids on the tire swing and all of them piling into the hammock for story time. Eliza was careful; the audio of her reading copyrighted material was obscured with music, unless it was one of her own picture books.

"If they want me to plug their book, they can pay me," she said.

She said the same on her video blog but in other words.

"Hey, authors! Want me to read your book to my children in an upcoming post? Smash the like and follow and head to my website to fill out an application. You're the best!"

And then she and her kids all shouted, "We love you!"

The shameless plugs made Bailey feel as if she needed a shower, but she was also impressed.

She had some time with Harper and Mason while Kaiden and Eliza were filming Kaiden doing chores on Morris's fence and enclosure.

"Is Daddy staying over?" asked Bailey casually.

Harper answered immediately, her voice high and pipping like a bird's.

"Daddy doesn't live with us."

Mason gave her a hip-check.

"Ouch!" said Harper, more angry than hurt. "Why'd you do that?"

"Don't talk about where Daddy lives."

"Why not?"

"Because... I don't know. But we aren't supposta."

"I forgot."

"Because you're a pea-brain."

"What's that?"

"It means your brain is only this big." Mason indicated a very small amount between his thumb and index finger.

"It is not!"

Harper had confirmed Bailey's suspicions. The kids' father did not live here and these two squabbled like all kids.

Eliza's head came up from the fence and she glanced toward them.

"Who wants to swing in the hammock?" asked Bailey.

The two were delighted to follow her to the backyard, out of earshot, where she swung them until Eliza and Kaiden appeared.

"We're filming in the house with these two next. You can head back to the office."

"Sure. I'll get to work editing." It was a new responsibility and one she was much better at than managing emails. The requests from fans were endless and the endorsement offers were so plentiful, Eliza could afford to be choosy.

"Great."

She found Aubree bundling the tulips for tomorrow's market. The daffodils had about had it, but there were still some late bloomers.

"How are you doing, since... you know, the guy at the coop?" asked Bailey, referring to the attack.

Aubree's reply was curt and meaningless.

"Fine."

She hesitated then took a step closer. Aubree cast her a side-eye but did not object.

Bailey cleared her throat and tried again. "An assault like that, well, it can take a person time to process. Sometimes years. And it can be good to talk about it. If you ever want to speak to someone—"

"I don't."

Bailey backed off and opted for small talk.

"Did you pick all of these?" asked Bailey, eyeing the pile of blooms on the sorting table.

Aubree glanced up but made no answer.

"Want some help?"

The girl did not immediately accept. She was suspicious—a trait Bailey admired. Old enough to know not everything was what it seemed and not everyone had good intentions.

Bravo.

"Don't you have work to do in the office?"

"I can spare a few minutes." Bailey surveyed the table of fresh cut flowers. "Farmers' market was today. So what are these for?"

"Mom sells them to other vendors who sell them on Sundays. Albany, White Plains, and Union Square in the City. Where's Mom?"

"Still filming in the house."

Aubree glanced toward the entrance, as if checking that they were alone.

"He's not my dad."

Bailey's mouth dropped open, and she sucked in a breath as Aubree peeked up at her and then back to her hands, tying the next bundle.

She stared at the girl, stunned speechless. Aubree had just opened up, and what a revelation!

Was this the truth or her opinion? Bailey had to know but did not want her eagerness to shut down this moment of intimacy and the chance to bring them closer together.

She was considering her words when Aubree spoke again.

"At least I don't think he is."

Bailey's palms went wet and her skin itched.

"Why not?"

The girl wrapped a bunch of blooms together and tied them with a jute cording before plopping them in the black plastic bin.

Finally, she spoke.

"Look at them and look at me. They're all blond and they all have blue eyes. Their hair is..." She lifted a hand and plucked at a curl, tugged, and released. The curl sprang back into place. "... Well, not this."

Her hair was a completely different texture. And Aubree's eyes were brown. She looked nothing like Kaiden.

"Lots of families have different hair and eye colors. Skin colors, too."

"But they don't have a seven-year gap in their ages."

The girl was clever.

"That's not so uncommon. It can happen for a lot of reasons."

"Name one," said Aubree, thumping down a bouquet with enough force to knock off a petal. She plucked that bloom away and added a new one.

"Well," said Bailey, "sometimes couples get pregnant by accident on the first go and other times it doesn't happen for them because of a medical condition with either partner."

Aubree's eyes widened. "Is that true?"

"Yes. The point is, couples can seek medical help. Did your mom have trouble getting pregnant with Mason or Harper?"

Aubree narrowed her eyes and the muscles at her jaw bulged. Then she returned to her work.

Bailey's skin tingled as the pause stretched. She'd touched on something. But what?

"I don't know anything about that."

But the teen wouldn't look at her. And the denial rang false.

"Another reason for physical differences is adoption. If your mom adopted you, you'd look more like your birth parents."

Aubree's reply was abrupt and sharp. "I'm *not* adopted."

"I see." Why was she so hostile? Another nerve touched?

Aubree knew something. And she knew to keep it to herself.

"Well, if you ever want to talk about anything, I'd be glad to. Talk, I mean."

The girl nodded but did not look up.

"There's other reasons I think he's not my dad," said Aubree, her voice now so low that Bailey barely heard her.

"There are?"

"I remember someone. My real dad. I remember him, and he looked and smelled different."

"Different how?"

Aubree gnawed on her lower lip. Finally, she said, "His cheek was stubbly and my dad can barely grow a beard. And I think he had dark hair or something."

"Dark. Not blond?"

"Like mine. Thick, wavy, brown."

"I see. You remember that?"

"I think so."

It was possible, Bailey decided. She could remember a different man, her real father. But why would Eliza keep that from her?

"You think Kaiden isn't your mom's first husband?"

"I don't know. She never said she was married before."

You didn't need to be married to get pregnant. Bailey knew well enough that young girls sometimes found themselves expectant mothers when still just teens. It made her wonder how old Eliza was fifteen years ago.

"Have you asked your mom?"

Aubree grimaced as if even the suggestion caused her discomfort.

"I think I'd start there."

"I tried," said Aubree, bundling another bouquet. "She tells me that Kaiden is my dad and that's that."

"But you don't believe her?"

Aubree shrugged, eyes downcast and fingers nervously tugging on the bow she'd finished tying.

"I see. Well, have you seen your birth certificate?"

"My... No. Never."

"That's a legal document. And it should list both your mother and father's names."

The girl's brow furrowed and Bailey could almost hear Aubree thinking. Finally, she gave a tiny shake of her head. "I don't know where she keeps stuff like that."

"Is there a safe in the house?"

"No."

"Then it's probably in her office in one of those locked filing cabinets. But I can't help you get into those."

But she'd planted the seed and with luck the girl's curiosity would cause her to steal the keys or break in. The trick was being there when that happened, while avoiding blame.

"I know what those sorts of documents look like. I'd be glad to help you."

Aubree stared, her expression giving nothing away. Bailey held on to her placid smile and forced herself not to shift.

When the silence stretched too long, Bailey thought she'd gone too far and that she might just get herself fired before she'd even gotten into the house.

Aubree was suspicious of her offer. What if she told her mother about it?

Regret twisted her stomach, bringing a painful stab.

"Let's get these flowers bundled," said Bailey, smoothly changing the subject. "All a variety or do you make some a single color?"

Aubree's shoulders relaxed and she glanced at the mound of cut flowers. "All one color or three of each color, to total twelve."

"Got it."

Bailey did not speak again but just hummed a tune as they worked on opposite sides of the sorting table. She bundled and used the guillotine-like flower stem cutter. Then she passed the bunch to Aubree, who tied the bouquet and stored them in the buckets of water.

"You guys must have been up early to cut all these," said Bailey.

"Tory does it. Mom doesn't work in the sun any more than she has to. Says it's bad for the skin. Wrinkles."

"Oh, I see. But Tory doesn't mind?"

"What does she care? Sun damage is the least of her worries."

"Really? What do you mean?"

"Her face is already wrinkly and she's... well, she's not very pretty."

"Being pretty is important to some. Not to others."

"It's important to me."

"I think that's true of most young women. Less so to older ones."

"You mean after they get a boyfriend or married or whatever?"

"Not all women marry or want to. Even the ones who have children."

That revelation caused Aubree's mouth to gape.

"Then how... You need a mother and father."

"You need a woman and sperm. That may or may not involve encounters with a man. Not all babies are born into traditional homes of a mother and father. You know that, right?"

"I guess. Yes. I mean, are you talking about a girl that's gotten herself into trouble?"

This made Bailey wonder how much Aubree knew about reproduction and what kind of hell she'd get into if she told her something her mother didn't want her to know.

"That's a common reason. Yes."

The bouquets were arranged and stored in buckets and it was time for Bailey to head back to the office.

Aubree cleared her throat. "I think Mom wants another baby."

SIXTEEN

Why did Aubree think her mother wanted another baby?

Bailey was about to ask the girl to explain, when she heard someone whistling.

Aubree grimaced.

"That's Dad," she said and turned her attention to coiling the twine.

Kaiden appeared in the wide door gripping the handle to an empty cart.

"Mom says to get the flowers... " His words trailed off as he noticed Bailey and cast her a huge smile. "Ah, here's beautiful Bailey."

Aubree's expression turned grim as she muttered, "Being pretty is important to some. Not to others."

No creature on the planet was better at throwing your words back at you than a teenage girl.

"And beauty is an arbitrary metric assigned to a person based on societal norms." Bailey had heard that from her bunk-mate in prison.

Aubree gave her the same look of confusion Bailey had made when she'd first heard this.

Kaiden sauntered in, oblivious, and the three loaded the little wagon.

"Okay. Take 'em to the spring house," said Kaiden to his daughter.

The Watts kept much of the fresh produce and cider in the little stone outbuilding constructed over a natural spring.

Aubree's gaze shifted between them, but she did as she was told. What was making the girl so somber faced?

Kaiden watched Aubree's departure, then stepped up beside Bailey as she brushed cut stem pieces into a trash bin.

Kaiden watched her work, not offering a hand.

"Any plans for a celebration tomorrow?" Bailey asked him.

Kaiden's brow wrinkled, as if the question confused him. "Not that I know of."

Now Bailey was frowning.

"What?" he asked.

"Tomorrow is Mason's birthday. Isn't it?"

"Oh, I don't know their birthdays. She has their real birthdays and then the ones she uses for the video blog. I didn't see a cake inside."

That made sense. Protecting the kids' personal data was wise.

"No, wait. We already shot that," he said.

"So when are their real birthdays?"

Kaiden opened his mouth, glanced toward the ceiling, and then shook his head.

He either didn't know or wasn't willing to share.

"Don't you know?"

He snorted. "Listen, I didn't come in here to talk about the kids."

The kids, he'd said. Not *my* kids.

"Got it."

He rested a hand on the table only inches from her hip.

"Well, then what about your wedding anniversary? You have any special plans?"

Anyone who followed Eliza's posts knew that she and Kaiden were married in mid-June, and celebrated on the solstice.

"We usually have a special dinner on the porch. So I guess we'll do that. Got a month yet. Right?"

He didn't know. Kaiden Watts did not know his kids' birthdays or his wedding anniversary.

On the blog, he always made some incredibly thoughtful gesture for his wife on their anniversary. Out here in real life, he didn't know their plans or what he was making her.

"That'll be nice. Listen, I have to get back to the office."

"What's your hurry?" he asked.

Bailey caught movement and spotted Eliza standing in the doorway. They made eye contact.

"All the flowers loaded?" she asked.

Kaiden startled and jumped away from Bailey as if scorched, then spun around. "Aubree took them."

Eliza flicked her attention to Bailey. "Didn't expect you here."

"I gave Aubree a hand."

"I see. That's why she finished early and without Kaiden's help. But it's also why I can't get any footage of Aubree and her dad bundling flowers."

Bailey's smile vanished like frost in May.

"I'm sorry. I didn't realize."

"You don't have our shooting schedule." Eliza sighed. "But I'll get it to you. It was a nice gesture to help our daughter. Going forward, I'd prefer you get your own work done."

Bailey made a retreat worthy of the confederacy at Gettysburg, scampering off with her tail between her legs.

Once she'd been so anxious to meet Kaiden. Now she thought he might get her fired. Best to stay clear of the man.

She got to work, finishing her lengthy to-do list before leaving the office after six with her first paycheck. The sky put on a beautiful light show. Purple, pink, and orange clouds reflected the waning light and warned of imminent showers.

On her walk home, a cold blast of air confirmed her suspicions. They were in for a storm.

Bailey just made it before the first spattering buffeted her single window as a dark curtain of rain swept over the field.

She stood in the open doorway watching as something brushed her leg. She jumped back, yelping.

The tomcat cast her a glance before zipping in out of the storm. She closed the door as the deluge struck.

The rain pounded the flat roof. The deafening beat was as loud as the percussion section of a college marching band. As the storm buffeted the prefab structure, Bailey wondered how safe this shack might be.

Was it anchored to the ground or just sitting on the concrete blocks? Were the trees far enough back to keep them from cleaving her place in two?

Bailey moved to the center of the room as the howling wind momentarily obliterated the drum of the pelting rain.

That's when the lightning and thunder came together, a seemingly simultaneous flash and boom!

Bones shot under her bed.

Something crashed behind her place.

Trees falling?

It could be a tornado. They had them in Upstate New York. One had laid the trees down like matchsticks.

She dropped to the floor, crawling under her bed with Bones, and hoped her truck was not underwater.

Were Eliza and her kids all right?

Should she go check on them?

The next flash of lightning convinced her to stay put.

The thunder came several beats later. The storm was

moving on. The rain ebbed, less violent now as flashes and booms continued to roll off to the east.

Well, the farm needed the rain. She crawled out to sit on the mattress, facing the window only two feet in front of her. Bones howled from under the bed.

Bailey fished the remains of a leftover burger from the fridge, broke it into pieces and put it on a plate on the floor. A gray paw reached out, dragging the meal under the frame.

"This keeps up and I'm charging you rent."

Bailey was midway through preparing her dinner when a knock came at the door.

She froze and stared at the blue box of macaroni and cheese.

If that was Eliza, she'd see what her assistant was cooking. With one swipe, she knocked it into the sink.

Would she see the cat?

If it were the intruder... She grabbed her walking stick. But he wouldn't knock. Would he?

Bailey went to the window, again wishing there was a peep hole in the door. She couldn't see the front step.

The knock came again, insistent. Louder.

She lifted her walking stick and opened the door, peering out into the night.

SEVENTEEN

Eliza stood on the concrete block that served as a landing, still looking camera ready, with her hair in a loose braid and draped over a fringed knit shawl. A dark green, flowered maxi dress and ankle boots completed the look.

"Hi." Bailey tugged up the stretched-out collar of her sweatshirt feeling drab indeed. "What's up?"

"Just checking on you. Any leaks?"

Bailey stood blocking the door. Which was worse, the cat or the junk food? Oh, the plastic containers. She was so doomed.

"All dry inside?" Eliza asked.

"Yes, so far. Would you like to come in?"

"Just for a minute."

Bailey stepped back as Eliza swept in. She scanned the ceiling for leaks as Bailey checked the floor for a cat. Bones had vanished. Bailey pushed the empty tin further under the bed with her foot.

"Looks good. That's a relief."

"That was some violent storm," said Bailey. "I heard something fall behind me."

"I'll check on that tomorrow. Listen, the Wi-Fi is down, so the cameras are out. Have you seen anyone?"

"Nobody," said Bailey. "Did Richard find anything else out?"

"No. Whoever attacked my daughter is still at large."

"You filed a police report?"

Eliza first looked surprised and then her brow knit.

"Of course I did." It sounded like a lie. Eliza was more proficient at lying than her daughter, so there was no way to tell. "And I apologize for snapping at you about helping Aubree. I was just having a bad day."

"Oh, that's not necessary." Not with the current power dynamic, she thought.

Bailey waited to hear the real reason Eliza was here, because she'd bet a month's pay it wasn't to apologize or to check on her. Was this a good time to get some answers?

"Listen, Aubree told me something, and I think you should know."

"Oh?" Eliza arched a brow, intent in her focus.

After getting such pushback on the homeschooling question, she proceeded with caution.

"She said she doesn't think Kaiden is her real father."

Eliza's head jerked up and she gaped at Bailey, eyes wide with astonishment. At last, she pursed her lips and gave a little shake of her head, dismissing her daughter's concerns.

"Nonsense. Kaiden is their father."

"She's pretty convinced."

"I see. Well, I'll speak to her." Eliza narrowed her eyes. "When did she tell you this?"

"When we were bundling the tulips. She looked upset."

"So she just blurted out, 'Kaiden isn't my father'?"

"Sort of. Yes."

"Teenagers. If they don't have anything to get angsty over, they invent something. I might do a bit on that."

That would be easier than just speaking to her daughter like a mother should, Bailey thought.

"Listen, I just heard from a national morning show." Eliza had finally moved to the reason for her visit.

She mentioned the name of a popular, long running program filmed in New York's Rockefeller Center. Bailey knew it. She doubted anyone with a television wouldn't.

"Wow. That's great!"

"Yes. It's not the first time. But usually, I have longer to prepare. This one is an unexpected vacancy they need to fill. Someone dropped out and they asked me. But it's tomorrow at nine. I wondered if I could convince you to watch the kids, while I make that appearance."

Tomorrow. Her one day off.

"It's a big ask, but we could really use the appearance fee, and it will give my feeds a boost. Always does."

"My place is a little small for four."

"Oh, no. You'd be at the house."

Elation welled inside Bailey and she nearly jumped in joy. Instead, she pressed a hand over her thumping heart.

"Of course. I'd be glad to help. What time?"

Eliza gave her the details and shoved off. Bailey returned to the congealed, neon-yellow mess she'd fixed for dinner.

The house! Tomorrow, she was invited into the Watts' inner sanctum.

She'd get more answers and one step closer to Eliza's inner circle.

* * *

The alarm woke her at five. Groaning, Bailey rolled toward the table that was only an arm's length away and silenced her phone. Her eyes popped open.

Sunday morning. The talk show.

She threw the bedding aside and flew through her morning prep as Bones demanded to be fed, to go out, and then come back in.

Did she now own a cat?

Bailey arrived at the Watts' home thirty minutes later and found the house ablaze with light and Kaiden's truck missing again.

Was filming his only reason for being here?

She knocked and Aubree let her in wearing a plastic cape, like the ones used in hair salons.

"Thank goodness. Mason is driving us crazy," she said. And then over her shoulder, "Mom! Bailey's here."

The reply was muffled, but Aubree stepped aside and Bailey crossed the threshold. She was finally inside.

The foyer held the familiar red bench with the spindles and the long back. Made by the Amish down in Pennsylvania, according to Eliza's posts. Above it was the row of pegs. Each held a coat and the rainbow of fabrics delighted. Below the bench were cubbies and baskets for the kids' shoes and wellies.

She paused to take it all in. The wide pine floors glowed. This hall led straight to the back door and centered the house with the dining room left and the living room right. The rag carpet and red bench brightened the narrow space. She knew every piece of furniture in the living room, from the couch to the armchair where Eliza did her quilting and embroidery. Beyond the dining room, the busy open kitchen awaited.

Bailey frowned. The living room was picture perfect only on one side, the side she always saw in the posts. Opposite the couch were silver reflector umbrellas on tripods, lights on stands, and clamps.

To the right was a rack filled with clothing. Boxes and baskets held hats, slippers, and shoes. Their wardrobe department.

On the shelves sat art supplies, paper, wooden toys, and a few children's books.

Properties department, she realized as she followed Aubree into the kitchen.

Here again the room seemed flawless on the side that held the worktable, stove, and window facing the backyard's enormous maple tree. But on the other side, between the electric heater and the microwave, the counter was piled with pots and baking equipment. The ingredients stored in mason jars on open shelving beside the farmhouse sink made a picturesque backdrop, but the real storage existed on this opposite side, as did a canvas captain's chair. And beside it...

Was that a television?

It was. And a laptop with a large monitor. The television was muted but already on a prime-time station showing the morning news preceding the program Eliza would be appearing on.

No wonder she didn't want employees in here. This was a stage set. Not a home.

Aubree lifted Harper down from the chair and took a seat.

"Bailey, take them upstairs," said Eliza. "They can play quietly in either of the two front rooms. Not Aubree's. We are live at nine-thirteen for six minutes. I need absolutely no interruptions during that time. Is that clear?"

"Yes. I understand." Her head was bobbing as if on a spring.

"Okay you two, off you go with Bailey. You mind her. You hear?" Something in her tone made both children stop wiggling and stand at attention.

"Yes, Mama," they said in unison.

"Go on."

Bailey ushered them out but turned back to see Eliza applying makeup to Aubree's pretty face. Subtle, expertly employed. The girl would not look washed out, but rosy and fresh as the flowers at their farm stand.

Mason headed up the stairs that had once appeared in a Christmas morning bit with the little ones peering through the spindles.

"Are we going to your bedroom, Mason?" asked Bailey.

Mason stopped and scowled at her question. Didn't he want to play in his room?

"But Mommy said we could play upstairs," said Harper.

Confusion followed. Bailey trailed after Harper who was ascending behind Mason, using her hands and feet, as if she were a quadruped.

"Let's go to the farmer's room," said Mason. "Okay, Harper? We can play board games."

"Yeah!" Then she paused. "And dress up."

Mason did not object, but neither did he agree as they reached the landing. Bailey followed the pair into one of the bedrooms.

In the doorway, she scanned the interior and sucked in a breath.

Bailey knew this space so well. But this was not what she expected.

It wasn't a bedroom. At least not like any bedroom she'd ever seen.

EIGHTEEN

Just like in the kitchen and living room, only half of Mason's room held furniture. The other half was more tripods, lights, and reflecting screens.

From the doorway the room seemed split down the middle. One half was a colorful boy's room with a bed, desk, shelving, and a toy box. The murals showcased farm life, beautifully illustrated in bold colors. His father had crafted his "big boy" bed to resemble a horse stall, complete with the correct hardware.

Had that really been five years ago?

There wasn't a single wrinkle or fold in the log cabin quilt on the mattress. The pillowcases matched the red and yellow covers. His beloved blue dog sat next to a purple elephant. The pair seemed to be having a conversation.

"Did you make your bed, Mason?"

"I make it every morning," he said.

"You did a fantastic job."

"Oh, that's not my bed," he said casually and hurried to the shelving behind a silver square reflector, selecting one of the board games.

This wasn't a boy's room. It was another set.

"I want Candyland," said Harper.

"That's for babies," replied Mason. "You can pick next."

Harper folded her arms and Bailey prepared for a tantrum as the child's upper lip was protruding and her scowl darkening by the minute.

Eliza's warning replayed in her mind. Could a tantrum be picked up downstairs at the other end of the house?

But before Bailey could intervene, Mason nipped the approaching storm in the bud.

"You make a sound and we'll never be allowed to play here again."

Harper's arms fell to her sides. She cast a worried look toward the hallway. Then she trotted across the carpet, which covered exactly half the room, and closed the door so quietly, you would think there was a hungry carnivore out there.

She turned, index finger to her pursed lips, and made a shushing sound as she returned to her brother.

The game Mason selected, with its bright purple box sporting a well-fed panda, did not fit Eliza's standard for children's toys. In fact, none of the out-of-sight games, puzzles, or toys fit. There was molded plastic everywhere.

"Non-sustainable," muttered Bailey, confused. "Where's your chalkboard?" she asked Mason.

"It's in the hall," he said.

Yet the board always appeared to be in this room. On the side never shown.

"Wanna play?" asked Harper.

"Of course. I love games. And I'm good at outdoor games like hide-and-seek and kick-the-can."

"We don't have those," said Mason. He set down the game box and removed little yellow, pink, and green plastic parts.

Bailey frowned. Hadn't they ever played hide-and-seek?

Harper snatched a tiny plastic panda from the box.

"Hey!" shouted Mason.

Harper put her finger to her lips.

Mason dropped his voice to a whisper. "That's not a toy. It's a game piece. Give it."

Harper did not. But she did place it correctly, next to a small plastic farmer, which seemed to placate Mason.

These two were just normal kids, Bailey realized, squabbling and trying to get their needs met.

"Let's play," she said, determined to be the perfect sitter.

Over the next half-hour, they played a game in which a farmer tried to grow bamboo to feed a hungry panda. It was pretty fun.

Eliza was a hypocrite and now Bailey wanted to know where the kids really slept, played, and studied.

After the game was stowed away, Bailey asked to see the chalkboard.

Mason led them to the hallway, pointing.

"I'm only allowed to color inside the lines. I did this one." Mason pointed to a childlike version of Morris. "Mostly inside the lines."

He gave the artwork a critical stare.

Now that she looked at it, she saw this was too good for a boy who was almost eight.

"Does Mommy do the drawings, and you color them in?"

"Or Aubree. I'll get to when I'm older. Maybe."

"I can't touch it," said Harper.

The girl stared up at the board, which tugged at Bailey's heart. Imagine having all these chalks and this huge board and never being allowed to create.

Belatedly, Harper added, "Or else."

Bailey's brows lifted as she wondered what "or else" looked like to the Watts kids. An image of her father's belt caused her to shudder.

"A time out?" she asked.

"In our bedroom," Harper said, as if this were a terrible fate.

"I see. Where is your bedroom?"

Mason took that one. "Back of the house."

"Back? You mean downstairs?" Bailey's curiosity was eating her alive. "Can we go see them?"

"I don't want to," said Harper.

"I wanna stay up here," said Mason.

The double no from her two charges told her much about their actual bedrooms.

"Well, what do they look like?"

"It's just one," said Mason, heading back to his stage bedroom.

"One room? For both of you?"

"And Aubree. She has the bed. I've got the top bunk," said Mason, seeming to have some pride in this.

"Mine is bottom," admitted Harper, who looked sad but then brightened. "But if I do this..." She rolled to her back and kicked in the air. "I can make Mason's whole body jump off the mattress."

"Well, that's some consolation."

"What does that mean?"

"It means you don't get what you want but you get something else instead."

"No top bunk but kicking consolation?" asked Harper.

"Exactly." She was a bright little girl.

"Dress up!" said Harper.

Bailey followed the pair to Harper's room and found it much the same. A half-perfect fantasy bedroom with expertly crafted murals of butterflies that she now suspected were not painted by either Aubree or Eliza. And the enormous playhouse. But when Bailey approached this, Harper captured her hand and tugged.

"It's just for looking unless Mommy is filming."

No wonder the child seemed so delighted when she got to

play in her playhouse. She was rarely given leave to enjoy the custom-built play area.

Bailey continued down the hall.

Aubree's room had dust on the study desk and though perfectly made, this bed also had not been slept in.

She wondered what Eliza's patrons and sponsors would do if they knew the truth?

The NDA now made a lot more sense.

Where did Eliza keep her children, when they weren't being adorable for her fans? Bailey set her jaw, determined to find out.

NINETEEN

Mason had already refused to show her their bedrooms, but Bailey needed answers.

"Hey, Mason, can you show me where you guys really sleep?"

Mason shook his head. His lips were pursed as if he was sorry to disappoint her.

"Mom said stay upstairs."

"That's okay. Another time. Right?"

"Right," he agreed, and his face brightened with relief.

They headed back down the hall to Mason's film set, as Bailey had decided to think of it.

All these years, she'd been so eager to get on the inside track, see Eliza's perfect life and if the woman who was an internet phenomenon was as happy as she appeared.

But Bailey saw nothing but smoke and mirrors. This house, this farm, this world didn't really exist. Eliza's kids were no better or worse than anyone's children.

And no more precious.

Fate could be cruel. Bailey knew that. Did Eliza?

Or had she skated out of trouble at every turn and glided into a life she had not earned and did not deserve?

Bailey and the kids played another board game, Harper's pick this time. Mason was cheating, but he was cheating to help Harper win, so Bailey did not intercede.

Though cheating to help someone you loved was still cheating. And there should be consequences for not following the rules—but Bailey knew that was often not the case.

Mason straightened and turned toward the closed door.

Bailey heard it next, the sound of footsteps. Why was Mason so alert to his mother's approach?

There was a gentle tapping on the door.

"You guys okay in there?" That was Eliza's voice.

"Come in," said Bailey.

Harper leapt to her feet and danced across the room as the door opened.

"All finished. You can come downstairs for breakfast."

Bailey glanced at her phone. It was nearly ten, late for breakfast but early for lunch. Had these kids not had anything to eat yet?

Mason followed his sister out of sight.

"You guys have a good time?" asked Eliza.

"Oh, great. They love the games."

Eliza frowned. "You played the ones on this side of the room? Unfortunate. I'm trying to get them to appreciate sustainable products."

"Oh, I didn't know."

She shrugged. "As long as they stay out of sight when we're filming."

"It's like a different world," said Bailey.

Eliza pinned her with a critical stare. "Most things aren't to be taken at face value. My followers want the fantasy. Down-home wisdom, hard work bringing fair rewards. Happy kids. Happy families. As it should be. Don't you think?"

And so rarely is. But Bailey forced a smile. "That's exactly what I was thinking."

"We need room to film and I need a place that is camera ready. These spaces fit the bill."

"And they are charming."

"Did they draw on the chalkboard?"

"No. Neither one."

Eliza exhaled a breath. "Oh, great. I forgot to tell you not to let them and was worried about it during shooting. Silly, isn't it, what your brain latches on to?"

"It is."

Bailey's brain had latched on to one thing for nine years. Sometimes the sentiments moved to the back of her mind, but they were always there with her memories. Her stomach twitched, absorbing the gut-punch of recollections.

"Would you like to join us for breakfast?"

* * *

After their brunch, Kaiden appeared. Had he been filmed for the talk show segment?

"RV is all packed," he said.

Were they going on a camping trip? That might give Bailey time to do some exploring. The back of the house was high on her curiosity list.

She glanced at the back door, checking for a security system and cataloging the lock. Deadbolt. Very secure.

"Oh, great. Thanks, Kaiden." Eliza barely glanced at her husband before turning to her assistant.

Bailey sat at Eliza's table with her kids, as she'd always imagined. Here, amid this family, she saw her efforts rewarded.

"Bailey, I'd like you to handle replies on the posts tomorrow. I'll be out of range."

"Oh, certainly."

"Do you think you know my online voice well enough to mimic me for a day?"

She could replace Eliza for much longer.

"I mean, I think I could handle one day and then you can read my replies and see if I pass muster."

Eliza nodded. That answer satisfied her. It was tentative and held just the right amount of willingness to try, without sounding overly cocky.

Bailey thought she understood her boss better now, which *should* make everything easier.

"Great."

And given a few more inches of slack, she'd be in that tempting, unknown section of the house.

What was she hiding there?

"If you're back in time from your day off, I'd like you to meet us. I need some video shot with the entire family and I'd like a pan instead of stationary footage."

That was a hiccup. The morning of her day off had been spent babysitting and now her boss wanted her evening, too. Normally, Bailey would not be so accommodating. But this was Eliza Watts.

"You want me to drive to the state park?" Camping trips were always to an unnamed New York state park. She knew the lakefront, primitive campsite, and trails from the videos.

Kaiden snorted. "There's no state park."

Bailey frowned, confused.

"We don't drive to a park. Don't even leave the property. Draws too much attention."

Bailey could just imagine the commotion if even a tiny percent of Eliza's fans spotted the Watts in the wild. The theories on which park the Watts family used was always a hot topic in the Coop Group, Eliza's group chat and the Coop Chicks page. They weren't even close.

"We just move the Ultra Van to the river and set up there.

With the right angle, Schoharie Creek looks like a lake. Then I cut in footage from the state park up in Cooperstown. As long as the lighting is a match, it works."

"I see."

So the kids never went camping? They never took that beautiful vintage motorhome anywhere but to the river and back. Did they ever leave the farm?

"Easier to have everyone sleep in their beds. You know? And we can film lunch, then a costume change, and breakfast. After that we film some bits at the water, Finally, it's dinner and the campfire. Then we just walk on back. Afterwards, I post them in the correct order: dinner, fire, breakfast, and lunch."

Bailey's grandmother would call that a busman's holiday.

"Clever. What time would you like me to arrive?"

"Oh, whenever you get back is fine."

"Super." She turned back to her breakfast, discovering that the cold butter just tore the flapjacks. Other offerings included soggy apple fritters and leftover cinnamon rolls topped with honey from the hives and most of which now sat on the serving plate instead of on the buns.

Some food just did not do well when served cold.

Mason and Harper had no trouble polishing off their servings and asking for more milk. Bailey frowned at the earthy taste of the milk, eyeing her glass with suspicion.

"Don't like it?" asked Aubree.

"Weird. Kind of tangy. Is it all right?" Bailey said in a low tone, as Eliza zipped to the refrigerator to retrieve the pitcher of milk.

"Yeah. That's how it always tastes. Goats' milk isn't cows' milk so it's more..."

"Stinky," offered Harper.

"What's stinky?" asked their mom, returning with the milk and pouring some into Harper's glass.

"Mason," said Harper, pointing, and she toppled the glass.

Aubree mopped up the spill.

Eliza scowled and righted the glass, then poured half a portion. "Now you use two hands like a big girl."

"I am a big girl."

Harper was right. If not for her home schooling, she'd already be in kindergarten.

But she wasn't. She was here with her mom taking trips to nowhere and sleeping in some place other than her bedroom.

"Big girls don't spill their milk," said Eliza.

Her criticism wiped the smile from Harper's face. The child now looked on the verge of tears.

Eliza pressed a fist to her hip, narrowing her eyes on her youngest. "They also do not cry over spilled milk."

Harper's chin sunk another inch. Eliza turned away, summoning a bright smile for her assistant.

"All finished?" asked Eliza, not waiting for a reply before collecting Bailey's plate. "I'll see you later at the river. Thanks again for watching the little ones for me."

"I'm not little," insisted Harper, pounding one fist on the table and sending her syrupy fork flying.

Bailey rose. "Thank you for breakfast."

She headed out. If the family were still at the river tomorrow, she might explore the inner sanctum of the house. Her curiosity had already caused her a few missteps. She needed to be patient.

She had been so preoccupied, she didn't hear someone following her from the house until the screen door slapped closed. Bailey turned and found Kaiden.

"You want to see the inside of the Ultra Van?" he asked.

Her mind went instantly to the bed she knew was in there. Was he propositioning her?

"I guess I'll see it later on when I meet you guys."

"Eliza will be tied up for at least an hour. We've got time, you know. For a tour."

He lifted a strand of her hair and slid his fingers down the lock, then tucked it behind her ear. The intimacy of the touch made her shiver.

His gesture left no doubt what kind of tour he was planning.

"I don't think so."

Kaiden's eyes brightened at this refusal. Either he liked a challenge or did not understand the concept of consent.

"You sure?"

She arched a brow and nodded. "Positive."

"Why is that?"

"You're married to my boss."

His grin widened as he shook his head. She thought his reaction signaled disappointment until he spoke.

"I'm not married."

Now Bailey felt off balance as perception and information collided.

"What are you talking about?"

"Eliza and me, we aren't married."

TWENTY

Bailey tried to process Kaiden's shocking claim.

They were the perfect couple, for goodness' sake. Just how naïve did he think she was?

"That's crazy."

He grasped her ponytail and draped it over one shoulder.

"Not crazy. We aren't married because I'm hired help. Just like you."

She opened her mouth, then shut it again as she calculated the chances he was telling her the truth.

"She hired a husband?"

"Now you're getting it."

"Do her kids know?"

They called him Daddy and not just when Eliza was filming a video.

"Naw. They think I'm their pa. I've been working here since before she had a blog. Just coming around a couple times a week. Her dad had just passed. Bought the farm and then bought the farm." He laughed.

Bailey did not, because joking about losing a loved one just wasn't funny.

Kaiden's mouth twisted, disappointed at her lack of reaction, she supposed.

"Second longest running employee behind Tory. How about that?"

"When was this?"

"Oh, before Mason was born, so six years, I guess."

"Mason is nearly eight."

"Okay."

"She hired you as a husband?"

"Nope. Handyman. After her dad died, Aubree started calling me Daddy. It just sort of happened."

"Just happened."

He grinned. "She wants her kid to think she was mine. Male role model, she said. I have acting experience. It worked out and so she kept me."

"Doesn't that bother you? Deceiving them this way?"

"She pays me enough for me not to care. There is no job in this county that pays what she does. Gives me a raise each year, too. And a bonus."

"But why?"

"Doesn't want her kids to grow up without a dad. Or doesn't want the trouble of a husband, I guess. I don't know. None of my business."

"How old was Aubree when this started?"

He used his hand to show how tall she had been. "Four or five, I guess."

"You don't know their ages or birthdays. Do you?"

He scowled at her accusation.

"Why should I? They're not mine."

His callous disregard landed badly, further tarnishing his image.

"I know what she needs me to know. Why're you so interested in all this anyway?"

Bailey wasn't answering that question. But she added her own.

"But you don't live here. Doesn't that bother them?"

"Why should it? They don't know any better. They hardly ever leave this place. So they wouldn't know if a daddy lives with a mommy or not."

"She told me you have construction work elsewhere."

"That's what Aubree thinks, too. Imagine being nearly sixteen and never having been on the internet or had a date or any friends."

"Fifteen."

"What?"

"Aubree turns fifteen in December."

"Whatever. Anyway, it's like they're in prison here."

Prison? No, this was nothing like prison.

"Won't last though," he added.

"What do you mean?"

"Aubree's growing up. Defying her mom. Testing the limits and sneaking off."

Bailey already knew this. And her relationship with Aubree was strengthening.

Kaiden continued speaking, thumbs now tucked in the belt loops of his tight jeans.

"Once, she even stowed away in the bed of my pickup. Brought her right home, though. Don't need to get arrested for transporting a minor, though she is growing." He smiled in a way that gave Bailey chills.

"She's fourteen!"

"Relax. I can count to eighteen, all right."

Bailey grimaced, wrinkling her nose. This man, he wasn't the Kaiden she knew and had come to admire.

"Are you telling me the truth?"

He raised his right hand. "God's honest."

"Would Eliza want me to know all this?"

"She never told me not to tell you. I don't talk about what I do here. I mean, folks in town know I don't live here. And I don't live around here, so it's not a problem."

"And that's why you're hitting on me? You aren't married?"

"And because you're so darn pretty."

She ignored that, waving away his words as if they caused an odor.

"Doesn't change anything. We're both her employees and if she sees me messing with you, she'll fire me."

"Then don't let her see you." His smirk and confidence irked her.

"That's a hard no," she said.

"She won't care. I know that from experience. She does not care what I do or who I do it with as long as the kids don't find out about it."

He let that settle in, her reaction the same as when she stumbled into a spider's web and the sticky strands adhered to her face. She wiped her cheeks with both hands and stepped back.

"I'm real good in the sack. How old are you? Twenty-one? She said you just finished some internship or something."

Bailey didn't answer.

He extended his arms and glanced down at himself as if wondering if she was seeing what he was seeing. He was still incredibly sexy. But her opinion of him sank each time he spoke. Before starting here, she might have taken him up on his offer. But she had other fish to fry, and he was just another one of Eliza's props.

"Listen, you're not my type."

"How you figure?" he said.

"Every time I talk to you, I feel like I need a shower afterwards."

He grinned. "I'd love to wash your back."

"I'm not playing hard to get. I'm playing leave me alone. Got it?"

He pushed his cap back and tilted his head, brows lifted, giving her one more chance to change her mind.

"Sure. Sure. I don't sleep where I'm not wanted. Though I don't think we'd do much sleeping. You be sure to let me know if you change your mind."

"Will do."

He turned back to the house.

"Hey, Kaiden?"

He glanced over his shoulder in a move that seemed rehearsed. "Change your mind already?"

She ignored that. "Do you know who Harper or Mason's real father is?"

He shook his head. "No idea." He tapped his chin with his index finger, seeming to think back. "She came with her dad when Aubree was a little kid. No guy. Her dad was some advertising guy in NYC. He's the one bought her this place. I got that from Tory. Fresh start, I guess."

"And she has no other... attachments?"

"I've never seen another man here."

"Never?"

He shook his head.

That seemed odd. Didn't she get lonely? There were several reasons a woman of Eliza's age avoided men. Being married was only one.

And since coming here, she'd had two more children. Hard to do without a man around.

"But she was pregnant with Harper while you worked here, Mason, too. Didn't you ever ask her?"

"Eliza doesn't like personal questions, and I like this job. So, no. I never asked. You should take a page from my script or you'll be like the rest of her assistants. Gone with the frost."

Good advice, but she wasn't here to make employee of the month.

"What'd you do before coming to work here?"

"Stage actor. Or I tried to be. Did some Off-Broadway work. Played Pippin once. Joined a traveling production. Crappy engagement. Low budget. Always on the road. Terrible housing. No medical. Never thought I'd land this kind of banging gig."

"How did you?"

"I grew up around here. Saw the advertisement for a handyman. Did a few small jobs here. Built their first coop. Wired the barn." He stared at the production barn. "But now I got my own fan base. Not that she lets me chat with any of them. Won't let me even see my mailing list. Now you talk about underage, you should see the posts and offers she had to block."

Bailey had seen them, of course.

"Those girls wouldn't turn down the prize bull in the pasture."

She met his stare. "You ever sleep with Eliza?"

He gave a slow shake. "Not for lack of trying. But I respect a no trespassing sign, yours included."

Kaiden pinched his cap between his thumb and first finger and gave her a little tip and bow.

"Excuse me now. Gotta run a few strays to the shelter." He thumbed toward his truck where she could see the tops of several wire cages.

Her heart gave a little lurch. "A gray tabby?"

"Two mutts. And Ginger had her kittens. We got the reels. And their eyes are open, so off they go."

She released her breath. Bones was safe for now. And kittens usually fared well. As for the mutts, their chances were not as good.

She headed to her truck, dragged by sadness for the abandoned pets and again seeing behind the veil. This man was also of Eliza's making. The fun-loving, charming father and devoted husband did not exist.

An actor. She'd hired a handsome, stupid man as her surrogate husband. And all she demanded was he keep away from the social media accounts and her bed.

Kaiden just told her that Eliza came here when Aubree was quite young, which made her wonder. If Kaiden wasn't Harper and Mason's father, who was?

TWENTY-ONE

Bailey was halfway to her truck when Eliza's text landed, and her stomach dropped. How much more of her day off was her boss planning to commandeer?

She had to backtrack to the house passing Aubree, who dunked a stick and string tool into a dishpan of sudsy water. Eliza took some still shots as Aubree made enormous soap bubbles that Harper and Mason chased across the sun-drenched yard.

Bailey called a greeting.

"Did you need something from the store?" asked Bailey, anxious to start her one day a week off. It was already nearly noon.

Eliza motioned Bailey to the porch.

"I know I said whenever you got back was fine. But could you be back by five?"

And there it was. The creeping theft of her one day away. Her annoyance battled with her need to get closer to this family.

"I... Sure."

"Great. Just walk straight across the fields to the river," said

Eliza.

"Will do."

"Wonderful. Enjoy your time off."

She had to be back in just over five hours.

Bailey turned to go, then hesitated, thinking of what Kaiden had alleged and what Aubree surmised. Should she tell Eliza?

"Something wrong?" asked her boss.

Bailey considered carefully whether to share what Kaiden had told her and if this information might cause her any backlash. She wanted answers and that meant taking calculated risks. Winding Kaiden up might be worth the gamble.

"Actually... yes. Kaiden told me that he's not the kids' father. That he's a hired actor."

Eliza's hands rolled to fists, landing on her hips.

"He never said that."

"His words were, 'Never thought I'd land this kind of banging gig.'"

Now Eliza's mouth puckered tight as her gaze cut to the barnyard, in time to see Kaiden drive off.

"He was hitting on you. Right?"

Bailey nodded.

"And when you reminded him that he was married..."

Bailey nodded again. "He told me."

"Moron." Eliza huffed. Then she leaned against the whitewashed rail.

Bailey let the pus run out of the wound. No sense poking until it drained a bit.

Halfway across the yard, Eliza's younger kids danced, chasing bubbles.

Finally, Eliza threw up one hand in surrender.

"It's true, he's an actor, and also true that he'll chase anything with a vagina."

"I see."

Eliza folded one arm and rested her chin on the opposite palm, as if even the thought of him gave her a toothache.

"I'd fire him, but he's good with the kids. I pay him to be good, but from their perspective they have an attentive dad."

"But it's acting. Don't you think that will blow up in your face? Aubree already suspects."

Her boss's gaze tracked to her eldest girl. "She's too smart for her own good."

Bailey tried again. "When your kids find out—"

Eliza cut her off. "They aren't *going* to find out. He and I have agreed on a settlement. Once they're grown, of course."

"They'll still want to see him."

"The settlement includes his funeral."

Bailey gaped, speechless.

"Don't worry, they'll be adults. That means I have to put up with him for another ten years or so."

"But you're deceiving your followers. Your fans all believe he's their father. Isn't this illegal?"

Eliza stiffened. "It's not illegal for me to provide a two-parent home. To give my kids a decent male role model. They'd understand that."

"Would they, though?"

She glared at Bailey.

"And what happens to Kaiden? He can't audition for other parts. He's too recognizable."

"If he isn't as stupid as he looks, he'll be fine. Plus, no one who follows me would ever recognize him."

"How do you know that?"

"Well, he's not blond, for one thing. And he doesn't have blue eyes. Hair dye and contacts. And with the severance, he'll never have to work again."

Which meant the story about not being solvent was also a lie.

The silence stretched and Eliza pushed from the rail.

"So what will it cost me?" Eliza asked.

"Excuse me?"

"For your discretion on this matter. How much?"

"Oh." Now Bailey straightened. "That's not... I mean, I wasn't trying to—"

"But you will. You'll start thinking, how much is she paying Kaiden? Not his real name, by the way. And what will he get?" Eliza scrubbed her knuckles over her sharp jawline. "And then you'll think, 'I'm not getting enough to keep all this quiet.' And then you'll demand a raise, or worse, try and sell your little story. Remember, you signed an NDA."

"I don't think an NDA covers fraud."

She aimed a finger at Bailey. "If you whisper a word to anyone, you will be very sorry. I will haul your ass into court. You'll lose... everything."

Bailey backed down. Though really, she had nothing to lose.

"I don't want a payout or a raise."

"Well, what then?"

"The truth about their fathers, I guess."

"Tell-all book?" Eliza guessed.

"No, never. I just want to help here, and knowing this will help me be there for you."

Eliza deliberated, her eyes looking off in the distance. Finally, her gaze tipped down to her laced fingers, twisting as if writhing in pain.

"All right." She glanced at Bailey, her mouth grim. "They don't have a father. At least not in the traditional sense."

"I don't understand."

She made a humming sound in her throat... or was that a growl?

"I use a sperm bank and the same donor. All I know is that he was a pre-med student at Boston University in the early 2000s and free of genetic mutations. They shared a childhood photo and voice recording with me. Mason looks a lot like him."

Bailey didn't know what she expected, but this was not it.

"But why hire a man to impersonate their dad?"

She shook her head. "I didn't want them to grow up without one. A male presence is important for child development."

So was an education, thought Bailey, but she kept this observation to herself.

"And since we have such an active following, it's easier to not raise the debate over the decision to be a single mother. IVF is controversial, still. And I don't want any backlash on my kids because of my decision to do this alone."

"I think that's wise and brave."

That stopped Eliza for a moment. This woman did not have a confidant. Bailey wondered if she could be that to Eliza. She didn't trust her boss but that didn't have to be a two-way road.

"Brave? Really?"

"Yes. And Aubree's father? You used the same donor for her?"

Eliza hesitated at Bailey's question.

Knowing an answer beforehand made it easy to find out how honest a person was.

"Yes."

And there it was.

The lie.

She didn't know who Harper and Mason's donor was. But she knew Aubree's father. And that man could not be Harper and Mason's daddy.

"Thanks for being honest with me," said Bailey. "You don't know how important that is. I'll see you later."

"Bye now," said Eliza, still giving her assistant a critical stare.

Bailey left the property. She swung by the library, got her card, and rented the maximum number of DVDs allowed. A web search for Eliza's hired husband yielded nothing. After a quick trip to the grocery store, she returned to the farm.

Bailey spotted Eliza and Tory in the flower fields. The tulips were falling apart, bright petals everywhere. And, for reasons she didn't understand, they were snipping off the flowers but leaving the leaves.

If Eliza was in the fields, who was watching the kids? Kaiden's truck was still gone. Did Aubree have to do all the babysitting in addition to the homeschooling?

She'd already discovered there were no lavish, adorable bedrooms. No farm-fresh meals. No devoted father. No camping trips to the lake. So was it possible there was also no school?

That crossed the line. Bailey knew it.

Parents were given a great deal of leeway when it came to educating their kids, but they did have to meet a minimum standard.

Judging from the list Aubree had written, Eliza was failing in her duties as a parent. But supposition was not fact.

Denying a child an education would be enough to call child protective services. Have Eliza charged with neglect. Ruin her reputation as an all-star child-rearing expert, destroy her endorsement deals and put a major hole in her merch sales.

But, according to Aubree, such reporting got the last assistant fired.

Right now, the kids were alone in the house. Bailey calculated the risk. Harper would tell her mother if she saw Bailey. She was right at that age when tattling was as tempting as chocolate ice cream. Would Aubree tell?

She didn't think so.

What were the chances of getting inside and not being seen by any of them?

Bailey transferred her groceries to the ATV and drove to her place. There on the step was a cooler. Inside she found soft cheese, eggs, butter, and a glass bottle of milk. Goats' milk. She made a face. Maybe Bones would drink it. She collected the lot and stowed them with the rest.

On the return trip she spotted Kaiden's truck in the lot. She cut the ATV's engine as Eliza left the house, camera out, recording a bit with Harper and Mason.

Filming their departure. Aubree waved from within the van and Kaiden tooted the horn. Eliza laughed and loaded the little ones.

"We're all packed up!" she said to her mobile device.

The house was empty.

Bailey waited but they didn't pull away. Instead, Eliza and her kids exited the RV and walked toward the river as Kaiden drove down the road. When the dust settled, Bailey glanced at her phone. Twenty-nine minutes. That was how long she had to check the house and then get to the river.

She left the ATV, grabbed her walking stick, and ran the distance to the house, approaching from the railing away from the security camera at the door. This side trip took her a full minute and she was panting and out of breath when she reached the window they often left cracked open.

It was shut.

At the juncture of cool glass and the upper framing, Bailey pushed. The window slid up.

Crouching, Bailey ducked inside and then crept along the edge of the room, avoiding the entrance to the kitchen and the security camera above the sink. For a second she waited at the top of the stairs, but then headed for the new addition, hurrying through the living room and through the door that led to the corridor beyond. There were doors on both sides. Bailey chose the one on the left.

The door swung open and so did Bailey's mouth.

"What in the world?"

TWENTY-TWO

Bailey stared into Eliza's massive bedroom. The space looked like it belonged to a teenage boy gamer, rather than an organic farm influencer.

Against the wall of windows sat a laptop, secondary keyboard, and a series of three large connected screens in a curving multiple monitor arrangement. She prayed that none of those had a webcam with a motion sensor. A headset looped over the back of the massager chair and a microphone on a stand sat behind the keyboard.

Unlike Eliza's public space, the smoked glass desktop was littered with scraps of paper and cheap ballpoint pens.

Opposite the computer setup sat a queen-sized bed, unmade, and a recliner half-buried under clothing. Between the two was a doorway and a glimpse of a counter and sink. Bailey stepped closer.

The bathroom smelled of bleach and lemons and was appointed like one in a luxury hotel with a large soaker tub, a towel warmer, ample counter space cluttered with makeup and beauty products, a walk-in shower, and a toilet with controls that seemed to do everything imaginable.

"Fancy," said Bailey.

Eliza kept the rewards of her success tucked well out of sight in this private sanctuary and control center that could not have contrasted more sharply to her public spaces.

Instead of earth mother, this room cried start-up techie.

She took a mental measure of the bathroom and guessed it stretched out behind the end of the hallway.

A glance at her phone showed she had only fourteen minutes before she needed to head to the river.

Bailey hurried across the hall, turning the knob, but the door did not budge. A quick inspection showed a deadbolt fixed to the outside of the frame.

Did Eliza lock her kids in? Beyond being incredibly dangerous, it was also cruel.

She flipped back the bolt and entered a room half the size of Eliza's. The one window leaked sunlight along the edges of the drawn curtains. She flipped on the light.

Here she found no colorful murals, wooden toys, or homemade bedframes.

Instead, the walls were painted white. A single overhead light with a cheap plastic cover illuminated the interior.

A bunk bed, on the left, poked halfway across the room. A single bed squatted under the window.

She lifted a yellowing stuffed rabbit from Mason's top bunk. Most of its fur had worn off and two black buttons replaced the original eyes. Mason's real favorite toy, Bailey decided. The one featured on the blog was cuter, newer, less well loved, and for sale in the shop.

Bailey wondered what he called it.

These beds were made. Each had a single pillow, white sheets, a blanket, and an old quilt. It felt familiar.

She didn't want to remember, but her mind took her back to that other top bunk.

They held Bailey in the county jail for less than a month. She never contacted her parents, of course. No point. There would be no help there.

Why she had thought her correctional officer or the army would help her was a mystery. They didn't. Just slapped her with an OTH Discharge the same day the verdict came in. *Other than Honorable*, the army's way of washing their hands of her.

It took less than ninety minutes for the verdict to come in.

Bailey didn't hear most of what was said past the high-pitched ringing in her ears. But she felt the cuffs go on.

Transfer and processing happened the next day and she left the clean dormitory-style room in the jail for federal prison which was so far north it was practically in Canada.

Everything there was different. Older, dirtier, and louder than jail. The clanging and shouting accompanied her as the guards escorted her along the concrete floor.

She shivered in the thin T-shirt and beige short-sleeved jumpsuit.

"Prisoner, stop," ordered the guard to her left. The second

opened the barred metal door. The paint where the correctional officer placed her hand was worn away to the exposed metal.

How long did it take to rub away all the paint?

"In you go," said the officer holding open the door.

She didn't want to. The urge to run welled as she rocked to her toes. It was illogical. She knew it. There was nowhere to run.

"In. Now!" The officer's voice had lost its laconic note of boredom and sounded annoyed.

Bailey stepped into the cell.

Her new cellmate eyed her from the bottom bunk as Bailey stood holding her bedding, socks, underwear, second T-shirts, and blanket, all stuffed in a single pillowcase. There were two pillows on her bunkmate's bed and none on hers.

Behind her, the cell door clicked shut with more force than necessary.

The odor of unwashed bodies and mildew turned her stomach.

Both said nothing as the guards departed. When the tap of their leather heels faded, the heavy-set woman sat up.

"Ah, my new bunky. What's your bid, pumpkin?" she asked.

She was asking the length of Bailey's sentence, but that didn't matter. What mattered was dominance. The appearance of strength and the price of engagement. You couldn't stop a bully, but you could make it costly.

Bailey sized her up. The woman was larger, but Bailey had army training under her belt and this woman had more than a few rolls of fat under hers.

Bailey aimed an index finger from beneath the stack of bedding, pointing. "That's my pillow."

The woman pushed a strand of greasy hair from her forehead. "I'm Paulene."

"I want my pillow," Bailey said.

"You know you'll be sleeping this far from me." Paulene extended her arms, revealing a crooked elbow.

"Same," said Bailey and locked her jaw, targeting Paulene's bad elbow for attack.

"I will molly whop your ass." Paulene stood and was unfortunately taller than Bailey estimated.

Bullies were nothing new. From the streets, to the shelter, to the army, nothing changed.

"You sure you want me to snap that elbow... again?"

Paulene hesitated. Slowly, a smile appeared and then came a barking laugh. "I like you." She passed over the pillow. "So, what'd you do, kill somebody?"

"Not my fault," Bailey said. But it was mostly her fault.

"Yeah. Me, either." She shrugged. "Gave me a dime, though."

Bailey knew enough prison slang from her pre-trial jail stint to understand that a dime meant Paulene was serving a ten-year sentence.

Paulene rolled back on her mattress. Bailey had her bunk and climbed up, giving her a view of the stainless-steel toilet, a rust-stained sink mounted into the wall, and the locked door.

"Hey, pillow pal," said Paulene. "You like girls?"

She sighed, wondering if she would have to break that elbow after all.

TWENTY-FOUR

BAILEY—NOW

Mason's plush toy slipped from Bailey's fingers, its button eyes clicking on the floor. She'd taken two steps toward the door before squashing the urge to run.

Her breathing came fast as she reminded herself she was not locked in. But Eliza's kids were.

No reason for a lock otherwise.

She retrieved Mason's stuffed animal from the floor, placing it back on his pillow.

A poorly crafted rag rug filled the space between the beds, adding a splash of color. Bailey stepped closer to examine it and found it woven from the remnants of clothing. Had Eliza made this or Aubree?

Aubree, surely. Because if Eliza had made it, there would have been a video blog.

A glance from the window showed a drop of a few feet to the ground. Aubree's escape hatch. How soon until she climbed out to never come back?

Bailey turned a full circle. Noticeable in their absence were chairs, desks, a bookshelf, a toy chest, or shelves. The only other toy she spotted was a rag doll on Harper's bed.

Where was the school room? Where were the educational materials their mother featured and sold?

Maybe behind the door past the bunk beds?

Stepping through the door, she found a small bathroom with a litter box for Ginger, a toilet, plastic shower, and a single sink in a cheap particle board cabinet.

The shelf beside the sink held three toothbrushes, a hairbrush, and hair ties. Near the faucets lay a sliver of white soap. A little pink pouch rested on the top shelf.

Bailey opened it.

Inside she found a tinted lip gloss, eyelash curler, two hard candies, and a men's wristwatch, missing the band. The time read quarter to ten. Bailey scowled and shoved it away.

This was clearly Aubree's bag, set out of easy reach of her siblings.

She tucked the bag back.

The cupboard held toilet paper, cleaning products, kitty litter, and a box of sanitary napkins. Bailey closed the doors and left the bedroom, pausing only to slide the latch back in place.

It seemed Eliza was fine with her teenage daughter sharing a bedroom with the little ones. If there were no choice, Bailey might agree. But she had three rooms upstairs.

Bailey left the house via the front door and porch rail, pausing only to grab her oak staff.

Nine minutes to spare. She raced around the house, ignoring Morris who trotted toward the fence.

"Later, Morris, I promise."

Bailey ran back to her cabin, mounted the ATV, and returned it to the barn, finding Ginger crying. Looking for her kittens, thought Bailey, her heart giving a little catch of sympathy for the forlorn mother.

With no time left, she hustled over the straw between the rows. The strawberry plants were covered in hard green berries and white flowers buzzing with bees.

Beyond the vegetables came the small hay field, large enough to feed Morris and the goats, if the posts were to be believed. And more and more, Bailey decided, they could not be.

Eliza had her kids working as farmhands and actors, but these children had no protection from the Screen Actors' Guild. Farms operated outside such laws and Eliza took full advantage. And beyond the legal requirements, these were small children who needed an education and time to play.

Were the gates meant to keep crazed fans out or to keep Eliza's kids in? Perhaps Kaiden was right. Sooner or later Aubree would climb over that barrier and disappear. And Bailey guessed it wouldn't be later.

As she entered the grove of sugar maples, the family's sugar-bush, the black flies attacked. Bailey swatted and thrashed toward a clearing.

She heard familiar voices and popped out of the tree line onto tall river grass. Bright violet iris grew in clumps on the sloping bank and daylily buds waved on long stalks, promising flowers when summer came.

A hundred yards downriver, the top of the fiberglass camper beckoned.

Bailey glanced back at the woods. The flies had not followed. Too hot? She didn't know but was grateful. She'd need to find a way around the sugarbush on the return trip.

She arrived out of breath and five minutes late.

Bailey called a greeting and Harper and Mason shouted back.

When she reached the group, she found them set up on a mowed patch.

"There you are," said Eliza. "We're nearly ready for you. Aubree is going to keep the kids inside the trailer while we film the first bit." She turned to the paid male actor beside her. "Ready?"

He gave her that loving smile. "All set."

Eliza turned away and his smile vanished. Kaiden winked at Bailey.

Kaiden seemed to be enjoying his game. Bailey thought he was playing with fire.

Between the grass and river, Bailey spotted a stretch of sandy beach. There was no lake in the state that had a sandy bank. So this addition, like the chalkboard, was for display only because beneath the elegant surface lay brown mud and stone.

Bailey itched to poke beneath the sand that Eliza used to hide every reality in her life. With just a little more digging, what else might she discover?

TWENTY-FIVE

When the kids' shivering and blue lips began to interfere with the filming, Eliza called a halt. Bailey had already filmed the family splashing at the shore of the creek, gliding from the bank in the tire swing and squealing as they dropped into deep cold water.

The next reel was their parents wrapping the little ones up in big fluffy towels and cuddling them close as they rubbed the blood back into their extremities. Eliza wore a lovely flowing teal coverup and Kaiden looked fit and athletic in cut-off jean shorts and a tight T-shirt.

Bailey had a hard time keeping from muttering her opinion of this charade.

The next bit featured Kaiden and Eliza's meal preparations, while Aubree and the kids played cornhole with the set for sale on Eliza's merch page. The boards featured Morris and the chickens and goats with the Watts Farm branding. The first take was interrupted by Ginger, who came yowling up to her mistress.

"She's looking for her kittens," said Aubree, lifting the cat and cuddling it close.

"Put her in the RV," said Eliza.

Aubree stroked her pet and murmured comfort as she did as she was told. Bailey felt a heart-twisting sympathy for the little mama, unable to locate her babies.

Meanwhile, Eliza muttered something about having the cat fixed, but how kittens were good for likes.

Bailey filmed her boss expertly creating a gourmet meal using the spice mixture they sold. 'So easy that you should try this at your next cookout,' said Kaiden.

Everything took on that golden glow as the sun sank near the treetops and the microphone cover prevented followers from hearing the wind that ruffled the leaves or the cat howling from inside the camper.

The family gathered in canvas folding chairs around the fire to dine, using planks of wood as individual tables. The smell of woodsmoke and roasting meat made Bailey's mouth water, but she was offered nothing.

Filming ceased twice. Once because Harper toppled her table, causing her food to land in the dirt. The second was because Aubree swallowed a bug and failed to deliver her line on cue.

But somehow, they got the footage Eliza wanted and the remains of dinner were collected and tossed. The chairs were stowed and the fire tended. When Eliza was satisfied with the set, she gathered her props.

After sundown, the family sat on logs around the welcoming fire. Bailey and Eliza filmed the kids roasting homemade marshmallows that she claimed to have made herself.

Someone had made them. Just not Eliza.

"Check the links below for the recipe!" said Aubree.

Then they made smores with homemade graham crackers and dark, fair-trade, organic chocolate.

Kaiden announced bedtime and all the kids groaned on cue

and then obediently headed into the camper. Kaiden offered one truly terrible dad joke before they climbed inside.

The filming paused and Kaiden left the RV so that the kids could get into their pajamas to pretend to sleep in a camper that would be parked back beside the barn in an hour. As for their healthy camping breakfast? That had been served before Bailey had arrived, after lunch and before dinner.

Kaiden paused by the fire beside Bailey. "You know, in the firelight, your hair is almost the same color as Aubree's."

"Is it?"

"But not so curly."

While Eliza scrolled through her phone, Kaiden strolled down to the river. Bailey watched his dark silhouette and saw the telltale glow of a lit cigarette.

"Does he smoke?" asked Bailey.

"Not tobacco," said Eliza and then caught on and hollered at Kaiden. "Put that out right now."

The glowing ember vanished.

"He knows the rules," she growled. "No smoking and no alcohol around my kids."

Bailey sat in the chair beside Eliza, staring at the glowing embers of the campfire. She licked her lips, nervous to broach this subject but feeling unable to keep her mouth shut.

"Eliza, when do the kids have lessons?"

Her boss shifted her gaze to Bailey, pinning her assistant with narrowing eyes. Bailey felt like a fawn the moment it realizes it's been spotted by a bobcat. A shiver lifted the hairs on her neck.

The orange light gave Eliza's skin a ghoulish glow and deepened the lines that were invisible in daylight.

When she spoke, her voice held an unfamiliar clipped edge. "You've seen our material."

"I have. Yes. And it's selling well, more than ever with

parents looking to supplement those summer packets sent by the schools."

"Which is mostly busy work." Gone was the easy rhythm of her words and the smooth relaxed delivery she used on her videos. The annoyance was on clear display. "Don't get me started on the low quality of those ridiculous summer reading lists."

Designed to help kids maintain their level of learning, thought Bailey, but she said nothing.

Eliza exhaled through her nose and then laced her fingers. Bailey prepared for a lecture on public education which would not be worse than the one she was now giving herself about minding her own business. She really needed to stop getting distracted by how Eliza raised her kids.

"Bailey, farming is a group effort. And my kids learn a lot more here than they would doing hypothetical math problems."

"Agreed," Bailey lied.

Eliza clapped her hands, making Bailey startle. Then she rubbed her palms together as if washing them in the air.

"And this isn't your concern." Her expression dared Bailey to disagree.

Bailey broke eye contact as Eliza continued.

"So how about you focus on your responsibilities here and let me worry about educating my kids?"

Across the fire, Kaiden gave a slow shake of his head. He'd clearly survived in his job for nearly a decade by doing what he was told and minding his business. Bailey needed to do the same.

"Yes, of course." Her voice turned small and conciliatory. "I had no intention of interfering."

"Sounded like you did. Don't do it again."

"Eliza, I—"

Her boss cut her off. "Bailey, enough! You work here. You

are not part of this family. Just do the job and stop questioning how I raise my kids."

"I understand."

"Good." Eliza aimed a finger at Bailey like a gun and pulled the trigger.

Bailey did not like being at the receiving end of a gun. Even a pretend one. The implied threat raised her protective instincts, and she had to remind herself she was no longer in prison.

Or was she?

TWENTY-SIX

Now that Bailey had seen the inside of their façade of a home, she had more questions. Did Eliza's kids ever leave the farm? Was she some isolationist prepper, awaiting the apocalypse? Did she neglect her children's education out of grievances with public institutions?

Or was she just using her kids to get rich?

Unfortunately, she could not get answers from inside the barn office where she'd been stuck all week since her question about the kids' education.

Aubree continued to visit her cabin, becoming a familiar sight in the evenings. They watched rom-coms and coming-of-age flicks and ate junk food and broadened Aubree's glimpse of pop culture and the outside world.

On Saturday night, as the credits of the zany comedy rolled, Aubree gathered her jacket to go.

"You think you could get me some lip gloss, the kind that's tinted pink?"

"Sure."

"And a razor."

"Your mother might find that."

"She won't."

The girl was becoming a woman. Unfortunate that this meant changing her appearance with makeup and shaving away her natural hair. Bailey admitted to herself that she had done the same. Shaved her legs. Curled her lashes. All to appear older than her years. Sneak into clubs. Go out with guys with cars.

That was before she'd slept with a boy she'd trusted to not be like her father and to get her far, far away from her violent dad and enabling mom.

Funny how what you want rarely resembles what you settle for.

Bailey tucked the DVD back in the library's plastic case then grabbed her hoodie. Since the deranged fan had broken in, Bailey didn't feel Aubree should walk back alone, though she did get here alone because Bailey never knew when or if she was coming.

They walked together to the backyard. Aubree hesitated, restlessly tugging at a lock of curly hair.

"You okay?" asked Bailey.

She shrugged.

Bailey clasped Aubree's forearm. "I'm here for you. If you need me, just ask."

"Thanks, Bailey. I might."

Aubree headed along the house, opened the window, and shimmied inside, nimble as an eel.

Bailey waited for the window to close, then headed back, cloaked in darkness and her gray hoodie.

* * *

Bailey woke in the night, confused at what had roused her.

Then she heard the pounding again, just past the foot of her bed.

What in the world?

The pounding came again.

"Bailey? Wake up!"

That was Eliza. What time was it?

"Yes," Bailey croaked. "I'm awake."

"Open the door," ordered Eliza.

Bailey wondered if she needed her walking stick as she padded across the floor. If Eliza had caught her daughter sneaking back into the house, the girl might have spilled the beans.

"Bailey?"

Eliza didn't sound furious. She sounded scared.

Bailey released the lock and tugged open the door. Eliza panted, out of breath, her face pale, her brow etched with worry.

Bailey pressed a hand to her throat. "What's wrong?"

"Richard got an alert. I did too, but I didn't see anything. He did something to the video, enhanced it. He said someone was out here."

"Where?"

"Behind your cabin."

"And you came out here alone?" Bailey couldn't believe Eliza was actually checking on her safety.

"Hold on, Richard is on the line."

Eliza lifted her mobile. Her other hand was tucked in the front pocket of her pullover jacket. Did she have a weapon hidden in there?

"She's fine, Richard. You don't need to come." Then she spoke to Bailey. "May I come in?"

Bailey stepped back, thankful she had done the dishes. Two bowls and two dirty glasses might raise unanswerable questions.

Eliza closed and locked the door and Bailey wiped the sleep from her eyes.

"We're worried it's the same guy who tried to grab Aubree. The camera caught him in the woods."

"Oh, that might be good. If we can catch him."

"It would be except it's only black and white and the image is blurred because the guy was running."

Bailey drew the collar of her T-shirt closed around her neck with one fist and glanced toward the locked window.

"Is he still out there?"

"We don't know. We've checked all the outbuildings."

"We?"

"Richard and me. He's outside."

"I see." She hadn't come alone.

"We even checked Morris's shelter. There's nothing."

So she and her security guy had checked the donkey and goats before checking on Bailey.

Eliza tapped the speaker function on the call with Richard, then asked, "Have you seen anyone?"

"No."

"And Bailey, I hate to ask this because you seem like an honest person. But who can really know. You didn't have... company?"

Bailey gasped and then recovered enough to give an emphatic, "No!"

"Good. Glad to hear it." Eliza turned to go.

"Eliza, am I safe out here?"

She turned. "Well, I should think so. Even our more persistent fans don't know you exist."

"I'm still alone out here. No internet."

"You can text or call."

Bailey broke eye contact.

"What are you asking?"

She gathered her courage and said, "I'd feel safer in the house."

"It's where my kids sleep," said Eliza.

"You saw an intruder. And I'm alone here with a stick." She pointed at her staff.

Eliza hesitated, one hand on the knob. "Let me think about it."

"Thank you."

Eliza swept out and Bailey locked the door.

Her daughter had been attacked on her property. She was wise to check the outbuildings to see if some nut was waiting for a second chance.

But first?

Bailey growled, feeling as irrelevant as the tulip stems dying in the fields. It was hard to be so unimportant when this family meant so much to her.

* * *

Bailey saw Eliza before leaving the farm for her day off. They watched the video of the intruder together. The blurry image, in black and white, showed a person wearing a dark hoodie and dark pants, rushing across the field of view.

"Is that toward my cabin?" asked Bailey.

"Yes. And the river. As far as we can tell he never came near the house. Richard thinks it's that same guy. He's giving a copy to the sheriff. Whoever he is, he is up to no good."

"What will you do?"

"More cameras and a perimeter alert. It will notify us if a person is onsite. Costs a small fortune. But that attack was so terrifying. I don't know what I'd do if something happened to one of my kids."

Yet she'd scolded Bailey when she'd stopped the attack because she was early.

"A mother's worst nightmare," Bailey said.

Eliza nodded but said nothing, just dipped her chin and

broke eye contact. When she looked back, she was forcing a smile.

"Big plans for your day off?"

A flea collar for Bones, she thought, but said, "Grocery shopping. Maybe a movie."

"We prefer sunsets," said Eliza, sounding condescending again.

The pause stretched long enough for Bailey to feel uncomfortable. What was she waiting for? To be dismissed?

Yes, she realized with annoyance, she was.

"See you later," she said before heading out.

"Have fun," called Eliza.

Bailey drove away feeling the relief of knowing no one commanded her time for one short day.

She went to the public library to get more movies before heading to a sporting goods store in Latham, NY. Funds were low, so she used her credit card for the small inflatable canoe and new boots. She considered getting a handgun, but the thought of a background check made her bag that idea.

She enjoyed lunch at a pub with an icy glass of soda and a plate of wings while she caught a ballgame.

After the fourth inning, she drove up the Northway, buying fresh flowers, before stopping at the cemetery.

Later, she ordered dinner at a fast-food place, a strawberry milkshake with a cheeseburger and fries. Those kids did not know what they were missing. She slurped the melting remains of her shake, then tossed the wrappers.

Satisfied with the day's errands, she stopped for groceries, including a pink lip gloss and a razor. At the gate, she entered her code. The gate did not open.

She tried again and a third time, but the gate remained closed.

Finally, she glanced at the darkening sky.

Dusk. She'd come back late.

She glanced at the grocery bag holding her coffee ice cream and frozen dinners. There was nothing for it. She sent Eliza a text.

Can u open gate?

You're late

Yes. Locked out.

Gate locks at dusk

Can u open?

She knew that Eliza *could* open it, because she'd done so for her security specialist. A better question was, would she?

Bailey locked her teeth and waited for the reply, already knowing. That sinking feeling dragged her down in her seat.

Leave truck. Walk in.

Bailey debated telling Eliza she had several bags of groceries. And then she realized that Eliza would know that, of course. She didn't care. Her assistant had gotten back after dusk. But didn't she have the full day off? Not just dawn to dusk?

She wrote one final text.

K

Bailey waited. There were no three dancing dots. No reply.

She shuffled the items that needed to be refrigerated into her backpack. The food she did not want Eliza to see went into her two-wheeled collapsable metal cart with the inflatable.

Finally, she hiked in, pulling her cart while gripping her walking stick. As she crossed the yard, she felt, rather than saw, someone watching.

The zip of fear made her heart race. She sucked in air. The porch swing creaked. Someone stood and walked to the steps.

Bailey wondered if this was Eliza, her daughter, or the man she saw attack Aubree.

The person stood there, motionless. Finally, the silent watcher opened the screen door and stepped into the house. Once there, she turned, and Bailey recognized Eliza's pale blond hair.

Bailey lifted a hand in greeting. Eliza closed the door. A moment later, the lock clicked.

She stood there, staring across the yard in the gathering dark.

Did her boss appreciate what she had?

Did Eliza recognize how lucky she was to belong to a family? To have children to love and a home where she found peace?

Or did you have to lose those things to really appreciate them?

TWENTY-SEVEN

On Monday, Bailey retrieved her truck just after dawn and was at her desk at seven working on the new merchandise launch of premade mixes.

Eliza's special cornbread, chocolate cake, pancake mix, and salted caramel brownies would go live this week. They were all organic. No processed sugar. And she didn't produce a single one herself. Just worked deals with the manufacturer who paid to use her branding and slapped her label on everything. What a racket.

Her boss appeared after eight, once more dressed in baggy coveralls. It seemed this was all she wore lately.

Before Eliza could lecture or fire her employee for returning late yesterday, Bailey threw herself on the sword.

"I had a flat," she said.

"What?"

"My truck got a flat. I had to walk back to town and get a tow truck to come out."

"New tire?"

No, because that was something that Eliza could check.

"He drove me and the tire back to the station and fixed it. I ran over a roofing nail."

"I see."

"I'm so sorry. I should have sent a text. But it's your day off too, and I didn't want to bother you."

"You can call if you're stranded, Bailey. I could have driven you to town."

"Thank you. It's so great to know that you have my back."

She held her smile and Eliza stared, her head canted to one side.

Bailey felt certain that Eliza's circle included only herself and her kids. She had no room for outsiders.

Eliza turned back to business.

"Kaiden will be staying after Ada leaves today. Come up to the house then."

Bailey nodded. Kaiden was often here for the meal filming, but he left with the chef. Although not today. This was different. Something was happening.

Eliza breezed out of the room and Bailey scheduled the videos as usual. She watched each one, becoming more and more concerned.

Her boss was lining up all her content. Bailey recognized the signs. Something big was about to happen. But what?

* * *

Bailey didn't have long to wait to get her answer. She arrived at the house just after Kaiden's arrival and Ada's departure. In the foyer, she nodded at Aubree who watched from the upper railing as Eliza set up the shot.

Bailey and Eliza headed upstairs as her boss explained what she wanted, ran through the blocking, where Bailey was to stand, when she was to zoom, pan and pull back. Back downstairs, Kaiden sat in the living room, his attention on his mobile, paying neither of them any mind.

Then they mounted the stairs again, to begin in the upper hall. Bailey's heart was racing. What was going on? Were her hands shaking?

Aubree had disappeared, but then she noticed a door cracked open and the teen peering out.

"Ready?" asked Eliza.

Bailey lifted the phone and nodded then counted her in with three fingers.

Eliza used a hushed voice, intimate as she whispered to her followers about an announcement so big that she just had to include all of her friends.

Bailey moved before her boss, capturing it all.

Eliza motioned to her content followers to come along and Bailey remained motionless until Eliza was two steps below her on the stairs, looking back, smiling broadly.

She was so damned good at this.

They reached the living room and Bailey moved to capture Kaiden in the frame. Gone was his phone and he now sat rhythmically oiling a leather harness.

Bailey swept along after Eliza stopped, moving to her mark, where the video would capture them both.

"Honeybear," said Eliza.

Kaiden lifted his chin and smiled, then he set down the harness and gave Eliza his full attention.

"What's up?" he said, then glanced in Bailey's direction and said, "Oh, hey everyone."

"I have something to tell you," Eliza said to Kaiden, then turned toward the camera's steady red light. "To tell *all* of you,"

She grinned. Bailey's stomach clenched as she braced for what she feared might come next.

Eliza clapped her hands together and bounced.

Then she shouted, "We're pregnant!"

Bailey dropped the camera.

TWENTY-EIGHT

Kaiden stared at Bailey and Eliza stared at the phone now laying on the rug, still recording. The top of Bailey's head tingled and she couldn't feel her fingertips. For a moment she forgot to breathe.

"No problem." Eliza scooped up the device. "Still running. Just continue. We'll fix it in edits." She passed Bailey the phone. "Hold it steady. Wide shot. Right?"

Bailey's hands were shaking as she held the camera. A sour taste filled her mouth. She resisted the contraction of her stomach muscles, refusing to be sick.

Eliza is pregnant.

She was just going to keep having kids, raising them, as if everything was right with the world.

But it wasn't right. The anger surged next. A building tsunami, but Bailey forced it down. This was not the time.

"Oh, okay," said Eliza, retrieving the phone and pausing the recording. "Surprised you, didn't I?"

Bailey nodded, snatching a few shallow breaths through a gaping mouth.

"Babe, I gotta be out of here in an hour," said Kaiden.

"Don't call me babe," snapped Eliza.

Bailey wished she'd caught that exchange on camera.

Oh, Eliza's followers were going to go out of their minds.

Now the overalls made so much sense. She'd been hiding her pregnancy. Waiting until she knew everything was proceeding as it should, or because things were complicated. Or for a million other reasons.

How far along was she?

"Do you need some water or something?" asked Eliza. "Your color isn't good." Her head tilted as if trying to puzzle out what was happening.

It was the kick in the pants Bailey needed to snap out of it.

"I'm fine. Just... Wow. You're expecting! That's so great!" Had that been even close to convincing or had it leaned toward hysterical?

Bailey waited and Eliza's concern faded. She smiled.

"Thank you, Bailey. Now we need this shot and then I'll bring in the kids so we can film their reactions."

"Of course. I'm sorry. We can do it again, right now. From upstairs?"

"No. Just follow me from the doorway. I'll make it work."

Bailey did as she was told. She filmed the apparently genuine reaction of Eliza's husband, learning that his wife was pregnant, for the second time in ten minutes.

He scooped her in his arms and twirled her in a circle as she laughed. Then he kissed her like she was the most perfect woman in the world.

Bailey knew better.

After recording this staged impromptu announcement, Eliza checked the videos.

"I can work with that. Go get the kids. Don't tell them anything, just that I want them in the kitchen." She turned to Kaiden. "I hope we get something adorable from one of them," said Eliza.

Dismissed, Bailey trudged upstairs, her legs so weary she barely made the landing.

From the living room, Eliza and Kaiden continued their conversation.

"Harper usually gives you something," he said.

"Fingers crossed. But if not..." The rest was inaudible past Bailey's pounding heartbeat. She stopped in the hall, realizing she was crying.

Bailey swiped the damp off her cheeks and gulped. These were angry tears, and unwelcome. If her boss saw, she might ask questions. And Bailey couldn't let Eliza know why her joyful announcement brought her assistant such pain.

Aubree was nowhere in sight. Bailey knocked on the door to Harper's room. Mason appeared, staring up at her. Behind him, Aubree and Harper played with an expensive doll. The teen spotted Bailey and dropped the doll as if scalded. Had she been expecting her mom?

"She wants you all downstairs."

"Filming?" asked Mason.

"Is Daddy still here?" asked Harper. The hope in her voice nearly broke Bailey's heart.

The children headed downstairs. Eliza directed Mason and Harper to sit at the kitchen table for the best natural light.

"Aubree, you're between them, hand on each chair," said her mother. "Bailey, stand there, so you can get all of us in the shot."

Bailey had to squelch the urge to leave the recording paused so that her boss would miss the genuine emotions and be left with whatever she could coax on retakes. But that seemed spiteful and risky. Bailey was many things. But she was not petty or short-sighted.

"Ready? Start the recording please." Eliza counted them in.

"Kids, we have a big announcement."

Mason leaned forward and Harper continued to kick her feet back and forth in a rhythmic tattoo against her chair.

"We are expecting a new baby."

Harper clapped her little hands, but Mason groaned and slapped himself on the forehead. Clearly he recalled having a baby in the house before.

Eliza continued as if Mason were onboard with this.

"Mason, you're going to be a big brother again, and Harper." Eliza leaned down and touched the end of Harper's nose with her fingertip. "You, my dear, are going to be a big sister!"

"Hurrah!" shouted Harper, leaping to her feet on the chair and lifting her arms like an Olympic champion.

"I don't want it," said Mason.

This made Kaiden laugh. "Too late for that, champ."

He moved behind Eliza, cradling both hands around her under her belly, revealing a very noticeable bump.

Bailey sucked in a breath. How had she missed that?

"Well, nobody asked me," said Mason, folding his arms over his scrawny chest and thumping back in his chair.

Now Aubree took over. She gave her mom a big hug.

"Congratulations, Mom," she said.

Kaiden held out his arms. "What about me?" he asked her.

She allowed him to hug her, too, but quickly drew away. Bailey picked up a vibe. Had this idiot of a man hit on an underage girl who was supposed to be his daughter?

Kaiden scooped up Harper who was now repeating a chanting version of the word "Yeah" over and over, while stomping her tiny feet.

Eliza grabbed Mason and Aubree and the family shared an adorable embrace. Finally, Eliza turned to Bailey, or rather, to the camera.

"That's right! Our family is growing again. I'm already five months along and one of my sharp-eyed followers is bound to notice. So here's the official announcement! We're expecting a baby in October." She gave a delighted squeak. "I'm sorry I kept this from you, but I wanted to be sure that our baby is healthy. We'll have a live gender reveal party, soon. Make sure to like and follow because you won't want to miss this!"

She cradled her stomach, and Bailey gripped the phone tight, ignoring the roaring in her ears. Eliza kept talking. Kaiden laughed. Mason said something else, but Bailey heard nothing but her heartbeat.

Then Eliza was prying the phone from her and giving her that concerned expression. Bailey snapped back to attention.

"...all right?"

"Oh, yes. I think my blood sugar is low. Felt a little dizzy."

Eliza turned to her eldest. "Aubree, get her a glass of cider." Eliza smiled at Bailey.

Bailey accepted the glass and chugged the contents as if at a kegger. Aubree retrieved the empty glass and gave her a meaningful glare. If Bailey had to describe it, she'd call it a "get your shit together" look. She tried, sucking in air through her flaring nostrils and wondering how this changed things.

It did. For her, at least. The earth's plates had shifted. She needed time to regain her footing.

Bailey had to think.

"Anything else?" Bailey asked.

"No. We'll take it from here. Thanks for acting as our videographer."

Eliza waved her away and Bailey returned to the barn, almost making it before the eruption of tears. They splashed hot and angry down her cheeks and dribbled off her chin to soak the collar of her T-shirt. Bailey snatched the blue bandana from her rear pocket and mopped her face. She'd started carrying one to mimic Eliza but found the cloth more than a stage prop. It was useful to wipe away sweat, to clean her hands, and to soak up the agony streaming from her eyes.

In the office she sniffed and paced and raged. When she'd

exhausted both her reserve of tears and the twisting anguish, she plopped down in her office chair.

Her boss could keep adding to her family. Have as many damn kids as she liked. Money was no barrier. She had a great house, a thriving business. She'd figured a way to provide a father to her kids without the bother of a husband.

And if something happened to her lovely home or family, would she just rebound like a rubber ball?

TWENTY-NINE

AUBREE

On the second Tuesday of June, after her mother had gone to bed, Aubree slipped through her window and crept through the yard. Since that creepy guy had tried to grab her, she wasn't allowed out by herself.

But her mom didn't know about her visits to Bailey's place at night. And she was never finding out because seeing Bailey, laughing, watching movies, and eating junk food was the highlight of her day. It was so great to finally have a real friend. She'd even found a chance earlier today to let Bailey know she was planning to visit.

Aubree listened to the peepers trilling and cicada buzz. Nearly warm enough for fireflies now. But she saw none.

Headlights flashed, pinning her in their blinding light.

She lifted a hand to shield her eyes as the engine turned over.

What was happening?

The headlights bounced as the vehicle made straight for her.

Aubree screamed and dove away as the truck roared past. It

thundered down the drive and sped off, taillights glowing red. From the house, the porch light flicked on.

She froze on her belly in the wet grass. Someone stood at the door.

Her mom. Should Aubree call out?

She didn't because if her mother knew she was out of bed, she'd never get out again.

Crouching, Aubree dashed toward the large maple trees. From there she sprinted to the corner of the house.

A flashlight flicked on, the beam scanning behind her then swinging toward the road. Beyond the curve in the drive, the gate barred entrance. But anyone could drive out.

Aubree pressed close to the side of the house. From the porch, her mother spoke on her phone.

"There was someone trespassing on my property."

Aubree held her breath. Could her mother hear her heart slamming against her ribs?

"Yes, that's right. I can see the tire tracks on my lawn. A truck, I think. Didn't get a clear look."

Aubree glanced toward her mom and noticed something different about her mother's appearance. She gaped as her mom pivoted, turning in the direction the truck had taken. She was dressed in a loosely fitting T-shirt and pajama pants. With Aubree's suspicions confirmed, she glared.

Fueled by fury and the receding panic, Aubree reached her bedroom window, lifted the sash, and crawled through to her bed. She closed and locked the window, stripping out of her clothing and burrowing into her nightshirt as the door opened.

"Aubree?" whispered her mother.

She tried for a sleepy voice. "Yeah?"

Her mom didn't answer. She just walked to the bunk beds and checked Mason and Harper.

"Everyone okay?" she asked her eldest.

Her mother padded to her and leaned to stroke her forehead. Aubree pulled away.

"Why are you sweating?"

"Because it's hot in here," she said.

"I'll leave the door open. Goodnight, darling."

Her mother paused in the hall, one hand on the knob, then left the door open. Aubree flopped back to the mattress. She threw one arm over her eyes and exhaled, releasing the tension and the terror with several long breaths.

Maybe whoever was driving that truck had not seen her.

No, they swerved right for her. But then they'd veered off.

Why?

Someone had tried to kill her. Or had they tried to kill her mother?

* * *

By morning, Aubree decided to never mention the truck. Her mother had seen it, so she knew about the trespasser. She slept poorly and woke to the morning's grayish glow. Milking time.

Her mom appeared, with one hand under her belly and one gripping the pail of milk. Aubree groaned but tossed aside the blanket.

"How's Thistle?" she asked as they reached the milking shed. Her favorite goat had been losing weight.

"About the same," said her mother.

"I was thinking she might have an infected tooth or something."

"Could be."

"Will you call a vet?"

Her mom shook her head.

She never called a vet. She didn't believe in them. She believed in nature's medicine, whatever that was.

Her mom's phone chimed with a gate alert.

She watched her mother check the text and enter her pass-code—a new one, Aubree noted.

"Richard is here."

"Why?" Aubree hoped her mother couldn't see the hot flush that made her neck itch.

"Did you hear anything last night?"

"Like what?"

"A trespasser on our property."

Aubree rounded her eyes. "That man?"

"We don't know."

"Is Bailey okay?"

"Yes. I reached her last night. Richard and I are going to walk the property. Try and figure how he got in here."

"Okay. Can I come?" Aubree asked.

Her mom hesitated, glancing back toward the house.

"They're asleep," said Aubree, referring to her siblings. "And Mason is old enough to watch Harper. I was sitting at his age."

Her mom's mouth was grim, but she nodded.

They were on their way back to the house when her security consultant found them. His two assistants hung back, one on his phone and the other on a tablet.

If she kept quiet, her mom might forget she was here.

"We swept the barns and walked your property line to the north as far as the river," said Mr. Garrow. "Found the vehicle tracks."

"And?"

"Whoever it was came in on the north side. Cut the barb-wire fence," he replied. "That's how they got in."

"And went out the main gate."

"Right."

Even Aubree could see the tire tracks that cut through the tall grass. Had that truck been parked in the yard, just waiting for her? But that was impossible. No one knew she snuck out at night.

She wondered again if the driver was after her mom.

Should she tell them the truck was blue?

But then they'd find out she'd been sneaking out.

"I don't understand," said her mom. "They didn't take anything. They might not have ever left their vehicle. What the heck were they doing?"

Richard had no answer.

"We need those boundary alerts," said her mom.

"Working on it. Take a few days."

Bailey arrived. She spotted them and veered in their direction.

"Good morning," she said. The day held a chill and her mom's assistant wore a light gray hoodie zipped to her neck and had both hands tucked in her pockets.

"Bailey. There you are. Did you see or hear anyone on the property after my message last night?"

She stopped beside Aubree. "No. Not before or after. Did he come back?"

Eliza gave her a brief rundown of how the intruder beat the gate.

"I see," said Bailey.

Richard glanced at Bailey. "I'd like you to walk me back to your place."

"Did the truck come that way?"

"It didn't."

Bailey appeared confused as she glanced at Aubree's mom for permission.

"Go ahead," said Eliza.

Mr. Garrow turned to his crew. "Jeff, review every minute of last night. See if the cameras picked up anything too distant to trigger an alert. I want pictures of that vehicle. Plates if you can get them."

The larger man headed toward their work van.

"Stuart, check that the gates are working properly. Haven't been tampered with."

The other man strode off.

Aubree pushed down the guilt at not telling her mother about the truck nearly hitting her. If she did, she'd never get to visit Bailey again.

"You think we'll catch him?" asked Aubree.

THIRTY

BAILEY

Richard Garrow said not one word to Bailey as she led him to her cabin door, as requested. Once there she stopped, and still he remained silent, glancing around at the ground, her front step, and the shoddy front door.

"What's going on?" she finally asked.

"I'm piecing that together," Richard said.

"Was it the same man who tried to grab Aubree?"

"That's a possibility." He walked once around her cabin then stooped to study the muddy cinderblock step before her door. He stood and motioned with his chin.

"Let's go down to the river," he said.

She followed him.

He spent several minutes looking at the riverbank, studying some gouges in the mud and an area of flattened grass.

"You know what caused these?" he asked her.

She shook her head.

"Were you down here last night?"

"At the river? No."

He asked her to go through the events of the previous evening, which she did as they walked back to the yard.

"Eliza texted you last night at nine-forty-five in the evening?"

"I don't know the exact time. I was in the shower, so I missed the alert, but replied before turning in."

He paused within sight of the house. "Did she tell you her big news?"

Bailey blinked at the sharp detour in the conversation. Richard faced her.

"About the baby? She did! Actually, I filmed her announcement. She'll be posting that soon. Her fans will be over the moon." That would be true. The Coop would be all a flutter.

"But not you." He cocked his head. "You don't seem that happy for her. Why is that?"

Richard scrutinized her as the pain surged up like lava from a dormant volcano. She didn't look away, just held his critical gaze, staring directly back, struggling not to cry.

"I didn't see it coming. But, of course, I'm thrilled."

Richard snorted, his smile knowing. "That right? Thrilled?"

"Of course." She locked her jaw, refusing to look away.

He gave her a triumphant smile. "You're lying."

Bailey looked him straight in the eye. "Why would you say that?"

THIRTY-ONE

BAILEY—NINE YEARS AGO

Bailey dragged herself from the darkness, clawing back to consciousness from the void. Her heavy eyelids throbbed. Why did her throat hurt?

The foreboding pressed on her chest, filling her with a terrible sense of disaster.

Why did her body ache as if she'd been pummeled?

The answer came from the sound. The steady beeping she knew from long ago. A heart monitor.

Claudia!

Bailey forced her eyes open and found herself lying in a hospital bed, the white curtains drawn. With great effort, she lifted her arm, finding the IV line fixed to her hand with white paper tape. Her arm! Deep purple bruises pocked her skin. A tentative shrug caused a wave of nausea.

"She's awake," said a female voice.

"I'll get her," said another.

Bailey shifted her gaze. The slight motion caused a spike of agony behind her eyes. But she could see. A woman stood at the raised bedrail. A stethoscope looped sideways over her neck, and both hands were tucked into the front pockets of her pink scrubs.

"Welcome back. We've been worried about you."

Another woman in green scrubs stepped into her line of view. A mask looped over one ear, dangling beside her chin.

Bailey tried to speak and groaned, hand going to her throat.

"We just removed the trach tube," said the new arrival. "That's why your throat hurts."

Bailey frowned, causing another bolt of blinding pain.

"I'm Dr. Lopez. I've been taking care of you. You're in the ICU at Albany Medical Center."

Dr. Lopez rested a hand on her forearm. "Most of your injuries are superficial. Lots of road burn from the pavement. But you suffered internal bleeding, and we had to operate to remove your spleen. In addition, you've suffered a head injury, and we are relieved to see you awake."

Lopez flashed a penlight's beam into her eyes. Bailey winced.

"Pupils reactive," she said. "Can you tell me the month of the year?"

Bailey held up one finger. *January.*

"One? Oh, yes. The first month of the year. Very good. Who is the current president?"

Bailey couldn't remember. That was stupid. Of course she knew. But she could not recall.

"You were in an accident. Do you remember?"

"Accident?" she croaked, not recognizing her own voice.

And Bailey's befuddlement cleared. The collision flashed in her mind like a reel from a horror movie. The dark, empty road. Driving her heap to the box store lot because they could park there overnight. Living in her car for now. Safer than the shelter.

Headlights. She remembered impossibly bright headlights. Accelerating, too late. The crash.

Oh, no. What have I done?
"Where is Claudia? I need to see her!"

Bailey returned from her cabin and spotted Aubree standing alone on the front steps. The girl clung to the porch upright beam as if it were her last friend. Bailey gave a wave as she hurried back toward the office, not wanting Eliza upset by her absence.

"Mom's in the equipment barn with Tory," called the teen.

Bailey stopped. "Is she looking for me?"

"Don't think so."

Aubree lifted her thumb to her mouth and chewed on her cuticle. Bailey changed direction, heading toward the teen, pausing on the walkway.

"You okay?"

Aubree gave a half shrug.

"Did her security guy tell you anything else about the guy who was joyriding here last night?" Bailey pushed the ball cap back on her head.

"Intruder cut the fence." Aubree pointed toward the barns. "I heard that much."

"Was it the same guy? The one with the knife?"

"Don't know." Aubree's face pinkened. "For all my mom spends on security, her crazy fans still get in."

"It's frightening. And you never know what these people have in their minds. What they want."

Bailey watched the girl shifting, restless. Who wouldn't be?

"Aubree? You all right?"

"Last night, when that truck was here?"

"Yes?"

"I was in the yard."

"Oh, my God, Aubree. You saw him?"

"No. But I saw something else."

Aubree dropped her gaze to her clasped hands, her breathing rasping as if she was struggling not to cry.

The girl shuddered and Bailey climbed the steps, drawing Aubree to the wicker loveseat and sitting beside her.

Aubree's narrow shoulders slumped, and her chin tucked as she beat her jointed hands against her thighs. She looked miserable.

The girl pivoted to face Bailey, tucking one long leg up on the seat cushion.

"Last night, when my mom was on the porch, I was in the yard, and I noticed something strange. I mean strange about my mom."

Bailey's brows rose. She'd thought they were discussing the intruder.

"Aubree, honey, I'm not following you."

The teen's words blasted out in a harsh whisper. "She wasn't blossoming at all."

"What?"

Aubree rushed on.

"She was wearing a T-shirt tucked into her pajama pants and she was absolutely flat here." She drew her palm down her stomach. "Nothing."

"Nothing?" asked Bailey. "You're sure?"

"Positive."

Now Bailey was confused. "How is that possible?"

"It's possible because... I don't know but it's just like the last time—with Harper. She's just pretending."

"Pretending?"

"My mom is *not* pregnant."

THIRTY-THREE

"What?" asked Bailey, reeling from what Aubree had just said.

"It's just an act, like everything else around here."

Bailey sank back in her love seat. Of all the crazy scams Eliza had pulled...

"You're sure?"

"One hundred percent."

"But she can't pretend to have a baby. Her fans will go berserk."

"She's not pretending. She'll have a baby. But she's not the one carrying it."

"You mean she's adopting you kids but doesn't want her followers to know?"

"I don't know how she gets the babies." The teen lowered her voice and spoke quickly. "I don't know if she steals them or buys them. But I know that she's not Harper's or Mason's mother."

"Oh, this is terrible."

Before speaking again, Aubree glanced across the yard toward the second barn.

"With both Mason and Harper, she left to go to the 'hospital'." Aubree used air quotes on that last word. "And came home with a baby. My mother has loads of money. She could buy us or something."

Bailey looked over her shoulder and then back at the teen. "Aubree? Really?"

"Or she stole us. Or Harper, at least." Her voice rose on this revelation; she was on the verge of tears. "And I remember someone, I told you before. A man with dark hair. I think he might be my real dad."

"If you were stolen as a baby, you wouldn't be able to remember that."

"I know. But I do remember him. I can't explain it. But I don't think she's my mother."

"How could she do that?" asked Bailey. "A missing baby would be national news. Three missing babies, that would be a case for the FBI or something."

"Maybe she bought us on the black market."

Bailey scoffed. "Come on, now. That's kind of out there."

She didn't want Aubree breaking down. Not with Eliza likely to leave the barn at any time. So she offered an alternative. "There are other possible explanations."

"Like?"

"Lots of families adopt."

"We're not a family! And she's not adopting. Her belly gets bigger and bigger, but it's not a baby."

"What then?"

"I don't know. I think it's a pillow or something."

"A pillow?" That did not make sense. But there were other kinds of pads. "Aubree, could she be wearing a pregnancy pad? It's what actresses use, and they have weighted ones, so men and women can see what it's like to carry a baby."

"Yes! That's it. I've felt it when she pretended to be pregnant with Harper. It's kind of swishy. Not like when Thistle or Bonnie are carrying. Their stomachs are hard."

"I see. And last night you think she wasn't wearing it?"

"Yes. She'd gone to bed and must have taken it off. The truck caught her by surprise, and she wasn't wearing it."

Bailey thought about this allegation.

"You believe me. Don't you?"

"I believe you think that's what you saw. But maybe we can do better than that."

"What do you mean?"

"Maybe we find some evidence."

"How?"

"She'd need more than one size. Early pregnancy. Late pregnancy. And if she's done this before..."

"They're here somewhere," said Aubree, catching up. "We can find it." She leapt to her feet.

"I've got to get back to the office."

"Oh, please! You just stand watch, and I'll search her room. Five minutes. I swear."

Bailey glanced about the yard, seeing no one.

"All right. Five minutes."

Aubree scrambled inside and Bailey followed as far as the foyer, where she paused.

"Where are Mason and Harper?"

"I told them they could play in Mason's upstairs room." Aubree beckoned over her shoulder. "Come on! Hurry."

THIRTY-FOUR

Bailey stood guard in the children's bedroom window as Aubree darted into her mother's bedroom. From here, Bailey had a clear view of the sloping yard, springhouse, and barn where Tory and Eliza were supposed to be. If they left, Bailey and Aubree should have time to make it out the back door before they reached the house.

Aubree was on her hands and knees peering under the bed. Then she disappeared into the bathroom. Something crashed to the floor.

"It's all right," called Aubree. "Just the plastic drinking glass."

Bailey glanced back toward the barn and then across the hall as Aubree emerged from the bathroom and shook her head.

"Nothing."

"Look in her closet. Suitcases, boxes, drawers."

"You do it," said Aubree, taking her place.

"This was your idea."

"But you're taller and she has boxes on the shelves. Hurry."

Bailey hesitated. "Keep your eyes on that barn. Do not let me down."

Aubree sucked in a breath and nodded, using her index finger to cross her heart. "I promise."

Bailey hurried to Eliza's room and the walk-in closet. The room was stuffed with Eliza's wardrobe on hangers, on shelves, in baskets and in a full-sized dresser.

Bailey rummaged through the drawers first, finding some very sexy underwear, very practical underwear, and several new nursing bras with the tags still on them. The next held a jewelry organizer with earrings, bracelets, and necklaces all in order and none of which Bailey had ever seen. They were fancy, mostly gold in color and possibly actually gold. All this glitz seemed to have come from another life. Another woman.

The next three drawers held gauzy tops, shirts, and shorts. The bottom drawer held various kinds of jeans and coveralls. But no foam or silicone prosthetics.

There was nothing in the suitcase but smaller bags, totes, and a luggage scale. The baskets held scarves, jackets, hats, and more hats.

Three more bins lined the top shelf. The first was loaded with purses and clutches, all from various designers and none appropriate for a farmer. Like the jewelry, Eliza's bags pointed to a former life, a very different former life.

Bailey dragged down the next one and was surprised at the weight.

And there it was—a very large silicone baby bump in a hue that was a near-match for Eliza's skin tone.

Bailey touched the thing. It was cold but the navel looked exactly right. Beneath this was a stretchy, black Lycra sleeve. A tube into which the silicone likely slipped for easier wear.

"Bingo," she whispered. Then she called over her shoulder. "Aubree. Is it still clear?"

"Yes."

"Come look."

Aubree darted across the room and into the closet. She gasped.

"I knew it." She poked the silicone bulge.

Bailey slipped the sleeve back to the bottom of the bin and replaced the silicone bump. "She's wearing a smaller one now. This will be later."

"She's lying to us. To everyone."

"Yes."

"So, she's stealing the next baby, too?" asked Aubree.

"I don't know. But I'll help you find out."

From somewhere down the hall came a familiar voice.

"Aubree. Where are you?"

They froze.

"That's Mason."

Bailey pushed the bin back into place.

"I'll bring him to the kitchen. You go out the front door," said Aubree, then trotted away. "I'm down here," she called from the hallway.

"Harper won't give me back my..." The rest of what he said was garbled.

Bailey slipped out of Eliza's room and glanced across the yard. Eliza and Tory now stood before the barn. If she left the house, Eliza would see her and know she was not in the office.

The murmur of voices reached her. Aubree and Mason in the kitchen, perhaps.

"Front door and side railing," she whispered to herself.

Bailey charged across the living room and hesitated at the foyer. Depending on where Mason stood, he might see her leave. A quick glance showed all clear.

She slipped out the front door, holding the screen so it did not bang shut.

Was Eliza still in front of the barn?

Bailey hurried to the far rail and hopped to the ground. Now she'd need to wait for Eliza to return to the barn, head to the field, or reach the house. If Eliza went into the office, Bailey's goose was cooked. She needed a reason to be up here, and her mind raced with possible excuses.

Then a scream brought her upright. The high-pitched wail echoed with terror and lifted the hairs on Bailey's arms.

From far off, she heard Eliza shout Aubree's name.

Something was happening.

Bailey hesitated. If she ran to the kitchen, Eliza would know she wasn't at work.

A moment later, Eliza pounded up the front steps. The screen door squeaked and next came the beat of Tory's tread, slower, heavier, but not far behind.

Inside the house, the screams came again.

Bailey bolted down the hill and back to the office. Whatever this was, she could not have heard it from her desk.

She had barely gotten her sweatshirt off, her butt seated, and her computer working when the text landed. Had Eliza seen them? Bailey gritted her teeth and checked the message.

Open the front gate for EMS

EMS? Bailey rose and clutched her phone. Eliza had called emergency services.

What was going on up at the house?

Bailey tapped out her reply.

Yes. On it. Do you need me?

She waited. Waited. Stared at her phone, gnawing her lower lip as if it were lunch. There was no dancing three dots. No reply. Nothing.

Bailey left the office and stood in the parking lot between her truck and the one that had brought Richard and his two assistants. Where were they?

Last she knew one was assigned to check the gates and the other to review surveillance recordings. Had they seen her dart to the barn?

She craned her neck, trying to see what was happening at the house, desperate to go up there but afraid to leave her post.

Bailey gripped her phone, checking the front gate security camera as the seconds merged into minutes. Then she heard it. A faraway wail. Louder and louder still.

The front camera showed no one, but she still drew back the gate. The paramedic truck drove past the camera. She left the gate open because she didn't know if there were other EMS vehicles en route.

She motioned the driver to the house. They drove across the lawn as she ran behind the truck until it rolled to a stop.

A fit woman emerged from the driver's side. She wore navy blue up to and including her cap. Her shirt and hat were festooned with various yellow and red patches.

The paramedic opened a side compartment and heaved a large bag from within.

Her partner was already on the steps.

"This way!"

Bailey turned to see Tory motioning from the yard before the corner of the house.

They all changed direction and hustled after Tory.

A shiver puckered Bailey's skin as she dashed along.

What was happening?

Her daughter's scream brought Eliza at a run. She reached Aubree on the back porch. Intruder, was her first thought, but at the door she saw she was wrong.

Her daughter crouched over a body. Someone lay sprawled on the steps.

"Aubree?" She burst through the door.

Tory arrived a moment later, drawing up short in the open back door.

"Is that Richard?" she asked.

Until that moment, Eliza had not recognized him. But now that she looked more closely...

"Yes. It's him."

Tory crept forward. "He's bleeding." She squatted beside Aubree. "Looks like he crawled here."

Eliza followed the direction of Tory's extended arm to the glistening trail smearing the green grass. He had dragged himself to her doorstep.

And that meant...

Her heart jolted as her instincts shouted a warning. "Aubree. Where are your brother and sister?"

"Upstairs." Her voice was a squeak. "Mason's room."

She exhaled her relief. They were not in the yard or fields. Safe for now, she realized, the panic ebbing.

"Is he breathing?" asked Eliza.

Tory stooped, placing her ear close to Richard's mouth. Then she straightened. "Can't tell."

The backsteps ran with blood.

"What happened?" Eliza asked her daughter.

"I don't know. I just found him here. He's bleeding— everywhere."

Eliza picked up her phone and called 911.

"Get in the house, Aubree. Lock the front door. Find Harper and Mason. Do not let either of them come downstairs. You hear?" Her tone was sharp because she needed her daughter to understand how serious this was.

"But—"

Eliza cut her off. "Right now, goddammit!"

Her daughter's ears pinned back. "Yes ma'am."

Aubree spun away, fleeing as if her shorts were on fire.

Then Eliza sent Tory to fetch scissors and the sheets she'd left in the dryer while she sent her assistant a text. The gate was supposed to open automatically for emergency vehicles, but she couldn't take the chance.

This was so bad. It was going to hit the papers. No way to keep her fans from learning about this. And the authorities. An investigation.

She checked his pulse. It was thready, but she could feel the beat. Warm, sticky fluid coated her fingers, and she wiped them on her coveralls.

"You hold on, Richard. Help is coming."

So much blood. She knelt beside him.

Eliza leaned close to Richard's face.

"Who did this?" But he did not open his eyes or give any sign he heard her.

The blood. She shook her head, refusing to remember.

"Tory! Where are you?" Eliza yelled.

Her head gardener hustled out dragging a sheet.

"I've got to make some pads," said Tory. "Where is he bleeding?"

"I don't know. His back. But... I don't know!" The shock was receding, and horror flooded in.

She rolled Richard over.

His shirt was torn in several places. Eliza yanked it up, revealing a ghastly horror.

Tory stumbled to a halt at the grisly sight.

Richard's multiple wounds leaked blood with each beat of his heart.

Eliza scanned the yard again, searching for a threat. The intruder. The one with the knife. The one with the truck.

"Should we just fold it and press it to his wounds?" asked Tory.

Funny. Tory never asked her opinion when they were tending the plants, but people were different.

"Yes. Fold it and we'll both put pressure on the worst of them."

Tory stared at Richard's stomach. "Tough choice."

She laid the folded sheet across his middle and they both pressed. How long had it been? And how long did he have?

They knelt in silence on either side of his body. Eliza noticed his color, gray like the ash from a fire. And his lips were bluish purple.

"He's bleeding through the pad," said Tory.

They both pressed, leaning their body weight on the pad that covered Richard's ravaged body.

He was bleeding out right here on Eliza's back steps.

She glanced toward the yard again, scanning for movement, for danger. For help.

Finally, she heard it, the high shrieking sound of hope. The paramedics.

"Tell the ambulance people to come around the house."

Tory rose and hurried down the back steps, avoiding the pooling blood. Then she dashed out of sight.

Eliza stopped pressing to check for a pulse. Then she checked again.

Richard's heart had stopped.

Eliza shivered on the back porch steps. The sun was shining. It was warm out. Wasn't it?

Why was she so cold?

The paramedics rounded the house with Tory, Richard's security team and Bailey in tow.

The EMTs moved Eliza out of the way and took over care, beginning CPR and slapping electrodes on Richard's chest. She stood between Tory and her assistant, watching with surreal detachment. Was this actually happening?

Richard's men retrieved a stretcher from somewhere and the four of them lifted Richard onto the gurney and hustled away.

She, Tory, and Bailey followed them as far as their rescue truck, watching as they loaded Richard.

Eliza glanced at her coveralls and stretched her bloody fingers. Richard's drying blood.

Beside her Bailey stared, pale faced and breath rasping. When she turned to Eliza, her eyes were huge. "Is he gonna be okay?"

THIRTY-SIX

BAILEY

By early evening, the sheriff and his men finally left the farm. The weariness pressed down on Bailey's shoulders, rounding her spine as she slumped in one of the wicker chairs on Eliza's front porch.

The back porch was still a crime scene.

All three of the Watts children sprawled on the wide sofa. Harper sat curled in Aubree's lap and Mason huddled against his mom, sticking to her like Velcro.

The phone ringing in the kitchen sent Eliza hurrying to answer. Mason scooched over to lean on Aubree in his mom's absence. She wrapped an arm about his thin shoulders, her eyelids sinking.

Eliza returned, out of breath with excitement.

"It's a miracle. Richard is alive!"

Bailey straightened. She'd seen all that blood. He was soaked in it.

"How is that possible?" she asked.

"They used something, MAST pants? I don't know, but it kept him alive until they got to Albany Medical. But they have to..." Eliza glanced at her kids, who both sat wide-eyed as two baby chipmunks. "They have to make him stay asleep for a little while, so his body can mend."

Was Eliza talking about a medically induced coma?

As Eliza ushered the children out for their dinner, Bailey stared into the darkness beyond the reach of the yellow porch bulb and tugged the blanket more closely about her shoulders.

"Bailey? Would you like to join us?"

She would like to. In fact, it was all she wanted since she'd rolled through that gate.

"Mason, go set the table. Harper. You can do napkins and silverware."

The pair rushed off.

Eliza looked at her eldest girl. "You, too, Aubree."

The teen followed the others inside.

"Does Richard have family nearby?" asked Bailey.

"No. He has a daughter. They don't talk."

"Wife?"

Eliza shook her head. "She died."

"Oh, how sad. Accident?"

"Suicide."

That landed hard. "Even sadder, then."

Bailey stared into the darkness beyond the reach of the yellow porch bulb and tugged the blanket more closely about her shoulders.

"I don't think you should go back to the cabin tonight."

"Really? Thank you. I was dreading going back there in the dark."

"Sheriff said to take extra precautions. I'll have Aubree set up the cot in the office."

Why had she assumed Eliza meant she'd stay in the house? Her disappointment must have been obvious.

"You didn't think I meant you'd stay here, did you?" Eliza snorted.

"I-I did, actually."

"Bailey, you're my assistant. And I want you safe but I need to consider my family's privacy."

"I understand." What she understood was that her welfare was low priority.

"You'll be safe in the barn. It's very secure. Phone, Wi-Fi, and solid locks." She arched a brow. "Security cameras." The pause stretched.

Bailey had the distinct impression Eliza would be watching.

* * *

Bailey walked back to the cabin just after seven the next day, to shower, change and get a thermos of coffee.

Eliza watched her from inside the screen as she passed.

What had she done to make Eliza so hostile? Was it the attack or her budding relationship with Aubree? This might just be the pattern. Squeeze every drop of work out of each assistant before firing them.

Confused and worried, Bailey hurried to wash up and then headed back to the office.

Before reaching the barn, she received a call from the sheriff's office requesting she come sign her formal statement. She sent a text asking permission—*permission*—to leave the property.

Eliza's call came a moment after the text landed. Her boss did not hide her annoyance as she granted Bailey's request to leave. Feeling her position was suddenly as unstable as an overloaded canoe, she hurried to the station and through the process as best she could.

Back at the farm, Eliza had some news.

"Sheriff Rathburn is on his way over. Let him in."

"I just left the station. Why is he coming?"

"Do I look like his assistant?" she snapped.

Bailey glanced away.

"Find out if this shit has hit the news yet." Eliza stormed into her office and closed the French doors.

Bailey went to work and did not speak to Eliza until she ushered Rathburn in.

She rapped on the closed door and waited for Eliza to glance up, scowl, and motion them in.

"I'd like to walk the entire property boundary," said Rathburn. "Look for any *other* signs of incursion."

Eliza's gaze flicked to her assistant, her eyes narrowing. Bailey's face heated as she broke eye contact.

"That's not necessary."

"It might be," he said.

"Not today."

The sheriff ran his knuckles over the stubble on his cheek, watching Eliza. Was he mad at being told no?

"We had a report of a truck stolen."

Bailey's ears perked up.

"That so?"

"Yeah. The thief returned it. Owner made a report and then called to cancel. He assumed someone took it by accident."

"Let me guess. Keys on the dash?" asked Eliza.

Rathburn nodded. "But it was the same night as your trespasser, which you should have reported to us."

Eliza's gaze flicked to Bailey once more, knowing she'd spilled the beans. She was still glaring when the sheriff spoke again.

"I don't like coincidences."

Eliza's frown vanished as she turned to the sheriff. "You're right. I'm sorry I didn't call you. And now Richard's been stabbed. This attack has me rattled."

"That's understandable."

Bailey's boss tented her hands and then tapped the index fingers together like a tiny heartbeat. "Can you post a person on the road?"

He gave a slow shake. "I don't have that kind of personnel. We're stretched thin because of a transfer."

"I see. Anything else?" she asked.

"Not at this time except to inform you that I am releasing the crime scene."

"Thank you. I'll walk you out."

They headed away together, and Bailey returned to her desk.

Did the sheriff suspect Eliza was hiding something?

THIRTY-SEVEN

By the end of the week, Bailey had had enough of sleeping on a cot in the barn office and moved back to her cabin. Bones had left her a dead bird as a welcome gift.

Eliza's fans picked up the report of the attack at the Watts Farm on Friday and news outlets reached out for comment. Her boss refused all interviews as the story conflicted with her branding.

Instead, Eliza ignored the ugly in her life and shared the video of their "private" anniversary celebration. Bailey got to edit the videos of the happy couple, add music and overlay the closed captions. In addition, Eliza scheduled a special live online event the first Saturday in July for her highest tier members.

Meanwhile, Bailey struggled to get back in her boss's good graces with little progress as Eliza continued to be frosty toward her, and Aubree's visits diminished. The attack was further buried by Eliza posting her news the second week in July that they were expecting, which blew up their feed, swamping Bailey with comments and the barrage of attention from fans, followers, sponsors, and the news media. Everyone seemed out of their minds with joy for Eliza, and new sponsors appeared like coins tumbling from a slot machine.

With the days stretching long and hot, many of the crops grew ready for harvest. Eliza filmed her family picking produce and packaging the goods for market, Mason's and Harper's fingers stained red with the raspberry juice. The actual work was done by the migrant pickers, and they would be back for the cherries and blueberries.

By month's end, there was still no progress on finding Richard's attacker and Eliza's security guy remained in a coma. But the story of the attack was well and truly quashed.

Eliza announced a gender reveal party to take place on August 24th at her store. Her backers at the Farmstead Fanatic level or higher were invited to attend in person. And everyone from Harvest Helper level and up could join Eliza's livestream of the event. The numbers of patrons soared as followers upped their monthly contributions to score an invite.

The gender reveal meant lots of prep and Bailey struggled to get ahead of the workload.

She missed seeing Aubree.

"You okay?" asked Bailey after another week without a visit from the girl.

She shrugged.

"Mom caught me trying to sneak out a couple of days ago. She gave me hell. Called me irresponsible. Said I'm ungrateful and reckless. It was really bad."

"Did she hurt you?"

"What? No. Nothing like that. Just, when she's angry, she makes you suffer."

"Aubree, if you don't feel safe, I can call child protective services."

There was more than enough cause.

"No." Aubree waved her hands. "They don't do anything

except make things worse. Plus she'll know it's you and fire you."

Bailey agreed. Eliza was a terrible mother. And a terribly lucky one. For now. But that was because her followers didn't know what was happening here.

The NDA she had signed did not cover crimes and a piece of paper would not keep Bailey from exposing Eliza for what she was. A fraud.

For years this woman had amplified the good and dodged all threats to her perfect little life. No one had ever knocked *her* to the ground and then curb-stomped her.

The little ripple of disaster had rolled on by, leaving her world intact.

Again.

Back then, the news had reported a brief hospital stay. Then she'd walked—no, danced—out of there and into a new life. And it seemed she never looked back.

But she would look back. Bailey was determined to make her remember it all.

Plans needed to change.

Bailey watched closely, wondering when the larger baby bump would be deployed. It finally appeared the third week in August in what was supposed to be Eliza's eighth month. Just in time for the gender reveal party.

The larger bump was hard to miss as Eliza made a video emphasizing how big she was getting. Fans' comments poured in with advice and support. The sponsor rolls grew by the week.

Eliza had hit the big time.

Most of the following week Bailey's days were filled with receiving sponsor products deliveries that would be featured in upcoming posts, handling email requests and party planning. They filled the entire supply closet and now spilled into the sorting barn.

But when Tory Nichols called in sick the Thursday before

the gender reveal party, Eliza added something new to her already long day.

Come to house.

Bailey had learned never to ask why or keep Eliza waiting. It was best to drop everything and come running or get an eviscerating verbal take down.

On my way

Bailey found Aubree waiting on the back porch.

"What's up?"

"She wants you to take me to the milking barn. She's too busy."

"Sure. Glad to."

Together, they headed through the light rain to the milking shed. Bailey thought this a wise precaution since the attack by the knife-wielding creep by the chicken coop and the attack on Richard. Bailey carried her trusty stick. It was something, anyway.

They reached the pasture; Morris made a racket rushing toward them. They paused. Bailey's ears went back.

"Why aren't the goats in the milking shed?" asked Aubree, pointing.

The goats always waited to be milked inside the shed. But they were clear on the other side of the pasture. Morris continued to bray.

Bailey's neck prickled.

Morris threw his head, pawing the muddy ground. Certainty settled heavy in Bailey's stomach.

"Something's wrong." She gave Aubree's arm a quick squeeze. "Wait here."

Then she spotted the shadow moving inside the shed.

"Run!" she cried.

Aubree sprinted toward the house, screaming.

The man stepped from the shed, eyes fixed on his retreating target.

He was above average height, overweight, and wearing green sweatpants and a dark hoodie drawn up around his face.

The same man. Bailey was certain.

"Just go!" she shouted at him.

"Not without her," he whispered.

His rasping voice raised the hairs on her neck.

The man charged. Bailey raised her stick as he plowed into her, knocking her flat. Then he rushed after the teen.

Bailey rolled to her stomach. From her peripheral vision, she spotted Eliza leaping down the back steps, holding something in one fist.

Eliza bolted past her daughter. What was in her hand?

A flashlight?

Bailey gained her feet and lifted her walking stick to join the fight. Aubree flew up the porch steps and hesitated, clutching the porch rail.

With a click, something flew from the end of the device Eliza pointed. Two wires shot forward, darting into the man's chest and shoulder. Eliza pressed a trigger and the man toppled. His jaw snapped shut and his body stiffened. Blood poured from his mouth.

Had he bitten his tongue?

Eliza held the trigger, and he continued to spasm.

A stun gun, Bailey realized. The woman's weapon ban did not extend to herself. Bailey could not help but admire the ferocity of Eliza's protective instinct and her ability to defend her family.

Eliza released the trigger. The man sagged on the ground. When he lifted his hand toward the dart impaled in his shoulder, Eliza squeezed the trigger again.

This time, when she stopped, she said, "You stay down, or I'll hit you again."

He did as he was told, lying in the mud outside the milking shed.

"You're going to jail."

He smiled and then spoke, his voice sounded sleepy and dazed. "Still found you. I know where she lives."

The threat gave Bailey a chill. It wasn't as if Eliza could move the farm.

This guy was dangerous, and he'd try again. A restraining order would be useless. And how many others like him were out there?

This man brought into sharp focus that Eliza's social media presence drew more than likes and endorsements. It also drew predators.

Had Bailey thought to be the only one attracted by these seemingly perfect parents and their adorable kids?

"Mom?"

Aubree stood on the porch, arms tightly folded.

"It's all right, honey. Go sit with the kids. Tell them they're safe."

Are they? Bailey didn't think so.

Eliza did not take her eyes off the intruder as her eldest girl headed inside. The look Eliza aimed at her captive made Bailey shiver.

This woman wasn't just protecting her kids. She was protecting her livelihood, her fame, and a gold mine.

"Bailey," said Eliza, her voice eerily calm. "Phone the sheriff."

She looked up the number and then called.

The man groaned. "I got to move the arrow in my chest."

He rolled but Eliza hit him again. The smile on her face was chilling.

Of the two, Bailey believed Eliza was the larger threat to her kids.

THIRTY-EIGHT

The arrest and subsequent interviews had drained away all Bailey's adrenaline. She was running on fumes.

The deputy sheriff had driven the intruder away hours ago. Bailey and all three kids watched from the front porch as the sheriff and Eliza spoke in the yard.

Bailey might have been able to hear the conversation, but the creaking chains on the porch swing ruined her efforts. She debated calling Mason and Harper off the porch, but then she'd have to keep them both busy and quiet.

"Did he hurt you?" asked Aubree.

"No. Just knocked me down."

"Morris warned us," said the teen. "He knew that man was in there."

"Thank God for that donkey."

"I think Mom heard Morris, too. She was there awful fast." Aubree drew her knees to her chest and hugged them. "He was trying to kidnap me. Wasn't he?"

Rather than diminish the truth, Bailey nodded.

"You think he's the one who stabbed Mr. Garrow?" asked Aubree.

"Very likely," said Bailey.

Eliza waved the sheriff off at dusk and joined them.

"Bryan said he'll send his deputy out with our statements tomorrow. So we don't have to go to the station to sign them."

"I have to sign something?" asked Aubree.

"No, sweetheart. You're a minor. I'll read it to you. We make any changes and I sign for you."

Aubree, clearly not pleased with this, crossed her arms to sulk at the reminder that she was still legally a child.

"Do you want to change the gender reveal party?" asked Bailey.

"Why?" Eliza looked miffed. "They got him. We're safer now than ever."

"Until the next kook comes after me," muttered Aubree.

Her mother glanced her way but ignored the comment.

"Would you like me to contact a company to get the perimeter alert working?" asked Bailey.

"Richard will finish it," said Eliza.

Her confidence was mystifying since, after three months, Richard was still unconscious. Wishful thinking? Delusional thinking?

Eliza lifted her chin, daring Bailey to contradict. She glanced away, deferring to her boss.

"You should head home." Eliza turned to her kids. "Let's get some supper."

Mason and Harper slid off the porch swing and hopped through the open front door like baby bunnies. Eliza let the screen slap closed behind them without a farewell to her assistant.

Bailey walked home, past Morris who came to meet her. Bonnet stood looking out of the shed complaining loudly.

Would anyone remember to milk them?

Eliza appeared on the back porch.

"Bailey. Wait. Aubree needs to milk the goats."

What time was it? The sunset blazed, turning the western clouds pink. A glance at her phone told her it was quarter to eight.

Aubree was quick, leaving Bailey to trudge back to the cabin. There she heated some beef and barley soup which she shared with Bones, who took his meal inside. Afterwards, he curled on her lap. He did not object when she buckled a flea collar around his thin neck.

"Bones? Are you becoming a housecat?"

His answer was a purr. She stroked his head, feeling the tattered ear, scabby skull, and raised scars. Bones closed his eyes.

She felt a tugging in her chest. Was that happiness? Impossible.

Her phone chimed, making her jump. Bones leapt down and stood at the door demanding immediate exit after her affront to his rest.

The text was from Eliza.

Need the spreadsheet of confirmed attendees.

Was she out of her mind? Bailey didn't have those here, in her cabin.

On the office computer. Want me to get them?

The three dots rolled and rolled again and then vanished. Had she been about to order her back out to go get them?

Yes. Definitely.

* * *

On Friday, Eliza continued to post flowers and rainbows, avoiding the unpleasantness that had occurred as a direct result of her exposing her teenage daughter to unstable men. The quiet did not last long.

Bailey arrived for work on time and found Eliza waiting for her.

"Sheriff called. Aubree's attacker will be arraigned today. He said that he won't get bail."

"That's a relief. Is he the one who stabbed Richard?" Bailey asked.

"They're investigating," said Eliza. "He denies it, of course."

"When Richard wakes up, he can identify his attacker."

"Yes," said Eliza and broke eye contact.

Bailey suddenly wondered if Richard was brain dead.

"Will he wake up?" Bailey asked.

Eliza grimaced, then said, "They took him off that medication and he still hasn't come to."

"So it's no longer a medically induced coma?"

Eliza cast her an impatient look as if this was somehow Bailey's fault. "Apparently not," she said.

"I'm sorry."

"Richard is strong. He'll make it," said Eliza.

Bailey was much less confident. That much blood loss, it could cause brain damage. Couldn't it?

"Turning to business, Tory's still down with the flu. So I'm assigning you to help Maud at the market."

Bailey's heart sank. She'd been looking forward to the gender reveal party.

"Oh, but don't you want me at the reveal?"

"You've lined up caterers, party planners, the entertainment, and extra staff for the store. Why do you need to be there?"

Was this some kind of punishment? Did Eliza not trust her?

"Besides, Aubree and you are thick as thieves, and I need her focused."

And there it was.

"Oh. I-I see. Well... sure. Same time?"

"Up before the birds," said Eliza, using her cheerful voice, so familiar to her followers.

Bailey wondered if she should mention the extra unpaid hours that the farmers' market added to her Saturday.

At five, Eliza breezed out, graceful as a swan instead of a waddling duck.

"I'll save you some cake!"

Was it Bailey's imagination or did Eliza seem to derive pleasure from depriving her assistant of any perks? Why did she feel like Cinderella missing the ball?

* * *

On market day, Bailey was surprised to see the line of guests waiting at the closed store.

It was six in the morning and the event wasn't for hours. Had they slept here?

Bailey drove on, ignoring the tug of regret at all she would miss. She'd planned each detail, from the custom-made cookies —honey, of course, but elaborately frosted. Fresh baked goods, also for sale. The three-tiered cake. The raffles, the games, the videographers, and the big reveal delivered by drone. Tiny collectable, sustainable pink treats floating down on little parachutes to the party goers and only available onsite.

She wondered how many minutes before they began appearing for sale online.

At the market, she drove to the stand and unloaded the crates. The booth setup was much the same, except that August brought a larger variety of flowers from the cutting garden and added tons of produce for sale.

Maud whistled during setup and sold bundles of her own products, as before. The crowds were good and sales consistent throughout the day. As the market drew to a close, Bailey decided this long-time employee might give her some answers on their boss.

"When did Eliza arrive in the valley?" That seemed like a good opener. Not personal.

"Must be nearly ten years. Came with her daughter and her dad. He bought the Steuben place for her. Then stayed to help her get started."

"Just the two of them?"

"And Aubree."

"What about Aubree's dad?"

"Neil? Nearly forgot about him. He left after a few months and she filed for divorce. He didn't contest it."

Maud turned to the T-shirts, removing the example on the back of the tent from the wooden hanger.

"Where is Neil now?" asked Bailey, helping Maud fold her unsold inventory.

Maud's answer was a shrug. "No idea. Never been back and Eliza doesn't want to talk about him. I respect her wishes."

Bailey nodded, dropping the subject. She chose her next question with care, couching it with an observation. "I'm glad for Eliza that she found Kaiden. Were they married here in town?"

This time Maud's answer was not immediate. She broke eye contact and offered a shrug. Her hesitation made Bailey take notice.

"Dunno."

Maud's body language said otherwise.

Bailey made another observation and watched to see how it landed.

"No wedding photos in her online albums. So it must have been before she started her vlog."

"Second marriage. That's just practical. And she wanted more babies. So..."

So a husband was a natural way to start. Especially in a

small, conservative farming community. A good place for a do-over, if you had the money.

The loading complete, Maud drove the Watts' van away and Bailey returned to her truck.

She made it back before three to find the farm's store and main gate closed, the party well over and all the guests gone.

Bailey found Eliza at her desk, editing video footage. She waited to hear a thank you for organizing the great event or some information on the reveal. Had the drone drops worked? Had attendance been stellar? Was the party a success? But instead, Eliza offered her a brief nod and said, "Oh, finally."

Bailey locked her teeth and forced a smile. "How was the party?"

"Videographer you picked was a perve. Hit on Aubree. Had to have Mason do some of the filming."

"Oh, I'm sorry. He came well recommended."

"You can't trust recommendations."

"Did the drone drop work?"

"Fabulous!" Eliza's smile dipped and she presented a fake pout. "I'm so sorry you missed it. But I'm posting the video now, so you can see it all. Nearly as good. Right?"

The difference between seeing cake and eating it, thought Bailey, but she said, "Can't wait."

Eliza stared a long, silent moment, but if she was looking for sarcasm, she'd be disappointed. Bailey smiled on.

"Good to be off my feet. My ankles are so swollen," said Eliza.

But, of course, nothing of her lower legs was visible beyond the flowing skirts and red cowboy boots.

"I'll bet," said Bailey, forcing the corners of her mouth higher.

"Harper is thrilled it's a girl. She wants a little sister."

"That's so great. Congratulations on everything."

"Thank you, Bailey. You know, when the baby arrives, I'm going to need you to pick up the slack."

Before she fired her, Bailey thought. But she said, "Absolutely."

The pause stretched. Bailey's smile grew heavy, but she held on. All she wanted was to be off her feet. But Eliza kept her standing at attention as if she were a plebe at bootcamp. Was it her imagination or was Eliza engaging in more power plays these days?

This would be her second twelve-hour day this month.

"Day off tomorrow," said Eliza. "Any big plans?"

"I thought I'd visit Richard."

"Oh, that's nice." She nodded her approval. "I need to get up there. But he is unconscious, so..." She waved a hand and returned her attention to her editing.

Conversation ceased until Bailey said goodnight.

Funny how Eliza believed she had it all handled while Maud robbed her blind and her daughter plotted her escape.

* * *

On her day off, she drove to Albany to visit Richard Garrow in the ICU. Unfortunately, it was family-only and she received only a condition update. After two months, he was still listed as critical.

"Has he woken up?" Bailey asked the nurse.

"He's fighting. That's all I can tell you."

"Is there brain damage?"

"We just don't know."

That was the best she could hope for.

Once back in town, she headed to the library to research computer tracking software. Bailey had noticed Eliza's recent lax laptop security and saw a chance to install this app. Finally, she swung by Tory's place with some chicken soup, electrolyte drinks, and the tissues that contained aloe vera. But she found the woman's truck gone, the lights out. She got no answer to her knock and didn't feel good about leaving food outside, so she took it back to the farm with her. She briefly wondered if Tory had taken herself to the hospital and hoped not.

In fact, the more she thought about it, the more she doubted Tory was sick.

She called Maud and asked her to check on Tory. Later on, she got a text that everything was fine but no explanation as to where Tory had been. Not in her sickbed, that was obvious.

Bailey got the feeling she was being played.

* * *

On Monday morning, Bailey handled phone calls and emails from sponsors eager to have their baby products linked to Eliza's very successful organic brand. Her opportunity to install the new app came before noon when Eliza went to speak to a delivery driver and left her computer running. Bailey took the opportunity to install a program she'd purchased. The software recorded keystrokes. By that afternoon, she had Eliza's passwords and access to her secure files. She printed several spreadsheets and all of Eliza's passwords.

Bailey checked the financial records first, beginning with Eliza's video-sharing account. Her branded posts brought her between five and twenty grand each. And she was doing one or more a day.

She did the math. The Watts Farm drew thirty-one grand a month on branded posts on this platform alone. That was nearly four hundred thousand a year.

The other outlets told a similar story. No less than a thousand dollars a post and the highest performing ones, featuring Morris or the kids being adorable or Eliza baking up something amazing, bringing closer to eight. Add the sponsorship money with the merchandise and produce sales and Eliza's income topped a million dollars annually.

Bailey thumped back in Eliza's expensive desk chair.

Her boss had everything going for her. She owned an amazingly profitable business in an ideal setting. Her kids were great and her fake husband provided them a part-time male role model and her a farm hand. Without a cloud in her sky, Eliza's life looked as if it could continue under sunny skies.

But the clouds always came back.

THIRTY-NINE

Aubree finally made an appearance at Bailey's place on Thursday night. At first, she thought the tapping was just one of the larger moths, driven to a frenzy by the electric light. But it was Aubree.

She let her in with more than a few unwelcome nocturnal insects.

"Well, hello stranger. A little late for ice cream and a movie."

Aubree rolled her eyes and gave a heavy sigh. "I couldn't get out. She's checking everything before she goes to bed."

"Still?"

Aubree shook her head in disgust. "She used to just tuck in the little ones and that was it. But now she peeks in before she turns in."

"Maybe she suspects you're sneaking out. Or maybe she's rattled that a fan came after you."

"They caught the guy. It should be safer now than ever."

Bailey lifted her brows. "*If* that's the guy by the coop and in the truck."

Aubree seemed to think about that, glancing toward the door. "Are you scared to walk over here?"

"It's never dark when I leave work."

"In the winter it will be. Oh, but..."

"But what?"

"Mom said she's keeping you until after Halloween. But then..." Aubree shook her head.

"I see. Well, you warned me."

Aubree tented her brows and cast Bailey a worried look. "But you won't leave before that?"

"No way."

"I wish I could come with you."

Bailey gave her a sad smile, then scooped rocky road into two dishes and placed them on the table with the chocolate sauce, sprinkles, and the open bag of pretzels.

Aubree helped herself.

"I found out something from Maud," said Bailey, realizing then that Maud never entered the actual farm. Aubree seemed more interested in ice cream than conversation, but Bailey persisted. "She worked for your mom—"

Aubree interrupted, mouth full and a blue and a white sprinkle fused to her chin. "Forever."

"Well, at least since you and your mom and your *dad* arrived here in this valley."

That got her attention. Aubree wiped her face, her intent gaze shifting to Bailey.

"My dad?"

"Your *real* dad."

She pounded her fists on the table, making her ice cream bowl jump and the spoon clatter to the floor. "I knew it!"

Aubree sank back into the plastic chair. Now that Bailey knew how much money Eliza made and had, the cheap furnishings and creepy little box of a cabin irritated her even more.

"Maud said that your mom came here with her husband. She said his name was Neil and he didn't stay long."

"He just left?"

Bailey shrugged. "That's one way it could have gone."

"How else?"

Bailey shook her head. "No idea. Maud either doesn't know or won't say."

Aubree stared out into space and the cabin went quiet except for the occasional moth bouncing off the mesh screening of the open window as if it were a vertical trampoline.

She closed her eyes, chin sinking. "I remember yelling. They fought."

"Just yelling?" Bailey waited as Aubree shifted in her seat, suddenly uncomfortable.

"Once he pushed her. She hit him with something. Then... I don't remember." Aubree covered her eyes with the pads of her fingers.

"Well, that all sounds terrible. Maybe it's good he left."

The teen pressed her palms to the table and splayed her fingers. "I wish he took me with him."

"You don't mean that."

"Don't I?" Her chin lifted at the challenge.

"Your mother loves you."

She snorted. "She loves that I babysit. Do half the milking and more than half the fieldwork. Collect eggs. Put the kids to bed and get them dressed. Supervise their lessons. Bet she'll have me changing all the diapers like she did with Harper."

"That's a lot of responsibility for someone your age."

She cocked her head. "Is it?"

Bailey hesitated, realizing that Aubree had no frame of reference for what was or was not normal for a girl her age. She cleared her throat and returned to the topic of her father.

"What are you going to do, Aubree? To find your dad?"

The teenager shook her head, seemingly lost. Her mouth opened and then closed. She had no answer.

Finally, she clasped her hands together, as if praying.

"Can you help me find him?"

FORTY

On the first Saturday in September, Bailey gave Bonnet and the twin babies each a tuft of grass and Morris a carrot.

Where was Thistle?

She peered around the pasture but saw no sign of the white goat. She'd mention her absence to Eliza.

Bailey was in the office when Kaiden rolled in and parked before the barn.

She stepped out to tell him that Eliza wanted him in the house for the first setup.

"No farmers' market for you this week?"

"Not today."

"Good. I missed seeing your pretty face."

"Did you now?" She decided that flirting right back might be a good way to drop her intel on him. "You know who isn't going to miss me?"

He placed his hands on his muscular thighs, leaned forward, and widened his eyes, as if she had his full attention.

"Who?" he asked.

"Maud."

"And why is that?"

"Because Tory is less observant than I am. Or she's in on it."

He straightened; his expression of rapt interest was replaced by one of confusion.

Bailey had the feeling that Eliza had picked Kaiden for more than his looks. He was not the sharpest tool in the shed, which worked to her advantage.

"In on what?"

"Skimming. I watched her pocket at least nine hundred dollars last time I worked the market. Eliza hasn't noticed a thing."

"Impossible. She has an inventory of everything."

"But Maud is adding her own knockoffs to the mix, and selling them along with Eliza's merchandise."

"Did you tell her?"

Bailey shook her head.

"Why not?"

"Well, you've also worked the farmers' market with Maud. I've seen the videos."

"Yeah."

"Then you must have noticed it too."

He gaped. Then he recovered and lifted his chin.

"Sure I did."

"I knew it. If you didn't tell her, there must be a reason."

"There is."

But he didn't give her one.

"I'm sure you know this too. But... here, it's easier to show you." She pulled up the video of Eliza telling him that they were pregnant on her phone.

"So?"

"Well, you have 6.9 million views. The gender reveal had even more."

He shrugged, losing interest.

"Also, I'm not really sharing anything you haven't already figured out. Video streams earn around eight cents per view.

The sponsorship rate is twenty dollars per 1,000 visits. This video has two sponsors."

He stared at the muted video.

"This single post generated a hundred and thirty thousand in sponsorship. The video with the entire family has even more."

Kaiden straightened. "Where'd you get that figure, about the sponsorship?"

"Simple web search. Here, let me show you." She extended her hand for his phone; he unlocked it and gave it to her. She punched in the search terms and then passed it back. "See?" She pointed at the two of the result summaries.

"Damn her!" he bellowed. "And she pays me SAG minimum plus a thousand bucks for each post. That bitch!"

He took one step toward the house, and she grabbed his arm, forcing herself to tears.

"Kaiden, what are you doing?"

"Getting a raise."

"But if you tell her how you found out, that I told you—"

He cut her off. "I could figure this out on my own. I don't need some flunky schooling me."

"Right. Of course."

He shook her off, clearly insulted that she thought he'd bring her words into this fight. He was proud, and beautiful, and Morris had at least thirty IQ points on him.

"Why did you tell me?" he said, suddenly frowning.

"I think she's exploiting her kids. She makes them work in the fields, keeps them all in a single bedroom, and I don't think they're getting even a minimum education. I was hoping you could maybe talk to her about it. She might listen to you. You could make sure they all have bank accounts and are being paid for their work. Parents are supposed to manage their children's earnings until they can do that themselves."

"But lots of stage moms dip into the pot."

"That doesn't make it right. I don't think she's even set up accounts for them. And you understand what kind of money they're making. She can afford to see to their futures."

"This is bad. She's a bad mother."

"You'll advocate for them?"

"You best believe it."

She'd loaded the shotgun and pointed him toward his target. He marched off, red-faced and fists clenched, while she crossed her fingers that Kaiden would leave her out of it.

Aubree was dressed and waiting in the kitchen for the usual Saturday session with their dad. The meal Ada Schmirkus had plated yesterday sat on the counter.

Ada had spent all Friday afternoon in the kitchen with her mom preparing and filming the meals. It was Ada's hands on the fast-motion, overhead shots of the counter.

Now most everything was a day old, and her mother didn't bother to heat any but the first plates for them.

"Mom, did you call the vet?"

Last night, Thistle had been lying down and did not rise, even when they fed the goats their ration of grain. Today, her mom had handled the morning milking while Aubree got her siblings up and dressed.

"Not now, Aubree. I'm busy."

"Did you see her? How did she look?"

"Later, I said."

Aubree returned to her place at the table.

Harper and Mason were so excited to see their dad and to have a few minutes of his attention. Harper held her latest painting and Mason hoped to take him to see the dirt pile where he used his wooden toy trucks. Meanwhile, she felt like the single duckling dropped in a nest of swans.

Dark, curvy, and getting two new pimples, she did not fit in this flock of blonds. But her dad didn't enter with his customary smile and greeting. He stormed through the entrance, throwing back the screen door so hard that it slammed against the house.

"Eliza!" he bellowed.

Harper dropped her painting and Mason startled, his arms going straight out to grip the edge of the table as if to stop himself from falling. The two children scampered behind their mom.

Aubree's mom's jaw bulged as she went stiff and still. Only her eyes moved, going wide and then darting here and there. She seemed to be searching for something.

She pushed the little ones toward the kitchen door.

"Backyard. Now," she said and gave Mason a shove.

They hesitated at the door until their dad burst into the dining room, red-faced and panting. Spittle flew from his mouth, as if he had rabies.

Aubree sucked in a breath and the kids dashed out. Her dad stalked forward. The back door slammed. She wanted to follow Mason but was trapped between her mother and her father, who lurched forward like a mad dog.

"Millions. You're making millions. And paying me pennies!" he shouted.

Paying him? What was he talking about?

Bailey arrived, appearing behind Kaiden, her face drawn and her hands twisting together.

"Aubree, go outside," whispered her mom. "Kaiden, simmer down."

Babysitting again. Banished from all adult conversations.

Bailey was the only person who didn't treat her like a kid.

Her mother's assistant motioned toward the kitchen with her head. Aubree slipped past her mother and out of sight. But she didn't leave the house. Was her father going to hurt her mom? Should she call for help?

Aubree ducked into the foyer that stretched from front to back door as her dad shouted, "Admit it!"

The screen door hung by one hinge. Her father had nearly torn it from the frame.

Indecision froze her to the spot. Mason and Harper stood outside the back door, clinging to each other and staring with wide eyes.

"Answer me!" bellowed her dad.

"Kaiden, you calm down or I swear I'll call the sheriff."

"And I'll expose this whole thing."

What does that mean?

"I'll tell them all exactly what you are and what you did."

"I'm sorry, Eliza, he just asked me how many hits your announcement got. Then he did the math." That was Bailey's voice, higher than usual and carrying an unfamiliar tremor.

"You what?" shouted Eliza.

"*I* did the math!" shouted Kaiden. "Millions of views. You are making thousands of dollars on every goddamn post."

Something shattered. Aubree jumped. Was that the vase of cut flowers?

"Don't you speak to me like that in my own home."

Aubree furrowed her brow. Why had she said *my* home, emphasized the word as if her dad had no real place here? She knew he didn't live here. But some parents lived apart. At least that's what her mother said.

"I'll do what I like. I'm their father. Right?"

There was a long pause. What was happening?

"Don't touch me!"

That was her mother. Aubree took a step forward.

"Calm down. Both of you," said Bailey.

Her dad's voice was still loud and angry. "Don't tell me to calm down!"

Then another crash and a thump. It was too much. Aubree charged back into the kitchen. Her mother lay sprawled on the floor, hands braced behind her. Her dad loomed with fists clenched.

She shrieked at them. "Stop it! Stop!"

All three heads snapped around to stare at her, frozen like a tableau of violence. No one moved for several heartbeats.

Then her dad offered her mother his hand. She slapped it away and stood without his help.

Bailey moved to Aubree's mom. A single support in this battle between the two most important adults in her life.

"Let's discuss this," said her mother.

"Fine." Her dad raked his fingers through his hair and Aubree frowned. The roots of his hair were dark.

Why had she never noticed that before?

"Not here."

"Then where?" he said.

Aubree's mom pointed toward the front of the house. They stormed off, marching past the tilted screen and out of sight.

Aubree released Bailey's hand, hurrying to the open front door.

Her dad hustled to catch her mom and tried to clasp her elbow, but she shook him off. They disappeared into the barn office.

"Should we go after them?" asked Bailey.

"I don't know."

Bailey cast her a worried look. "He shoved her to the ground."

Aubree held back the whimper in her throat, but her vision blurred, making the yard swim before her eyes.

They crept to the front porch, slinking along like two members of some elite military team, using the ferns and support posts for cover.

"We could call the sheriff. Report your dad for domestic abuse." Bailey pressed a hand to the back of her neck.

But they didn't call. Just watched and waited, barely breathing.

The birds continued to sing and flit from branch to branch as if the world was not collapsing underneath Aubree's feet.

"Here they come," said Bailey, lifting a finger as the two emerged from the barn.

Aubree spotted her mother carrying a familiar satchel.

"Oh no."

Bailey diverted her attention to glance at her.

"What?"

"That's the bag where she keeps her gun."

"What? What do you mean? You think she'll hurt him?" Bailey sounded shocked.

Aubree chewed her lower lip. Indecision paralyzed her.

Bailey watched Aubree's parents. "They're taking Kaiden's truck."

"Should we stop them?" Aubree asked.

"How?" Bailey dashed to the end of the porch as the truck pulled out. "What is she going to do?" Bailey looked panicky and was breathing hard.

Aubree backed into the house as the fear finally found her, shaking her to bits.

Where were they going?

Why did her mother think she needed a gun? Was it for protection or...

But then she thought of her father. The real one with dark hair who used to carry her on his shoulders. The one who disappeared and never came back.

Had her mother done that, too?

And in her heart, she knew what her mother would do to any man who threw her to the ground in her own house. To a man who shouted at her and frightened her kids.

Her mother was strong. Too strong, maybe.

"Aubree? You all right?" asked Bailey.

"We gotta get Harper and Mason." If she was afraid, they would be terrified.

She knew that her mom would be back. But uncertainty gnawed. What if she took away this dad, too?

FORTY-TWO

BAILEY

Bailey gathered the weeping little ones in her arms and rocked them. Seated there on the backsteps, facing the yard, fields, and trees that flanked the river, she hushed and cooed and stroked the soft hair on their heads.

Aubree sat beside her, cradling her face in her hands as she stared into space with unfocused eyes.

"I want Mama!" wailed Harper and then buried her face against Bailey's shoulder.

"She'll be back soon."

Aubree cast her a glance.

"I remember this," she whispered.

"What do you mean?" asked Bailey, still swaying back and forth with the kids. "We all remember. It just happened."

"No. Before."

Bailey glanced past the blond head pressed to her.

"Before?"

Aubree nodded. "Them fighting. The police coming to the door."

"Are you talking about..." Bailey's words fell away and their eyes met. Aubree inclined her head. This wasn't about Kaiden.

This was about the man before him. The dark-headed man Aubree believed was her father.

"When?" asked Bailey.

"That time before we came here." Aubree stared at Bailey. "And I remember that... that he never came back."

This news caused Mason to wail. Both the kids now howled like coyotes, heads lifted and tears streaming from the corners of their eyes.

Bailey patted Harper's heaving back as the child choked on her tears.

"I want Daddy!" she cried.

"All right now. That's enough," Bailey whispered. "You're okay. I got you."

The kids wanted Kaiden. Ironic, she thought, because he obviously cared nothing about them. Though she'd told him the kids lacked any schooling and expressed her concerns they were being exploited, he confronted Eliza only about being cheated. He hadn't spent one breath challenging her about her care of the kids.

"Listen," said Aubree.

The two little ones both sat tall, straining to hear. Bailey recognized the clatter of a diesel engine and then the distant rumble of tires on gravel.

"That's Dad's truck."

Mason leapt off the steps and ran toward the drive. Harper scurried after him. Bailey and Aubree followed, coming around the house together, in time to see Kaiden's red truck pull to a stop.

The door opened on the driver's side.

And only Eliza climbed out.

* * *

Mason pulled up short at seeing his mom drop from the driver's seat. But Harper ran to her, howling like a rising wind. Her mom stooped to lift her to her hip.

Bailey and Aubree stopped behind Mason. Aubree's hands slipped protectively to her brother's shoulders as they waited for Eliza to reach them.

Once there, she handed Bailey her phone.

"Film this. Livestream. I can only do it once."

Bailey took the camera, warm from Eliza's skirt pocket. Where was the bag holding the gun? Where was Kaiden?

Eliza sat on the porch steps with the little ones flanking her, and Aubree, seated one step below, turned to stare up at her mom. Their arrangement reminded Bailey of a stage play.

Bailey moved as directed, capturing all three of the children's faces under the bright morning light with a background of empty furniture and red potted geraniums.

The shot did not include the screen door, hanging cockeyed by only one hinge.

It was a good setup, and Bailey didn't recall ever seeing content filmed here. That made it different. One look at the still image and her followers would know something had happened. They wouldn't be able to keep themselves from watching.

Eliza counted them in and waited two silent beats before beginning.

"Harper, Mason, Aubree, I have to tell you something that will be hard to hear."

The kids all had pink faces and red-rimmed eyes. They seemed aware that tragedy had already struck. Bailey had to keep herself from leaning in to hear Eliza's next words.

Her voice trembled. Gone was her usual exuberance. The shroud of sobriety hung over them with the boughs of the sugar maples.

"Your father has left us. I'll be filing for a divorce. Do you know what that is?"

The little ones shook their heads. They had no classmates whose parents had already introduced the word. Aubree knew it. Bailey could tell by the way she rolled her lips in and bit down, as if to keep from screaming.

"It's when a mommy and daddy decide that it is best for their family to live apart."

Of course, the two little ones looked baffled. Their mommy and daddy already lived apart. Not that any of Eliza's followers knew this.

"But he's coming back?" asked Aubree.

Eliza shoulders slumped and the tears swimming on her lower lids dribbled down her cheeks.

"No. He won't be coming back."

This caused Harper to wail as if she'd touched a hot skillet. She threw herself across her mother's lap to sob.

"But why?" asked Mason.

"It's because of a big word. I don't think you'll understand it. The word is infidelity. Your dad was unfaithful to me—to us." She looked right at her assistant now.

Bailey's mouth went dry. Did her boss believe she could be that stupid?

Then she realized that Eliza wasn't staring at her. She was staring at the camera, her followers.

"He doesn't want to live here with us. He wants a different life. And we can't make him come back. Even if that's what we want the most."

Mason choked on his tears now, swiping bravely at his eyes with the neck of his T-shirt.

"I don't want him to leave," he said, his voice rising to a crescendo on that last word.

"I know, sweetheart. I know."

Aubree had her head on her mother's opposite knee and her arms around her little sister. Harper trembled and let out a gasp with her sobs. Eliza drew her son close.

"We'll get through this together." Eliza looked at each of her kids and then rested her free hand on her stomach, the baby bump.

The four created a tableau of family grief. And the livestream captured it all.

Oh, this was going to drive her followers crazy. Kaiden better run because they would be after him, at least on social media.

But Kaiden didn't have an account. He didn't post on the video blog. And if what Eliza had told Bailey were true, he was not blond, did not have blue eyes, and his name wasn't Kaiden.

With one public announcement, Eliza had become a single mother with three kids and a baby on the way. Bailey couldn't help but think that Kaiden's departure was the absolute best thing that could have happened to this family business.

Eliza looked at Bailey, tears dripping down her face.

"It's a sad day here. But I'm thankful for all of you and your unflagging support."

Eliza made the slightest motion to her throat and Bailey stopped the feed then lowered the phone.

"That post will set records," she said, her voice cold and angry.

Eliza reclaimed her phone, then ushered the weeping children inside, pausing to glance back at Bailey.

"Do you know how to drive a backhoe?" she asked.

Bailey shook her head.

Eliza cast her a look of annoyance.

"Come inside to watch the kids. Keep them in the living room. I have to bury something."

FORTY-THREE

What was Eliza burying?

Bailey pondered this as she watched the kids playing with Mason's toy trucks in the dirt. Aubree sat beside her staring vacantly out at nothing.

Eliza had driven the backhoe out of the storage barn through pastures and out of sight.

"You okay?" asked Bailey.

Aubree shook her head but remained mute. Finally, she said, "She made him go."

"It's not your fault," said Bailey.

"No. It's *my mom's* fault." She spit the words. "*If* she even is our mom. And she told us at the same time she told her followers! Another grand performance." Aubree threw up her hands in frustration. "They're more important than we are."

"Have you seen her video blog?"

"A couple of times. She didn't shut down her computer, and I had a look."

"Have you ever done a search for the dark-haired man you remember?"

Aubree's chin dropped to her chest. "I don't know how to do that."

"I could help you find him."

Her eyes sparkled with interest. "You'd do that?"

"Yes, if he's your daddy, I think you should know what happened and why he left."

From the road came the low rumble of an engine.

Aubree stood. "She's back."

A moment later, the backhoe rolled into the side yard. Clumps of grass and clods of dirt covered the teeth of the back bucket.

Eliza waved and the little kids rose from their own excavations to wave back.

"I wonder what she buried," said Bailey.

Only the teen's eyes moved as she tracked her mother until she and the backhoe disappeared.

They were all waiting in the kitchen when she returned.

Eliza studied them in silence, picked up the closest plate of food, and threw it at the back door. The plate shattered and the kids wailed.

"Aubree, take them to their room."

Her daughter hesitated. Bailey half expected the teen to confront her mom. Instead, she lifted Harper to her hip and took Mason's hand, leading them away.

Eliza covered her face in her hands and squatted on the floor, silently weeping. Bailey watched, afraid to move.

Finally, Eliza lifted her head, her brows low and angry.

"*You* did this," Eliza hissed.

"What? I didn't."

Her boss aimed a finger at Bailey. "You did. You said something. I know it."

"Eliza, please—"

She cut her off. "Zip it."

Had Kaiden told her? It didn't matter. Bailey would deny everything. At worst, it would be a he said, she said.

"Years he never understood the income stream. You show up and bang, he's a tech wunderkind. I'm not buying it."

"I never said a word, Eliza. I swear to God."

Her boss dashed away the moisture from her cheeks and stood, fists clenched.

"Get out of my sight," snapped Eliza.

Dismissed, Bailey turned tail and hurried away.

"And Bailey?"

She hesitated at the screen door, stifling the urge to run.

"If you did this, I will make you sorry."

*　*　*

Late in the day, Bailey heard the diesel truck turn over. A few moments later, the gate chimed an alert. An hour passed before the next gate notification. Eliza drove Kaiden's truck right past the barn and toward the pasture.

Eliza used the tractor or backhoe in the fields. Bailey had never seen her drive a truck down there. So what was she doing?

Bailey itched to follow but didn't dare leave her desk.

When Eliza arrived twenty minutes later Bailey asked, "Everything okay?"

"Moved a deer carcass out of the pasture."

Bailey wrinkled her nose.

Eliza offered nothing more and Bailey didn't know what to believe.

"What's the chatter online?" asked Eliza, scooping up her laptop.

"Mostly support. Concerns from a few sponsors and offers from new ones."

"Send me the offers."

Eliza spent the rest of the day in the house with her kids and her laptop. Bailey wished she were a fly on the wall.

Meanwhile, in the virtual world, Eliza's bombshell announcement sounded like a tornado siren, blasting far and wide. Despite the epic numbers, she advertised to be certain all her followers received the stunning news. The response was immediate and overwhelmingly supportive.

People could be good sometimes and they could be gullible.

Hundreds of thousands of hits, views, shares, and comments. The tsunami of activity grabbed sponsors' attention and Bailey spent the afternoon forwarding offers from manufacturers of baby products, women's rights groups, and divorce attorneys who seemed frantic to represent her.

Bailey remained late trying to clear the inbox. But the emails were flying in faster than she could even read them so she gave up and headed back to her rabbit hutch.

There was no one in sight. At the side yard and pasture, Morris greeted her as usual.

Bailey scratched Morris under the chin.

"Where are the goats?" she asked. But the donkey just closed his eyes and drew back his big velvety lips in ecstasy.

Finally, Bonnet stepped from the milking shed followed by the kids and then Thistle, who trotted gamely along. A glance at their bags showed the nannies had been milked.

"There you guys are."

Morris accepted a treat, and Bailey turned to go but a voice stopped her.

"Don't feed my animals unless you're told to."

She jumped, then turned. Eliza loomed on the back porch.

How long had the woman been watching her?

"Oh, of course not." Bailey gulped. The silence settled about them like fog. "Uh, Thistle looks better."

Eliza's gaze flicked to the pasture. "Yes, seems to be back to her old self."

Bailey had a thousand questions but proceeded with caution.

"Where are the kids?"

Eliza's eyes narrowed and her mouth pressed into a thin line. Bailey had annoyed her boss again, but she held her look of interest against the obvious glare.

"Saturday is bath night."

But they had no bath in their room. Just a tiny fiberglass shower.

"Harper loves the tub." The lie was so smooth, it melted off Eliza's tongue like butter on hot bread.

Her smile held a secret. Bailey pretended not to notice as she eyed the villain in silence. The stillness choked her.

"How are they doing?"

"Bewildered, I think."

Bailey was desperate to ask what happened. Where did Eliza and Kaiden go? How did she end up alone in his truck? Where was Kaiden?

But pushing would get her fired. She was certain. And whatever Eliza said might be another lie. Or another threat.

Should she tell her boss that her oldest daughter believed her mom had hurt her dad? Should she assure her again that she wasn't responsible for Kaiden's outburst?

She felt her neck stretched and ready for the guillotine. Eliza, the queen of hearts, might cut her with a word.

Not yet. Please, not yet.

Her thoughts were so loud, it was a wonder Eliza couldn't hear them.

Eliza rested both hands on her new baby bump.

"I'm going to tell you a secret." She said this with no preamble and then added, "And you're going to keep it because if you don't I'll sic my lawyers on you. They're ruthless. Just like me."

FORTY-FOUR

Bailey stood below the backsteps wondering why her boss would share something with someone she didn't trust, had just threatened, and planned to fire.

She needed to be careful. Eliza might be hunting for a fall guy. Bailey could not take anything this woman said at face-value.

Her boss sat on the bench beside the kitchen window. She didn't speak, and Bailey's heart ricochetted around her chest. Should she ask her what the secret might be or wait?

Finally, Eliza said, "Kaiden is gone for good."

"Gone where?" asked Bailey.

"Settlement. He's greedy and shortsighted. Easy fix. We have a termination clause. So I fired him."

Was this the truth?

Eliza's steady gaze raised Bailey's skin to gooseflesh. If she'd fired Kaiden after so many years, she wouldn't hesitate to do the same to her. Or worse.

"He was shocked. Hurt, too, I think. Realized too late what he'd lost. It couldn't have been all acting. He's not that good."

"I know the kids love him."

"My followers, too. He's got charisma, that's for sure. I paid him a bonus to keep him off social media. Last thing I need is him popping up on a morning talk show. Told him if he breaks our deal I'll press assault charges, and I reminded him I have a witness."

Bailey let out a breath. Eliza needed her, for now.

"And he did this stupid thing in front of my kids. Burned that bridge to ash."

"He accepted everything?"

"Didn't give him an option, except arrest. I made a formal statement with the sheriff and showed it to him. Threatened to press charges."

She had neatly yanked the rug from beneath Kaiden. The spectacle terrified Bailey. Eliza was a formidable opponent.

"So after a respectable time, I'll start interviews again. Everyone's replaceable." She let that settle without adding the unspoken words, *including you.* Bailey kept her head down.

"He's such an egotistical ass, I'm glad to see him go before this little one can remember him." She cradled her belly and smiled.

"I'm sorry."

"Don't be. I'm getting more sponsorship opportunities than ever and the video watches are generating record income. Tomorrow I'll sort those offers and consider which will work best for my branding."

It seemed Eliza had figured out a way to turn Kaiden's removal into yet another money-making machine.

"You think he'll come back?"

"He won't."

Eliza stood. Bailey thought she overplayed the difficulty of getting to her feet.

"Is there anything new with Richard?" asked Bailey.

"'Unchanged,' they say. Hopefully Richard doesn't come out of this a vegetable. Got enough of those around here."

Was that supposed to be funny?

"Meantime, I found a new security guy."

Another reminder that, to Eliza, people were interchangeable. She was wrong, though. Some could never be replaced.

Eliza paused at the back door. "See you Monday, Bailey."

* * *

Eliza's words about Kaiden's departure were prophetic. The sponsorship deals were phenomenal, and she took many. By October the tops of the maple trees had turned golden, the free products arrived and the sponsorship videos, unboxing videos, demonstration videos, and pregnancy updates continued as the deliveries changed from pregnancy items to baby clothes, toys, cribs, carriers, car seats, monitors, and every conceivable type of stroller. Did they know there were no sidewalks on the farm?

The kids were generally cheerful with sad moments that did not last as long as Bailey would have expected after the loss of the only dad they ever knew. Kids seemed more adaptable than adults, handling changes that would fracture a grown person into tiny sharp slivers.

Eliza posted some sad posts because they were popular.

The tears grew less frequent as the Saturdays came and went without their father. Eliza made each so special, and the younger kids enjoyed themselves with the new tether ball set, and an inflatable bouncy castle at the store for Morris's birthday party. Their mom confided to her followers she was trying to set a new normal. And she asked for advice, which she never looked at and Bailey had to handle.

Aubree, at least, was not distracted. She grew more sullen and surly, still furious with her mother.

"She did not behave this way before *your* arrival," said Eliza to Bailey after Aubree stomped away.

"I think it's more Kaiden's departure."

"Is that what you *think*, Captain Obvious?"

The venom in Eliza's tone kept Bailey silently working the rest of the day. It was always easier to kick the dog. But it was hard being the dog.

The following Monday, and the week of her official due date, Eliza declared she was too close to delivery to help in the fields.

Morris featured in more videos as Eliza shared tips for making simple, quick, nutritious meals and posted content she'd stockpiled for this occasion.

But she did post two new videos. The first was of the apple harvest, which was stellar. Tory and the kids had picked baskets full for Saturday's market. And Bailey filmed the fallen apples being turned into cider at a local mill.

Harper could not reach even the lowest apples on the tree and so she stole one out of Mason's basket, with her brother unaware.

The images were lovely and dear and lacking the part when Mason caught Harper red-handed and shoved her, spilling both baskets and bringing Harper to tears.

The second spot was of the nursery, newly painted by a local handyman.

"Pale lavender is such a soothing color. This one is called..." and the plug, color title, brand, and link were all neatly furnished.

Bailey filmed Eliza's tour of the room. The sponsor's crib sat empty and waiting. The long pan included dozens of endorsed products, all new and neatly stacked. Bailey zoomed in on the mobile, filmed Eliza demonstrating the features of the monitor, and highlighted the changing table stacked with bags of diapers. Eliza pointed out the eastern exposure and a nice view of Morris and the goats.

Bailey, filming the video, watched Thistle headbutt one of the twins away.

The migrant pickers arrived for the actual harvest of the pears and apples.

Eliza and Tory tackled the mountain of orders, giving Bailey an opportunity to speak privately to Aubree.

Since Kaiden's departure, her eldest had not performed for the camera and Bailey had been witness to more than one loud fight. Aubree wanted to speak to her father. Her mother flatly refused. As their relationship worsened, the tension grew. And Eliza continued to blame Bailey for the rift.

Despite Eliza's rancor, Aubree needed a friend and mentor, and Bailey was happy to fill that role.

Most of Eliza's previous assistants had lasted only a few months and Bailey had been here just over five. Time was running out.

FORTY-FIVE

The sheriff appeared again on Friday.

Bailey let him through the gate and shortly afterwards was called to come and sit with Aubree. She passed Rathburn on the front porch. He gave her a long up and down look, as men do, but lingered on her feet.

"New boots?" he asked.

"Not really. Had them awhile." She'd bought these with her first paycheck and returned the borrowed ones. These were a better fit, and did still look almost new.

"Like 'em?"

"Yeah. They're comfortable." Bailey continued on her way and found Eliza and Aubree in the kitchen engaged in a silent battle. There had been some kind of exchange judging from Aubree's cross-armed sulk and Eliza's evident fury.

In the backyard, Mason and Harper darted by the window, taking running starts at the new tetherball and giving it mighty whacks.

Eliza left them to see to the sheriff.

"Want me to fix you something to eat?" asked Bailey.

Aubree shook her head. "Not hungry."

Her appetite had left with her father and the girl was losing weight. At a time when she should be insatiable, she was full of grief.

She slumped on the bench, tracing the woodgrain pattern with her index finger as her brows dipped over stormy eyes.

"You miss your dad a lot, huh?"

Her finger stilled. Aubree wrapped her arms around herself and nodded.

"He isn't my dad. But he sorta is. The only one I ever really had at least."

"I understand grieving the loss of a loved one."

Aubree was young and despite Bailey's revelation in her attempt to console, the teen's focus remained on her own problems.

"He promised, if she ever sent him away, that he'd come back for me. But he hasn't."

Bailey knew Kaiden wasn't coming back and, if he did, he wouldn't be allowed near Aubree.

"I'm sorry. But if they are divorcing, they have deep problems. Ones that take time to work out."

"*She's* the problem. She's doing it again."

Now the teen had Bailey's complete interest. "Meaning what?"

"I've been remembering things from before. Big fights with my dad. The other dad, my *real* dad, in a different place. Then we came here with him and my grandpa. I remember him. My mom's dad helped with the planting and he built our first greenhouse." Aubree stared into space with sightless eyes. "But my dad didn't stay. They had the biggest fight ever, all three of them, and then my dad drove away. Just like now. He was... gone. You know?"

Bailey did know, yes. All too clearly. The memories made her chest ache.

"Was this when the police came to your house?" asked Bailey, recalling what the girl had told her.

"No, after." Aubree swept the hair off her forehead.

"I see."

"And she's so mean! Why can't I leave the farm? I'm not allowed to drive. Not even the tractor. And none of us can ride in the truck or the RV. Why doesn't she teach us stuff? Not just how to milk goats and preserve food. I hate it here."

There was a point, Bailey knew, when teens felt oppressed and stifled by their parents and their rules. Aubree had reached that moment. Without college as an escape, the launch to adulthood could be fraught with peril. Whether she appreciated her mother or not, Eliza provided a safety net, regular meals, and a clean, warm place to sleep. Aubree might be angry, but she didn't understand what waited out there for a girl without people to look after her.

But Bailey did.

"Your mom is protecting you."

"She isn't!" Aubree threw up her hands in frustration. "She just wants us to do what *she* wants. Says if we don't, we'll be homeless."

"The farm is most of your income."

"I don't care! I want my dad and she drove him off, just like Kaiden. Plus, she's always lying to us. To everyone!"

"About what?" asked Bailey.

"About being pregnant. About Thistle. About my dad and about what happened after they drove away."

"Thistle? What's wrong with Thistle?"

"She's gone."

Bailey was confused.

"But I saw the white goat this morning."

Aubree shook her head. "That goat arrived today. She's not Thistle."

"You sure?" Bailey asked.

Aubree's nod was adamant. "Mom got rid of Thistle just like she got rid of Dad. But he wouldn't just leave and never come back."

"Men do."

Her eyes glittered. "Yeah? Why did she come back in my dad's truck? He loved that truck. He would never leave it behind. He'd never leave *us* behind."

Aubree bolted down the hall so fast, she was a blur. Bailey followed as far as the front steps, where Aubree reached the sheriff.

"Can you help me find my dad?" Aubree asked.

The uniformed officer turned toward her.

"What's that, honey?" he asked.

"My dad. He left a month ago."

The sheriff glanced at Eliza, who gave a nearly imperceptible shake of her head.

"We need him back."

Eliza cast Bailey an impatient look, pressing her hands to her hips. "Aubree, go inside."

"He's missing," said Aubree.

"We are aware of the situation," said the sheriff.

"Well, what are you doing about it?" asked Aubree.

"Go inside now," said Eliza and then pinned Bailey with a look. "Get her inside."

What did she want her assistant to do, pick her daughter up and carry her like a naughty toddler?

The teen pointed toward the barn. "His truck is still here. How did he leave without his truck?"

The sheriff cast away a long breath. Then he faced Aubree and said, "Your dad is fine, young lady."

"Have you seen him?"

"I have not."

Eliza pointed to the house. "Inside. Now."

Aubree faced her mom, her face pink and nostrils flaring. "What did you do with Thistle? I know you took her."

"Honestly, Aubree. A milking goat is a milking goat. What does it matter?"

"Where is she?"

Eliza rolled her eyes upward. "I replaced her because she's not producing milk."

Her daughter burst into tears and fled toward the animal enclosure.

Eliza turned to Bailey. "Look after her."

"Of course."

It was ever and always what she wanted.

Eliza was losing them. Didn't she see that?

No. She did not. But there were some jobs a mother just couldn't farm out.

FORTY-SIX

AUBREE

Aubree's face felt hot and her breathing came in angry blasts. She leaned on the wooden planking of Morris's pasture, her emotions see-sawing between fury and embarrassment. Her mother was so mean! And her father was gone and no one was even looking for him.

"Aubree?"

She stiffened and then recognized Bailey's voice. She relaxed, letting her shoulders drop.

"You need a hug?" asked Bailey.

Aubree burst into tears. Bailey drew her into a warm embrace, rocking her. At least one person understood her.

"Aubree!"

She stiffened at her mother's sharp tone.

Bailey stepped back. Her mom stood before them, her face red and her mouth tight. Bailey cast her an apologetic glance and left them.

"Inside, young lady. Now!" The barked command got her moving.

Her mother marched her up the steps, gripping her arm so tight it hurt. In the foyer, she released her.

On the stairs, her brother and sister hid behind the spindles, having somehow managed to get inside without notice. They stared, wide-eyed in fear. Aubree faced her mother. Whatever their mom was going to say, they could hear it, too.

"What was that, young lady?" asked her mom.

"Where's our dad?"

"He left us."

"You made him go."

Her mom's voice quavered. "I didn't. I swear."

"I don't believe you. I don't believe anything you say. You're a liar."

"This is not how you were raised. Speaking out of turn. Embarrassing me in front of Sheriff Rathburn."

"I don't care!" Aubree shouted.

Mason's gasp gave away their hiding place. Their mom turned, spotting them peering through the rails like criminals in lock-up. The pair fled upstairs.

Aubree faced her mom. "I hate you!"

* * *

Ever since that guy tried to grab her, Aubree's mom refused to let her go to the milking shed alone. Aubree didn't want a nurse-maid but at five that evening, Bailey arrived to escort her.

"I don't need you to walk me," she said and then felt guilty at seeing Bailey's disappointment.

"I'm sorry. Do you mind my company?"

"It's not you. I just want to be alone sometimes, is all."

"I get it. But Aubree, someone tried to grab you—twice. And someone stabbed Richard. It's not safe alone out here."

"He's in jail."

Bailey waved away her words with one hand. "They don't know if the man they arrested is the one who did that to Richard or who attacked you at the coop."

Bailey understood her frustration, but she was hired help and had to do as she was told.

They headed out together. At the fence, Aubree paused and Bailey continued to the milk shed, giving her what privacy she could.

The donkey stood by the fence, dozing. She whispered his name. He lifted his head and brayed his greeting. She placed a hand on his velvety nose, and he quieted.

"There's my best buddy."

She'd been right here when Morris arrived in the pasture. In the early days she would ride him. Now her feet dangled all the way to the ground, and she felt too heavy a load.

"You want to walk to the river tomorrow? Have a bath?"

He nuzzled her. Aubree gave him another scratch and waited as Bailey checked the shed for intruders, as her mom had asked.

"All clear," she said and left her alone.

The two remaining kids stood in the milk shed with Bonnet, bits of straw clinging to their hides. Outside in the pasture, the white goat watched the others.

She glared at the imposter, who remained well out of reach.

"You're not Thistle. So I'm going to call you Gristle," she said, narrowing her eyes at the interloper.

Why would her mother switch this goat for Thistle? And then it struck her, and the tears flowed faster as she rested a hand on Bonnet's head. The goat stared up at her.

"She died, didn't she, Bonnet? She died and Mom thought we wouldn't notice."

Her brother and sister hadn't. But they didn't do the milking. To them, a white goat in the pasture was a white goat. But Aubree knew the difference. So did Thistle's twins.

She was going to confront her mother about the goat. If she got any straight answers, she'd ask again about her dad. If her mother lied to her, she was going to find the answers herself.

* * *

On Saturday, Eliza was one day past her due date. Maud arrived in the gray pre-dawn for the farmer's market load up. Aubree shivered as she hurried to the barn to find her mother with Tory and Maud, who loaded the van.

"Aubree, who's watching your brother and sister?"

She ignored the question because the answer was obvious. No one was watching them.

"Can I go with Tory and Maud today?"

"Absolutely not."

"You said when I was older."

"And you will."

"Fourteen is old enough to sell apples."

"We'll discuss this later."

That meant no. Her mother would never let her leave this stupid farm. The way she shut them up here, you would think they were all wanted for some crime.

Aubree stomped away. The grass in the yard defeated her show of annoyance, but she continued as if she were wearing tap shoes and pounding on a wooden stage.

Now Aubree was glad she hadn't told her mother about the truck that tried to hit her because, of course, that would be her fault, too. Then her mom would find out about her night visits to Bailey and take the only thing that she enjoyed.

She and Bailey watched movies and ate normal food. Aubree remembered vanilla sandwich cookies. She'd had them as a baby, before her mother brought her here.

Had she stolen her from her real mother? Was the woman she remembered and the dark-haired man her real parents?

She couldn't wait to tell Bailey her new theory. She'd know what to do.

FORTY-SEVEN

BAILEY

Bailey returned to her cabin before dusk, which now fell just past six in the evening.

Not long after dark there was a gentle knock on her door.

A lift of the shade and she spotted Aubree. Bailey opened the door and offered an ice cream sandwich. The teen wasted no time eating the treat. Afterwards, she scraped the remaining chocolate off the pads of her fingers with her front teeth, then washed in the sink.

Bailey noted Aubree's smile fading and the silence grew heavy.

"What's up?"

"Bailey, I think... I think my mom is hiding something."

"Besides the fake pregnancy, you mean?"

She nodded vigorously and glanced at her hands, tearing away her thumbnail.

"You're the only one I can talk to. When I ask my mother anything she just orders me around or lies to me."

Bailey wondered if Eliza had noticed the changes or if she thought Aubree's surliness and sulking were just a normal part of teenage life. As routine as the pimples on her chin.

They weren't. This was more. Bailey saw the shifts, even as Eliza discounted them.

"I'm sorry," said Bailey, thinking it was past time for Eliza to face the emotional mess she'd created by lying to Kaiden, and her kids.

She held Eliza responsible. For years she'd posted an ideal-ized version of a very flawed family while not doing enough to protect her children from the crazy, dangerous stalkers that would predictably find them.

Her kids were innocents in all this mess. Like the kids in the goat paddock, they were at the mercy of their mother.

Eliza didn't deserve them.

"Can you check back on the gate camera recordings?" asked Aubree. "See if after they drove away together that day, my mom came back in his truck alone?"

"Sure. What am I looking for?"

The girl continued to tear at her cuticles, picking until they bled.

Bailey offered a tissue, and Aubree wrapped it around her bleeding thumb.

"Did you see the white goat in the pasture?" asked the teen.

The change of subject was jolting. "Thistle?"

"That's *not* Thistle. Thistle was a good mother until she got sick, and that goat won't let them near her. And look at her bag. It's not full."

"You asked your mom about it? What did she say?"

"She said she got rid of her. That she was a bad mother.'" Aubree squeezed the tissue around her thumb. "It's a different goat. She admitted it. But she won't tell me where she took Thistle, and she won't tell me what happened to Dad."

"I see. You don't trust her."

"How can I? Will you help me?"

"You think you can trust *me*?"

That stopped the girl for only a moment. "Yes. I trust you."

"All right. I'll check the camera and let you know."

* * *

Aubree slipped into the office on Monday during Bailey's lunch break after the morning filming.

"Did you check the recordings?" she asked.

"They left the front gate together," Bailey said. "She came back alone."

"So he did leave?"

"I'm not sure. She could have dropped him off somewhere. But your dad has a cap on his truck bed. Camera can't pick up what's in the truck bed because of the cap."

"You think she brought him back?"

"He hasn't contacted you."

Aubree picked at the scab on her thumb, comforted by the sting of the skin tearing. Aubree had told her that her dad had promised he'd call.

Bailey rubbed her hand over her jaw, looking uncertain. "Can I show you something?"

She led the way to the equipment shed and pointed at the rear of the backhoe. Aubree stepped forward and studied the narrow rear bucket.

"She used this the day she came back alone. Has it been out of the barn since?"

"I'm not sure." Aubree leaned forward. "What is that on the teeth?"

"I think its dried blood. A lot of it."

Aubree staggered, only just keeping her footing.

"You think she hurt him?"

"She wouldn't," said Bailey. "Would she?"

"He might have been in the truck bed," said Aubree, pointing at the damning evidence. "He might have been unconscious." Another possibility landed, and she gasped. "I think... maybe...maybe she killed him."

"Aubree. You think your mother is capable of killing her husband?"

She did think that exactly.

Her stomach twisted and she pressed a hand over her mouth, fearing she might be sick. She dropped her hand.

"Help me search."

"For what?" asked Bailey.

"His grave."

FORTY-EIGHT

Bailey got a pre-dawn call on Wednesday. Her first thought was that Eliza figured out what she and Aubree were doing. But she braced herself for anything.

She tapped the phone and tried for a chipper voice. "Good morning."

"I'm about to livestream my followers." Eliza's words were rushed.

Bailey's heart spasmed against her ribs. It felt like she had a woodpecker inside her chest.

"Okay."

"It's time. The baby is coming."

Bailey sank back into her mattress in relief.

"Oh, gosh. What should I do?"

"My water broke three hours ago, so I'm on my way to the hospital in just a few minutes."

Bailey absorbed the unexpected stab of jealousy. Her fans believed Eliza was about to deliver. But her boss, her eldest daughter, and Bailey all knew that was a lie.

"I know it's not even sunup," said Eliza. "But I need you to watch the kids until Tory gets here, which will be late afternoon sometime. Family member is ill."

"I didn't think she had family."

"She *had* a brother. Nephew's down in Margaretville."

"I see. Is it serious?"

"Surgery of some kind. Unexpected but he's doing well. Post-op, I gather. So can you do it?"

Bailey made her wait. Aubree had told her that this woman was preparing to fire her and now she wanted her help?

"Of course."

"Oh great. I'm in the barn. See you soon. Okay?"

* * *

Bailey reached the office a half hour later without a shower or coffee.

Eliza held her phone as she spoke to her followers, framed in her picture window in the morning light. Her cheeks were flushed, and a sheen of sweat made her appear to glow.

Had she done some physical exercise to achieve that look or was this all makeup?

Eliza cast Bailey a quick glance, then returned her focus to her recording.

"But I wanted to share this miracle with you. Every birth is a miracle and every child a priceless gift."

On that they agreed. Every child was irreplaceable. And Eliza was lucky enough to have three and soon four. She didn't deserve them. Not one.

"Okay, great. I've gotta run. Don't worry, I have a friend to drive me, because... you know." Here she paused, seeming to choke back tears at her situation, giving birth amid a divorce. Then she rallied, lifting her head. Forcing a smile. "I'll keep you all posted. And don't forget to share your awesome ideas for baby names. If I choose yours, you'll be getting a special thank you. Gotta run. I have a baby to bring into this beautiful world."

She wasn't naming a stray kitten. Why would she let followers make such an important decision?

Bailey's annoyance deepened into something harder and more dangerous.

Was Eliza going to ask her to participate in this sham?

What would her fans do if they learned the truth?

Eliza wasn't pregnant. But she was a murderer.

Now Aubree believed it, too.

Eliza ended the livestream and tucked away her phone. Then she headed to the safe.

Bailey watched, spotting the first two numbers on the dial. She made an assumption and saw she'd figured out the pattern for the next number. She didn't need to see the last one. Four numbers. Four dates.

She backtracked to the door and made more of a racket opening it.

Eliza turned, smiled, and opened the door to the safe.

"Thank you for this." She drew a bank deposit satchel from a shelf. The heavy-duty locking canvas bag usually held the cash from the markets zipped inside. But today was not market day and the sack bulged.

"How you feeling?" asked Bailey.

"I'm great. I spoke with Tory. She'll be here closer to noon."

Eliza held her silicone baby bump and twisted her face into a grimace.

Bailey tamped down the rage at this act and rushed forward. "Should you sit down? Do you need me to drive you to the hospital?"

Eliza relaxed her facial muscles and chuckled. "You've never been through this."

Bailey's smile went tight.

"It can take hours. I'm heading to Albany Med. Expect me back sometime tomorrow."

"Do you want me to bring the kids to see you there?"

"Oh, no. That's unnecessary."

Which made Bailey wonder where she was really going.

"I'd rather have them meet Charlotte here."

"Charlotte? You have a winner?"

"Yes. No one submitted that one, so easy choice." She pressed a finger to her lips. "But it's still a secret from my followers."

And from her family? And her patrons, followers, and fans? And the naming contest? Also a sham.

"I'm expecting a call today. You'll need to take the details. Give them my private email address."

"Who from?"

Eliza mentioned the name of one of the biggest producers of baby food in the country.

"You're not going to use their products. Are you?"

"No." Her eyes twinkled. "They want to launch a line with my brand! All organic."

The way money just fell out of the trees and into her coffers left Bailey speechless.

"I'll reschedule. Tell them to send the contracts. I'll look them over."

"Will do."

But first she and Aubree were going to search that mound of earth. Nothing like a murder to change even her children's opinion of Mommy dearest.

"So you want me at the house until Tory arrives?"

"Oh, actually, I'd love you in here taking the calls and handling comments. That livestream is going to bring huge engagement. Wait until they all see I'm in labor."

She chuckled, seeming to have forgotten to act as if she were having contractions. "I'm all packed. Car seat we picked is already installed. Try to keep up with the comments and tell Tory I said thanks."

Bailey waved her off, wondering if she might get Aubree away in the daylight to explore possible burial sites.

Eliza didn't bother to appear to be having any more contractions. She just climbed into her truck and drove away.

The urge to follow built like floodwater against a damn. Bailey was desperate to know exactly where and how her boss was going to come up with a newborn baby.

FORTY-NINE

FOURTEEN YEARS AGO

"Push, honey. One more big push." The ER nurse stood at the foot of the examination table between her spread legs.

The sweat on Bailey's body covered her skin like oil.

"I see the crown. Push."

The muscles in Bailey's legs trembled and her stomach ached. But she pushed. Everything changed in an instant. The baby slipped from between her legs, and she fell back, her body pulsing with fatigue.

She'd waited until well after her water broke. Well after the contractions came faster and faster. Only then did she head to the hospital, knowing they could not turn her away.

At nineteen, she had no insurance, no job, and her parents had disowned her as soon as they learned she was "knocked up", as her father called it. Not that she'd want to raise a baby in that house. She was going to be a good mom. A protective one. And nobody would lay a hand on her little one.

"A girl." The nurse held up her baby, still wrapped in the white caul and giving a shuddering cry.

Bailey reached.

"Let's clean her up first." The nurse stepped away and her partner moved between Bailey's splayed legs.

The contractions began again. What was happening?

She groaned as her body clenched.

"Here comes the placenta," said her new attendant. "You're doing great, hon. Nearly there."

She mopped the sweat from Bailey's face with a cool, damp towel. Bailey's eyes drifted closed for a moment and then the contractions came again.

"Is Bobby here?"

"Who?"

"Her father."

She couldn't ask for her husband. They'd never gotten married. Bobby said marriage was for suckers. They should stay together because they loved each other. Not because of some stupid piece of paper.

Bobby also had opinions on becoming a father. But he'd change his mind when he saw their daughter. Twenty-two wasn't too young to be a dad. And he could still party with his brothers. She wouldn't stop him.

But she'd had to quit work because of her pregnancy, and they'd lost the apartment. Since then, they'd crashed on his friend's couch. But Bobby hadn't been around much. She didn't know where he went and was afraid asking would just make him mad again. It worried her.

"I'm not sure. If he's in the waiting room, we'll bring him back."

If.

He'd said he was just parking the car. That was hours ago.

She closed her eyes. There was still hope. She was sure he'd change his mind.

The placenta slipped from her and they cleaned her up. Gave her ice chips and covered her with a warm blanket.

Her baby's cries brought her eyes open. Her breasts contracted at the sound. Instinctively she reached for her girl.

"Here she is. All clean."

They placed the baby on her chest. She was pink and tiny with a crown of reddish fuzz on her head. Bailey lifted one little hand and counted her fingers. Her baby stared up at her with big blue eyes.

"Hello, there. I'm your mama." Tears leaked from the corner of her eyes.

"Do you have a name picked out?" asked the nurse practitioner.

"Yes. Her name is Claudia."

FIFTY

Tory arrived before noon to watch the kids. According to Aubree, Tory usually let the teen get the kids to bed and never ventured past the living room to check on them. So she and Aubree had agreed to search for a grave immediately after lights out.

Aubree showed up at Bailey's door just after ten, wearing knee-high rubber boots and carrying both a shovel and a flashlight.

Bailey glanced past her at the low clouds sweeping before the moon. A gust of wind rippled across the hayfield. The weather was changing.

"You ready?" asked Aubree.

"Let me get my stuff."

She stepped aside so Aubree could wait inside, then hurried to tug on hoodie. A glance at the teen showed her trembling and on the verge of tears.

Bailey hesitated. "You sure you want to do this?"

Aubree's chin sank to her chest and she cradled her middle. Finally she peeked up from beneath dark, damp lashes. A ragged breath and a choking sob revealed she was crying.

"Oh, come here." Bailey reeled her in. The teen relaxed her head onto Bailey's shoulder. As Aubree cried, Bailey imagined all the things that might have been.

Finally, Aubree drew back and pressed her fist to her lips. Bailey waited for Aubree to dash away the tears and snatch a few ragged breaths.

"Do you want to go back to the house?"

She shook her head, sending her curls bouncing. Finally, she met Bailey's gaze.

"What if we find him?" Aubree asked.

"We call the police."

Aubree twisted her fingers with the opposite hand.

"I don't want her to go to prison."

"Well, if she hurt Kaiden, that's what will happen."

"But what about me and Mason and Harper?"

She didn't answer.

"Bailey?"

She grimaced. "They'll send someone from the county to take you."

"Take us where?"

"Foster care facility. After that, you'll be placed in foster homes."

"Together?"

"It's possible."

Aubree's eyes grew wide. "But it's also possible... what? They'd separate me from my brother and sister?"

"It happens," said Bailey, shifting in her seat.

Aubree's voice rose. "Then what?"

"Depends. If your mother comes home, she can take care of you."

"And if she doesn't?"

"Well, foster care might turn into adoption. For the little ones especially."

"What does that mean, for the little ones? What about me?"

"Teens mostly end up in group homes. They're harder to place because most couples, well, they want..."

"They want babies."

"Ideally. Yes, or younger kids."

Aubree went silent, staring into space with sightless eyes. Finally, she snapped her attention back to Bailey.

"This is my mother's place. Her father bought it for her before he died. So it will be mine and my brother's and sister's someday. If Mom went to jail, it would be ours."

"No court will let a fourteen-year-old own property or take custody of her siblings. You'll need a guardian, at least. Preferably a relative."

"We don't have any."

Bailey tried for a sympathetic look. The poor kid really had no good options.

Aubree's expression turned stormy. "I wish *you* were my mother."

Bailey blinked but said nothing, letting the idea blossom in Aubree's mind.

"You could be!" insisted Aubree. "You could be our guardian and we'd be your wards."

Where had she learned about wards?

Aubree rushed on. "You know how to run the social media stuff. And we'd help you. Do all the same kind of posts. And I know how to grow things and care for the animals. Tory will help, and Ava. Maud will run the store and market. Just like always."

"Aubree, you need to go to school. Have friends your age. Not take over this business."

"Well, I'm not letting them separate us."

"Listen, even if the worst happened, you'd be able to go to school. A real school. You'd have friends. And you could get a part-time job. One that pays you wages."

The teen smiled. Was she imagining some ideal version of her future?

It wouldn't happen.

The girl finally lifted teary eyes to meet Bailey's gaze.

"I want that, but not if I lose Mason and Harper." She stared at her feet, head hanging, shoulders rounded, indecision making her insides ache. "I don't know what to do."

"If your mother hurt Kaiden, you want to know. What you do then is up to you."

Aubree grasped Bailey's hand. "If she did this, I'm going to tell. And then will you take us?"

FIFTY-ONE

Bailey knew that Aubree hoped she'd agree to take over if the worst happened and wondered how best to turn the girl's utopian family fantasy to her advantage.

"I don't know." Bailey thought her voice held just the right amount of hesitation.

"Please," said the teen.

"Take you?"

She nodded, squeezing Bailey's hand so tight it hurt.

"Yes. I'll take all of you."

Aubree launched herself into Bailey's arms. She hugged the teen and then patted her back.

"Honestly, I already feel a part of the family. I couldn't imagine you kids going into the care of a stranger."

"That's so great," Aubree said.

She rocked her until the teen drew back, flushing in embarrassment.

Bailey lowered her voice. "You know we could be wrong. Kaiden might be fine."

"He's not. He would have come for me." The tears continued to stream down her face in silver threads.

Bailey raised her brows and nodded. Then she glanced at the door. "You ready?"

Aubree gave a definitive nod and stepped out to collect her flashlight and shovel. Bailey lifted her walking stick and ventured out into the ever darkening night.

They headed toward the growing fields, stark and nearly empty now. The temperature was dropping, the cold breeze making her shiver.

Bailey shoved her hands deeper into the front pockets of her hoodie. She kept her walking stick caught in the crook of her arm. Aubree carried the shovel as they walked in the furrows of the vegetable patch under a yellow October moon, the air so crisp, she could see her breath.

They paused at the end of the row.

"Which way?" asked Bailey.

"I thought about where she might have... you know. If she did, I mean."

Bailey let Aubree struggle to reconcile what she suspected, allowing time for the possibility to sink in. The girl thought her mother was a killer. Bailey did as well, though no one would believe either of them without evidence.

Still, the girl faltered. The words murdered and buried gave her trouble. That was understandable. Bailey had witnessed a murder, and it was not a word she used lightly. Truthfully, she was relieved that Aubree came up with the possibility. It made this next part easier.

Bailey paused and tapped her index finger on her chin, thinking. "She went toward the river with the backhoe."

Aubree nodded. "Let's go."

They left the fields, their frosting breath trailing behind them like smoke, and continued toward the river.

A glance showed the house out of sight.

"Flashlight is okay now, I think," said Bailey.

Aubree flicked it on, pointing with the beam of light at a downed tree. She didn't move.

"You okay?" asked Bailey.

"I was thinking, if I turn around now, I can still pretend that my dad isn't missing. That he'll be back." She shone the light at Bailey then immediately lowered the beam. "Am I a terrible daughter to think that my mom..." She gave a squeak that might have been a sob.

Bailey tried vainly to restore her night vision.

"Aubree, you don't even know if she *is* your mom."

That observation caused the hand holding the flashlight to dip even further.

Above them, the moonlight winked on and off with the fast-moving clouds. The air felt heavier. Colder. Bailey sensed a storm.

Aubree located the twin ruts of a vehicle. Ahead sat the orchard and the sugarbush beyond.

They listened but heard only the peepers, cicada, and rustling of small creatures in the underbrush.

Bailey could smell the rain.

"Here," said Aubree, indicating the flattened grass. She swung the flashlight beam back and forth over the place where someone had left the road.

"Wider than truck tires," noted Bailey.

"This way." Aubree led her to remnants of a stone wall in the woods suggesting the boundary of a former pasture.

The darkness closed in. The hairs on Bailey's neck prickled.

"What's that?" She pointed her walking stick at the mount of freshly turned earth.

Aubree swung the light where Bailey indicated then answered in a whisper.

"It looks like a grave."

FIFTY-TWO

From somewhere across the river came the first roll of thunder.

"Should we head back?" asked Bailey.

"No." There was a conviction in her denial that Bailey admired.

The girl was naïve, sheltered, and hardworking. But she was also manipulative, sneaky, and determined.

"We should go before the storm gets too close. Trees are a bad place to be in a thunderstorm."

As if to punctuate her words, lightning flashed.

Aubree began counting. When she got to fifteen, she stopped.

"Three miles away. We have time."

"To do what?"

"Dig." She headed for the turned soil, propped up the light, and lifted the shovel, raking the dirt down the mound.

A flash illuminated their surroundings for a moment, turning the tree trunks a vivid pink. This time the thunder was louder and closer. The storm was coming.

"We have to go." Bailey retrieved the flashlight.

"Not yet."

Aubree prepared to deploy the shovel as Bailey held the light on a mound of earth partially buried in the fallen leaves.

An icy wind blew, and the first droplets of rain splashed on the tree canopy above them. Within a few moments the downpour grew deafening.

They huddled together as the rain pounded, bringing down the autumn leaves. Drenching cold droplets soaked Bailey's hair and ran down her face. Wiping the water away did nothing.

She raised her voice to be heard over the torrent. "What's that?" She pointed.

Aubree peered into the darkness as Bailey moved the flashlight's beam.

Something white passed the moving circle of light. Bailey dropped the flashlight, and Aubree lost her grip on the shovel as both staggered backwards. Aubree's hands flew to her mouth as she nearly toppled into Bailey.

They both stared at something unearthed on the ground as the rain fell in sheets.

Bailey lifted the light as Aubree stood, transfixed.

There in the circular beam lay a thin, white thing.

The teen gave a cry.

"Aubree?"

The girl didn't look at her, but just shook her head and muttered, "No. No. No."

"What is that?" asked Bailey.

There, sticking up out of the wet earth, was a two-foot-long narrow object, white as chalk. Too pale to be a tree branch but not too bleached to be...

"Is that a bone?"

Together they made a slow approach, as if expecting something to leap out at them.

Aubree sank to her knees in the mud. The rain half-blinded Bailey, who now held both her stick and the light.

The rain ran down the girl's dark head, straightening her

curls. She grasped one end of a long bone and gently worked it from the damp earth.

"It's old," said Aubree, examining the bone. "It's too clean to be…" She turned her attention to Bailey, who knew what she was asking.

"Yes. That's been in the ground quite a while. Maybe years."

"It's a long bone." She lifted her head.

Bailey stared at the gruesome object in her hands.

"Is it human?" asked the girl.

"I don't know. It looks like maybe… What do you think?"

The teen shook her head, soaked through, and looking small and lost. The worst had happened. She'd found a grave.

"Not Kaiden," Bailey said. "Too old."

Aubree reverently lowered the bone to a mossy bed beside her.

"If it's not him, then…" Aubree's nostrils flared as she stared at the bones. Bailey could almost see her abandon hope as her suspicions hardened into conclusions. "She did this before."

"What are you saying?"

"I think that's my real father."

FIFTY-THREE

Bailey and Aubree shivered in the cold rain as they stared at the undeniable evidence of death.

The teen pressed her dirty hands to her thighs. Bailey imagined her need for answers warring with her need to flee.

"No more," said Bailey. "Let's go now."

Aubree remained beside the bone as rain dripped from her hair. Finally, she accepted Bailey's hand, taking hold. Bailey tugged her from the mound. Aubree gazed back into darkness and the unmarked grave.

Out in the field, the rain fell in stinging darts. By the time they reached Bailey's place, they shivered from the cold. Outside, the storm continued to rage.

Bailey propped her stick and the shovel behind the door and gave Aubree her only towel.

The girl rubbed the water from her hair, curly again despite the deluge. And then she wrapped the towel around her shoulders.

"I'll make tea," said Bailey. Her electric teapot took little time to deliver enough boiling water for two cups of tea with sugar.

Bailey held her cup in two hands, inhaling the steam.

Aubree didn't touch hers, just stared into space.

"We have to go back," said Aubree.

"No. But maybe we need to call the sheriff?"

Aubree didn't respond.

"Drink some tea. Your lips are blue."

The teen drank her tea.

"I don't want to call," she said at last, then lowered her empty mug to the table. "Not yet."

Bailey reached across the surface, capturing Aubree's icy fingers and giving a squeeze before drawing back.

"I found something else," Bailey said.

Aubree's gaze flicked to her, and Bailey read caution in her eyes.

"I know how to get into your mother's safe."

"What good will that do?"

"Maybe there's information in there about the name of your real father."

Aubree looked uncertain.

"You could find out if Harper and Mason are really your brother and sister."

"They are. I don't need a paper for that."

"But it would also tell you where you each came from and if Eliza adopted you or..."

"Or if she stole us."

Bailey inclined her head.

"Proof. Then they'd have to believe me."

"Either way, you'd have more answers. After, we call the sheriff's office. Show them what we found."

"I don't trust him," said Aubree. "Can't we call someone else right now?"

"Sure, State Police, I guess. But you won't be able to look in the safe."

"Because they'll take us."

"Just for a little while. Until I can come for you all."

"Then we have to wait until we see what's in that safe," said Aubree. "Because I need to know who we are."

"I can't get into the office until after seven in the morning because of the alarm system."

Eliza had changed that after Bailey had been in the yard before sunup. It made Bailey think Eliza suspected her of sneaking around the office when she wasn't there. Which was exactly the case.

"Can you slip out at that time?" asked Bailey.

"I let the chickens out in their yard at daybreak, so that should be easy."

"Won't Tory come with you?"

"If she does, I'll slip out afterwards. Meet you in the office." She glanced at her analog watch. "Holy cats! It's after midnight. I have to go."

"I'll walk you."

"It's pouring."

"I don't care. I don't want anything to happen to you."

Bailey walked her to her bedroom window as the rain continued to fall. She waited for Aubree to get inside before heading back through the windswept fields. The clouds parted and the rain moved off. Bailey could see her breath and was shivering when she reached the cabin. Before her lukewarm shower, she set her alarm.

Tomorrow was another important day. What would Aubree think when she saw what was in her mother's safe?

* * *

In the morning, Bailey avoided the puddles between the neat rows of mounded earth. Bailey spotted Tory standing in the overhead light before the equipment barn. It wasn't even sunup. Why was she here so early?

Bailey lifted her hand to wave.

Tory tracked her progress but did not wave. A moment later the gardener lifted the mobile phone that Eliza did not believe she had, and appeared to be making a call.

Bailey didn't like that one bit. Who was she calling? Or was she taking a video? Bailey looked away and hurried toward the front barn, anxious to be out of the woman's view.

She waited there, hoping Aubree would see Tory. There was no way to warn her that the woman was watching. Finally, Bailey heard the tractor start up and rumble from the equipment barn.

Aubree appeared a few minutes later.

"Tory came with me to do the milking and when I helped Mason gather the eggs," the teen explained. "I watched from my room until she finally left. Got to start the fall tillage."

Bailey motioned with her head. "Come on. We gotta get this done before Tory comes back to the barn."

Only when inside with the double French doors closed and locked did Bailey release the tension in her neck and shoulders. Then she showed Aubree the combination on the note she had written and taped to the bottom of a beeswax candle in a glass jar on her mother's desk.

Aubree held the upended candle and read the numbers aloud, not noting the handwriting that was close, but not exactly like, her mom's.

"You sure this is the combination?" asked Aubree.

"I know it is."

She glanced at the series of two-digit numbers. "Weird. It's our birth years. But not this one." She pointed to the second pair.

Bailey thought Aubree might wonder why a mother needed to write down a combination so easy to recall, but instead the teen fixed on the numbers on the scrap taped to the candle's bottom.

"Here's mine, then this one, then Mason and Harper. Why this date?" asked Aubree.

"I don't know."

"It's between mine and Mason's."

"Anniversary?"

"No. She was already married. At least I think..." She lifted her worried eyes to meet Bailey's. "You think they weren't married when I was born?"

"I think that she's using birthdays."

"But there's four."

"Yes. I saw that. Did your mom lose a baby?"

"Lose...?" Aubree held her fist pressed to her mouth and nodded. "Mom went to the hospital once. We didn't live on the farm then. We lived... I don't remember where. Somewhere with sidewalks and I had chalks. There was a blue mailbox on the corner."

"Sounds like a city. What happened?"

Aubree squinted, as if that would make the memory clear.

"It was summer, and they went to a grown-up party at my grandpa's house. My other grandpa's. I was at a friend's party. But they never came. Everyone got picked up but me. They couldn't reach my mom."

The teen leaned back against the counter, gripping the edge tight. Her attention seemed fixed on the rustic ceiling fan.

"My grandpa Avery got me the next day, that's my mom's dad. He said Mom was in the hospital. She came home the next day. She was crying."

"Where was your father?"

"He came home right after mom came back from the hospital. That's when they had the first big fight. Then we all moved here, I think. After he left, my grandpa said he had to go away."

"But where did your dad go?"

"They wouldn't tell me."

"Then you started this farm?"

"Yes. How did you know?" asked Aubree.

"She's had the blog for nine years. You were five when she started."

"So where were we before? And where did my dad go?"

Bailey inclined her head toward the safe. "Let's find out."

Aubree first turned to the office door, locking it. Then Bailey spun the dial twice and then stopped at Aubree's birth year.

There was no hesitation as she moved to that second date, the one that Aubree did not recognize. Then she reversed to Mason's birth year, Harper's next, and with a click, the bolt released.

Bailey explored the files and folders, offering many to Aubree with a running description. The teen seemed shocked to hear that her little videos for various products gleaned her mother between ten and twenty thousand dollars per ninety-second endorsement.

"She's using all of you kids and according to these bank records, she hasn't started a conservatorship for any of you."

"A what?"

"By law, parents must set aside earnings generated by their children. I don't know if the law applies to farmers or social media influencers."

"Influencers?"

"That's what you *are*, Aubree. You have six hundred thousand followers on YouTube and over three hundred and fifty thousand on Instagram."

"I do?"

If the girl had a cellphone, she'd know this. Bailey showed her two of her most popular videos.

"Does that say two million views?"

"Giving Morris a bath in the river. Very popular." Bailey closed the app. Likely Aubree's wet T-shirt and soaked cut-offs didn't hurt those numbers. "Kids under thirteen can't have pages. All three of yours are run by your mother and by me."

"I'm fourteen!"

"I know. She's exploiting you."

Aubree's grim expression was punctuated by the pressing of her lips.

"Anything about my dad?" she asked.

"Not yet. But here's her checking account. She left with a check for twenty-five thousand dollars today. And there are three others in the same amount, stretching back to the day she made the announcement she was pregnant. See?" She pointed out the check stubs. "So however your mother is getting this baby, she's paid for it."

"Didn't steal us?"

"Bought you, I think."

Aubree bracketed the checkbook between her palms.

"That might be worse."

Bailey held up a paper. "She's already signed a contract to use the new baby in a line of branded baby food."

"We aren't related. Any of us."

Bailey did not disagree. It was hard to see things as they were instead of how you hoped they would be.

"What about my dad?"

"I don't know. There's nothing in here about the fathers. No payoffs. And I can't find your birth certificates. They have a space for the father's name."

"We have to stop her. We should go to the state police. Show them the grave and tell them that she killed my dads and she's buying us from our real mothers."

"What about the new baby?" asked Bailey. She didn't want Aubree to forget they'd soon have an addition to the family. "Are you going to leave that innocent little infant with her?"

"No. We have to wait until she's home. Then we all go. We can take the Ultra Van," said Aubree. "Except..."

"What?"

"Mason and Harper have never been off the farm or in a moving vehicle."

"Never?"

"Me, either. Not since I was super little."

"Well, first time for everything."

The knock on the outer door of the office made them both freeze.

"Bailey? It's Tory. Why is the door locked?"

FIFTY-FOUR

AUBREE

Aubree shoved the file folder back in the safe and Bailey spun the lock. Then Aubree climbed under her mother's desk as Bailey went to the door.

"Everything all right?"

That was Bailey's voice, Aubree knew. She pulled her knees closer to her chest and hoped her feet didn't show beneath the desk.

"Why is this locked?" Tory's voice held a definite edge.

"I didn't know it was. Did you need something?"

"I'm looking for Aubree. Have you seen her?"

"Not recently."

"I saw her heading down here earlier."

"Yes. But she left. Said she was going to see Morris."

Aubree thought she'd believe Bailey if she wasn't right here. She was a very convincing liar.

"I looked. She isn't there."

"Is she missing?" asked Bailey, her voice rising in concern.

"I'm going back to the house," said Tory. "Oh, what if it's that man again?"

"That guy's in jail. Could be another one," said Bailey. "We need to call the sheriff."

Aubree squirmed. What was she doing? She'd be in so much trouble.

"Let's not panic," said Tory.

"Another one of her crazy followers, I'll bet," said Bailey.

"I told her this would happen. She dangles her kids out there like bait and sooner or later a big fish is going to gobble them up."

"I'll come with you," said Bailey, then added, "Did you search the vegetable sorting barn?"

"No."

"Let's check there first. Hey, what about the treehouse? She goes there sometimes, you know. For privacy."

That would give Aubree time to get out of here and to the treehouse. Was that why Bailey mentioned it? Giving her a place to go?

She could sit up there with her legs dangling. Tory would see her. Aubree waited until their voices faded and then ran for the backyard.

She didn't have to wait long for discovery. Once she was back in the house, Tory seemed to relax.

* * *

In the late afternoon, Aubree waited on the back porch for Tory to return from the apple orchard and walk her to the milking shed where Bonnet already waited. The other goat was not producing milk and was ignoring the twins. But Bonnet had adopted them since her kid had been sold.

If Aubree needed any more proof that her mother switched goats, this was it.

"What happened to Thistle?" she asked her mother's gardener.

"What do you mean? She's right there?"

"That goat is not Thistle."

Tory glanced away. "I don't know about that, maybe she's just sick. Good idea to call the vet, maybe."

Aubree scowled at the obvious lie. Why did everyone but Bailey treat her like an idiot?

"You want me to call?" asked Aubree.

"No. No. I'll mention it to your mom when she gets home."

Sure you will.

At sunset, Ada arrived to take over as Tory had her own sheep and dogs to look after. Bailey logged the gate activity, saw the migrants out, and then headed to the main house for dinner.

Because Eliza wasn't there, Ada invited Bailey to share supper with the family.

They had just finished an amazing hot meal of tender pork chops, fresh apple sauce, and hot German potato salad when the gate alert pinged. The monitor in the foyer revealed Eliza's truck gliding through the gate.

"Mama's home!" shouted Harper, bouncing up and down in excitement.

"With the baby," added Ada. "Your new little sister."

Bailey was not at all surprised when Eliza arrived at the front door livestreaming the introduction of the infant to her siblings.

Bailey wisely stepped out of any shot. Eliza's brows lowered at seeing her assistant in her house, but she refocused on showing Harper and Mason scrambling to get a look at the bundle she held.

She was not an expert, but Bailey thought the little face

visible in the swaddling belonged to a baby who was several days old and, though Eliza had the glow of a new mother, she lacked the dark circles or general look of depletion.

Eliza moved backwards without a word, passing the mobile phone, still streaming, to Bailey.

She kept filming as Eliza, now in the center of the frame, dropped to one knee and drew back the swaddling. A glance told Bailey this was live.

"This is your new sister," she said. "This is baby Charlotte."

The lump in Bailey's throat refused all attempts to clear it by swallowing. The welling tears made her vision swim. But she kept filming as little hearts floated up across the screen. The number of viewers climbed, going from 54k to 185k as Harper asked to hold Charlotte.

Bailey followed the family into the living room, where they gathered on the sofa. The look of wonder on Harper's face was solid gold for Eliza's brand. And then she realized that Aubree was not in the shot. She lifted her gaze from the screen, keeping the lens pointed at Eliza. There was Aubree casting her a grim look, with her arms tightly folded across her chest. Disapproval bristled from her. This could be very bad. If Aubree picked this moment to confront her mother, every plan they had made together was ruined.

Bailey shook her head and then inclined it toward Eliza, silently urging Aubree to join the family.

She huffed and then stormed forward. But before she entered the range of the camera, that charming, gregarious teen emerged. Aubree should be on the stage with those kind of acting chops.

Eliza smiled as she handed the baby to her eldest daughter, saying, "Here's your big sister."

Aubree settled between Mason and her mother and held the baby.

"Hey," said Mason. "I'm the only boy!"

They all laughed and for just a moment, Bailey forgot that this was mostly an illusion. Their performances were so genuine. If she didn't know better, she'd think this was a happy family.

"It might be a little harder now," said Eliza, casting a glance at the camera. "Running the farm without your daddy to help us."

Bailey could almost feel the private subscriptions skyrocketing.

Eliza had enough money to hire an au pair and full-time tutor for each child if she chose to. Instead, she seemed to prefer having Aubree do all the childcare, milking, and work in the fields.

It wasn't fair and it wasn't honest.

After twenty minutes, Bailey had to brace her arm with the opposite one to keep it from trembling. Finally, Eliza announced that it was time for baby Charlotte's nap. But she promised to be back for her first feeding. She reminded the audience that only her Pro-level followers would see Charlotte's first bath.

Bailey ended the livestream wondering how Eliza was going to breastfeed when she hadn't delivered.

Only a moment after the feed ended, Eliza's phone rang. Bailey still held the device and glanced at the screen.

"Caller ID?" asked Eliza, rising and holding the baby on her shoulder, her other children abandoned on the couch. Mason used the empty space to try to push Harper to the floor. Aubree noticed but did not interfere.

"It's Albany Medical," Bailey said.

"Give it to me." Eliza extended her free hand and accepted the phone. "Yes?"

She listened, eyes drifting toward the ceiling.

"That's right. I see. That's great!" She lifted the phone and spoke to Ada and Bailey. "Richard is awake," she whispered, her expression bright.

Then she returned the phone to her ear. "Unfortunately, no. I can't right now."

Another pause.

"Thank you. Tell him that I'll see him tomorrow. You have a blessed day."

She ended the call and smiled at Bailey. "That's great news he's awake."

"And talking?" asked Bailey.

"They didn't say. Just that he's groggy. But he's awake! I've got to call Bryan."

Eliza's first move was to call the county's sheriff.

FIFTY-SIX

ELIZA

Eliza woke in the night to the silence of a still house. A glance at her phone told her that it was well past Charlotte's feeding time. Had Aubree fed her? She used to handle some of Harper's night feedings. But she would have heard the baby cry. Wouldn't she?

Uneasy now, she swept from the bed. Newborns' cries weren't terribly loud, but she had the monitor beside her bed.

Eliza rushed across the hall and threw open the door to the children's room and flicked on the light.

Before her stood a still, vacant space and three empty beds. She stared in horror at the rumpled covers and an open window.

With a hand pressed to her mouth, eyes wide and heart thundering in her ears, she stood paralyzed by the silence.

Charlotte!

She rushed forward, finding the crib empty.

Mind racing, she scrambled to understand what was happening.

Gone. Where are my children?

She screamed into the empty space, calling their names.

Just a prank. They had to be under their beds.

But the space was as empty as the room.

Eliza ran through the house, screaming until her voice failed.

The downstairs—empty.

The upstairs—empty.

When the icy dew numbed her feet, she finally stopped running. She dropped to the grass, not remembering leaving the house.

Her phone. She had to call for help.

Eliza charged back into the foyer.

* * *

The yard was alive with red, blue, and white flashing strobe lights.

Eliza opened the door to find Sheriff Rathburn and two uniformed officers mounting the front steps.

"My kids are gone!" she cried.

"When did you notice them missing?" asked Rathburn.

"They're not in their room." Had he asked her something? "They're gone! I looked everywhere."

The sheriff swept past her with his men. They divided, one charging upstairs, one to the kitchen, and Rathburn through the living room toward the family quarters.

After a few moments the three assembled in the living room.

"Outbuildings?" asked Rathburn.

"No. I only searched the house. Their window is open."

"Could they have just gone out themselves?"

"With a baby? No. My kids wouldn't do that."

"Did you speak to your assistant?"

How had she forgotten Bailey? "No. Maybe she has them. Maybe they're in her cabin." Eliza started running.

The sheriff shouted for her to stop, but she charged out the back door and across the yard in bare feet, her legs pumping as she flew through the field.

She reached the cabin just ahead of Rathburn, who was burdened with a utility belt. The lights were off.

Eliza pounded on the door. "Bailey! Bailey! Open the door!"

"Key?" he asked.

She shook her head. "In the office."

He hit the door with his shoulder, splintering the frame.

The cabin was empty except for a horrifying amount of junk food. What else had her assistant been hiding from her?

Sheriff Rathburn swiped his palm over his stubbled cheek. His serious expression signaled impending doom. The darkness descended, and she knew, even before he spoke, that the devil was at her door.

"She took my kids."

* * *

Rathburn draped a lap blanket over Eliza's shoulders. A call to Tory and Ada yielded nothing. Bailey was not answering her phone.

They stood on the walkway leading to her front door.

"Outbuildings are clear. She's gone and so are your kids. So she took them or was taken with them. Either way, we need to get out an Amber Alert."

Yes, that's a good idea.

"Is her vehicle missing?" he asked.

"I don't know. She has a truck. White, um, old. I'm not sure the make. She parks it in the office lot."

"That vehicle is outside the barn," said Deputy Sheriff Arias, pointing at the truck.

"Eliza, we have to know the vehicle make for the alert."

"Maybe she's still here."

He turned to Arias. "Check the grounds to the river. Perpetrator might have used a boat."

Arias jogged away.

Eliza rushed across the lawn to the corner of the porch until she saw the gravel lot before the barn, spotting her truck, Kaiden's, and Bailey's.

She gripped in the fabric of her nightshirt, squeezing the garment in an echo of the pain in her heart. Where were her kids?

"All vehicles accounted for?" asked Rathburn.

"The backhoe and tractor should be in the barn. Should be but..."

She scanned the yard, praying this was all some mistake. That the kids were here on the property... somewhere.

Then she spotted what was missing.

"There!" She pointed. "The Corvair. It's gone!"

"Describe it," said Deputy Sheriff Arias.

She did. The make, model, year, license number. It hadn't been off the property in four years. Was it even road-worthy?

"It's not registered. Oh, God. There's no safety belts. We have to find them!"

"Description of the children, photos, and what they were wearing."

This all took an eon, but Eliza gave them what they needed.

Deputy Sheriff Arias typed the details onto her tablet, then glanced at the sheriff.

"Alert sent."

FIFTY-SEVEN
ELIZA

Albany, NY—nine years ago

He had to be carried to the truck and poured into the passenger seat like the shots he'd poured down his throat. But he'd roused when she screamed at him, which she did the minute they were out of sight of his parents' house.

"You promised you were done with this!"

She glanced across the cab to find him slumping against the side window.

"Hey!" She poked him.

He startled. Had he been asleep or passed out?

Now he blinked at her with bleary eyes and slurred his words together. "Wha's wrong?"

"You passed out!"

"Na, I dint." He glanced around the dark interior. "Wha's that sound?"

"Seatbelt alarm," she said, rolling her eyes.

He clipped the belt on the third attempt. The chime ceased.

Her fists clenched the wheel. "I swear to God, I will leave you, baby or no baby. You should be driving. I'm nauseous from the pregnancy." Only twelve weeks along, and the morning sickness was roaring.

She turned onto the rural route to their development. A shitty townhouse they wouldn't be able to afford if he lost his license and couldn't get to work.

He'd promised on his mother's life that he'd quit. Be a good dad for their daughter and this baby. She'd just expected him to grow up when she did. He hadn't.

Why did every family gathering at his parents' house include a keg of beer and end with shots of whiskey? That wasn't normal. Was it?

The road signs whizzed by with the last of the streetlights.

"What happened to quitting? To cleaning up your act?"

God, how many times did they have to go through this same tired script? He'd beg her forgiveness. He'd make promises. Things would improve, until that first drink. Because there was never just one.

"Christ! Maybe if you'd lighten up—"

"Lighten up? Lighten up! We're having a baby in six months. You're going to be a father again. Time to crawl out of that whiskey bottle—"

"All right. I screwed up. Won't happen again!"

But it always did. His blackouts scared her so much she'd begged him to go to rehab. But he wanted to quit "his own way."

She was so stupid. Giving him chance after chance. Turned out his own way meant drinking in secret before he came home and making excuses to go out on weekends. Then he'd leave late for work on Monday because he'd been at the casino watching football and drinking with the guys.

"Bullshit. You're going to be a shitty father—again."

"Our daughter doesn't think so."

"She's five. She thinks fart noises are funny."

"They *are* funny."

"You're both children."

"You used to think I was funny, too."

"Well, one of us had to grow up."

"Don't act so high and mighty. I met you in a damn bar."

The truck drifted over the double solid. A horn blast alerted her, and she swerved back to her side of the two-lane highway.

"Easy. Jeez. Watch the road," he said.

"This damned truck is too big. I can barely reach the pedals."

"Seats adjust."

"Yes, but I don't know how to do that, do I?"

"Presets. I'm one. You're two. Just push the button on the door."

She did and the seat moved in, up, forward. Now she could see over the enormous hood of the full-sized truck he insisted on. She'd wanted the one with automatic braking, but he wanted the 4WD, a heated steering wheel, and LED headlights.

"Better?"

She didn't give him the satisfaction of a reply.

"I never drove this stupid thing. We should have gotten the SUV."

"I like trucks. Okay?" he said.

"No, it is not okay. SUVs are family friendly. But you still act like a high school kid at a kegger."

"Is it the trucks or the drinking? Make up your mind."

She was wasting her breath. She knew it. He wouldn't remember a thing she said because his drinking gave him black-outs nearly every weekend and now holidays.

"Slow down," he said.

"Oh, shut up. I'm driving." She pressed the accelerator, and they rocketed down the highway.

"Fine. Then watch the road." He motioned toward the windshield. Then his head dropped forward then jerked back.

"Are you sleeping?" she yelled.

"Resting my eyes." A moment later he was snoring.

Had he just passed out in the middle of an argument? That was a first. Meanwhile her blood pounded in her ears.

The flash of something before them registered too late. There was no time to hit the brake before the truck slammed into the object before her.

The airbags exploded, punching her in the face.

They thundered on, blind. She yanked the wheel, sending them skidding sideways and ricochetting off the guardrail.

She sat there in the stillness of the night. The high-pitched ringing seemed to be coming from inside her head. She sat in stunned silence, afraid to move.

What had just happened? Everything seemed fuzzy and confused.

Her passenger punched the airbag. She turned to watch him. Why did her neck hurt?

He threw open the passenger door.

"Wait!" She reached into the vacant space.

He vanished into the darkness. Hot, humid air rushed in, sending the white powder from the airbag explosion swirling. She coughed, fanning away the dust.

She released her belt and followed. "Wait!"

The smell of burning rubber filled her nostrils.

Above her, the yellow caution light flashed on and off and on and off, mocking her. She'd never even seen it or the intersection.

"What'd we hit... what?" She didn't know.

He staggered before the truck grill.

"A deer," she whispered. "Please let it be a deer."

Ears ringing, she stumbled to the railing on wobbling legs, her wet dress sticking to her skin. The world was silent except for the metallic buzz inside her head.

He used the hood to steady himself as he continued toward the driver's side. She was surprised he could walk that far. But then he swayed and dropped to his knees and sprawled, face-first, onto the asphalt.

The damage on the grill and bumper was minor and she considered driving home before someone happened by.

But how would she get him back in the truck?

Pressing a hand to the slight baby bump, she limped along, battling the dizziness as she headed for the break in the metal guardrail.

At the shoulder's edge, a bloody body sprawled on the grass.

Not a deer.

Her trembling rattled her teeth.

Below the road, the hillside sloped to a pasture. At the bottom, the barbwire and posts were torn and tangled around the smoking vehicle, which was now upside down and bent in the center.

Was she dreaming? Nothing seemed real. Her movements were clumsy and slow. Squatting beside the body, she checked for a pulse and found none.

The gravity of what she had done swept away the haze.

Shaking now, weeping and choking on blood and tears, she dropped to her knees beside the bloody heap. A person. Just moments ago, this was a person. And moments ago, she had not taken a human life.

Her words were meant for the victim but also for herself.

"I'm sorry. I'm so sorry." She clawed in her pocket for her phone, dialing 911 and reporting the accident.

The death.

She hesitated, glancing from the body on the shoulder to the man lying before the pickup's grill, and made her decision.

It was her best hope. Only hope. With a single tap she placed the call. They answered on the second ring.

Stammering, she reported the accident.

"We hit someone. They're in the road!"

The dispatcher asked questions and promised help. She

found herself standing at the roadside, staring down at the crumpled car. Its frame was folded in the middle, reminding her of a crushed beer can.

Then she saw something pink. Fuzzy. Lying beside the vehicle. Both hands flew to her mouth. She scrambled down the hill, sliding on her backside.

In the rear of the crushed compartment was a car seat, a child seat. Blood.

"Oh, no. Please no."

But her prayers were unanswered. It was a child. Had once been a child. She knew, even from four paces, that the little one was dead.

She'd killed a child.

Eliza cupped both hands to her mouth to stifle the scream.

FIFTY-EIGHT

ELIZA—NINE YEARS AGO

Eliza knew what the abdominal cramping and lower back ache meant before the paramedics arrived, and she knew it was too soon. Too soon for her baby's lungs to develop.

At the ER, she was sedated. When she woke, she lay shivering in a hospital bed. Every nerve in her abdomen vibrated with a pulsing, red-hot pain.

It hurt to breathe.

At her side, a heart-monitor blipped. The IV bag dispensed its liquid into a tube connected to her hand and secured with white paper tape.

She groaned. The pain seized the center of her consciousness. Nothing else mattered.

A call button looped around the bedrail. She reached and gasped again. But her fingers curled around the plastic lifeline, and she pressed the button. Kept pressing it. Mashing it as she bit down until her cheeks bled.

The nurse arrived and retreated and returned. For the rest of the night, she woke to agony, interrupted by a shot that melted the pain like candle wax before a blow torch.

She blinked up at the nurse.

"Where's my husband?"

"Oh, well..." Her gaze cut away, then swung back. But she didn't meet her eyes. "He sustained only minor injuries. He's been released."

"Released? Why isn't he here? Who has my daughter?"

"You rest now." The nurse patted her shoulder and Eliza's eye lids drooped.

"Call my dad."

The nurse took down his name and number.

"I'll call him. You rest."

It was the morning when she began to piece together what had happened. The memories came in jagged shards. But she worked them together one fragment at a time.

She'd started bleeding. The paramedics had been frantic. The hospital corridors flashed by in a blur of florescent lights. The operating room was icy cold. They'd sedated her.

The deep abdominal pain had her grinding her teeth as she clamped a hand to her abdomen.

The next shot sent her melting into unconsciousness.

She woke when the detectives arrived. They stood at her bedside, next to the bag of her urine. She didn't care.

They introduced themselves as she blinked at them. Detective Leather Blazer and Detective Bald.

"You were in a two-vehicle accident July 4th around 10pm on Route 151. Do you remember that?"

Of course she did. Eliza shook her head.

"Neil?"

"He's suffered minor injuries."

She exhaled her relief as her eyes winked closed.

"And he's in custody."

Eliza opened her eyes. Custody? Did that mean arrest?

"Your vehicle struck a hatchback carrying two passengers."

"Two?"

"That's right," said the bald detective. "Could you tell us what you remember?"

"We hit something."

"Did you see it?"

"Not until after. I called 911."

"Yes. Dispatch call received 10:12pm."

The pain was returning. Soon she'd need that shot.

"Did you see the victims?" asked Detective Leather Blazer.

"Victims?" asked Eliza, her heart monitor blipping faster and faster. She gave them her statement and the bald one took notes in a little book. When they finished, she asked for the nurse. The bald detective went to find her. The other stared at her with a somber expression.

"The driver of the other vehicle, Naomi Bow, survived. She is in guarded condition. I regret to inform you that her daughter was pronounced dead at the scene."

Eliza's voice faltered as she asked, "Wh-what was her name?"

"The child?" The detective checked his notebook. "Claudia."

"Age?" she asked.

"She was four, ma'am."

That was nearly the same age as her own daughter, Aubree.

"Is my husband under arrest?"

She held her confused expression waiting to see if changing the seat presets had worked.

"Yes, ma'am. He is."

"DWI?"

"Manslaughter."

The nurse arrived with the shot. Eliza sank gratefully into blackness. But she clawed her way back to consciousness because someone was calling her.

"Aubree?" she said, her word a croak. Where was her daughter?

"It's Dr. Loyd. I'm sorry to wake you. I'm the surgeon who operated on you."

Eliza opened one eye, bracing for the bad news, already knowing she'd lost her baby. Confirmation came a moment later.

"I'm very sorry to tell you that you suffered a miscarriage. Unfortunately, the fetus was too young to survive outside the womb."

Not a fetus. A daughter—*her* daughter. Eliza's obstetrician had told her the baby was a girl... would have been a girl.

"I knew."

"Did you? Well, I spoke with your attending up in Cliffton Park. I've informed her of your loss. We have a grief counselor who will be by to see you later on."

"Thank you."

"Would you like me to send one of our clergy?"

She shook her head.

"Do you remember meeting me in post-op?"

Eliza had never seen this woman before. She shook her head.

"I see. Well then let me tell you what we did. You came in hemorrhaging. You sustained a uterine tear. It's quite serious. Because of the pregnancy your bleeding was mostly internal. You suffered significant blood loss. Touch and go there for a while. But we had a great team. And you are a fighter." She smiled.

Eliza smiled back, though the tears were leaking down her temples and into her ears.

"Unfortunately, we were unable to save your uterus."

"What?"

"Your uterus. We had to remove it."

She tried to sit up and she cried out. "You can't do that."

"It was to save your life."

"But... But... Then I can't have children."

The doctor nodded. "That's true. But you're alive, Eliza. And I understand that you have a daughter at home."

The tears filled her throat and she choked on her sobs. The doctor patted her arm, offered sympathies, and hastily retreated as the nurse took over.

FIFTY-NINE

ELIZA—NOW

Eliza paced the yard. Deputy Sheriff Arias worked on the laptop, fixed to the dashboard, and Sheriff Rathburn sat on the porch flipping through Eliza's employee folder.

Where were her children?

She'd trusted Bailey with her kids. Trusted her with her business. Was it possible she'd been so badly mistaken? Or had whoever had taken her kids also taken Bailey?

Rathburn proposed that her assistant was a crazed follower.

It was a good assumption, since they'd arrested a man stalking Aubree. But Bailey was so affable and genuine.

She thought of all the videos she'd posted when she was sick or miserable. Back in the days when it was just her and her dad and Aubree. He'd passed when Aubree was six and Eliza missed him every day. He'd believed in her. Believed that she could take a rocky patch of land and a falling down farmhouse and turn it into a successful business. He'd bought the land and worked every weekend fixing the plumbing, the electric, and replacing lath and plaster walls with sheetrock. That was before the diagnosis.

His decline had been lightning-fast. A stomachache turned

to stage four cancer—everywhere. She'd lost him before the first harvest. Before she'd thought to use social media to increase their income. Before she'd discovered he'd given her his very last dime to provide her a fresh start.

He'd do anything for his child. And she'd done the same.

"Your husband has had no visitors," said Sheriff Rathburn.

"Ex-husband. Neil and I divorced after his conviction."

"I see. Would he have anyone on the outside who might kidnap your kids?"

Her ex-husband had a brother. But he lived in Alaska and worked on a fishing boat. He hadn't even come to the trial and clearly, he hadn't visited.

"No one. And Charlotte, Mason, and Harper aren't his children." They were hers. Each one was hers despite what some people would say. They'd say she wasn't a real mother because she couldn't carry those precious babies herself.

"He might just want to hurt you."

She shook her head, dismissing the notion.

"I read that he's serving concurrent sentences on two manslaughter charges," said the sheriff. "Vehicular homicide."

She said nothing, but her guts squeezed at the mention of all they had lost in that moment.

"He killed a child," said the sheriff.

She nodded. "Yes. Struck and killed."

"So why a double-charge?"

Eliza broke eye contact. Her chin dipped to her chest and a hand went to her stomach.

"I was pregnant. I lost the baby."

"I'm so sorry."

Why hadn't they bought the newest model of truck with automatic braking?

If they had that feature, Neil would still be a drunk, Naomi's kid would be alive, and Eliza could have gotten pregnant again after losing her baby girl.

Instead, a child was dead, she'd miscarried, and Neil was in prison.

She'd also lost her uterus and any hope of bearing more children. He'd been blind drunk. Another blackout.

It was why she hadn't let him drive. But that damned huge dashboard. It was impossible to see what was right in front of them.

After the crash, he'd left the passenger seat, running into the road.

The Fourth of July. Nearly, what? A decade ago? Almost. They'd been coming from his family's barbeque. Fighting— again. She'd never seen the car they hit.

By the time the police arrived it was too late. Too late for the little girl. Too late for her baby. And too late to deny her allegation that Neil had been behind the wheel.

He wouldn't remember. He never remembered. And his first DWI and his being blind drunk were the reasons she'd been behind the wheel in the first place. It was all his fault. And she had Aubree at home. She couldn't go to jail and leave her baby girl with Neil.

And the little girl, Claudia Bow, had been just four. Her teenage mother, Naomi, barely more than a child herself.

Eliza squeezed her eyes shut, trying vainly to banish the memories of that terrible night.

She shuddered.

"I want my babies back!"

"Just a few more questions. Is there anyone else who might want to do this?"

"I mean, yes. I have five million followers. More than a few have a screw loose. Look at the one you just arrested. I handle Aubree's social media accounts. You should see some of the DMs and comments. They're just sick."

"Any recent activity seem suspicious?"

"The usual. Bailey handles most of the comments."

"We'll need to see those."

"Of course." This all seemed useless. They needed to do something now.

"Does Aubree have access to them? Could she have a relationship with someone? Someone you aren't aware of?"

"She doesn't have a phone, computer, or access to mine. I change the passwords monthly."

She paced to the first big sugar maple and back. This giant had stood watch over this front yard for more than two hundred years. Had it witnessed whoever had taken her children?

"I need a list of former employees."

In her office, she handed over the requested information.

Her panic receded, and she could barely walk through the exhaustion that weighed her like some atmospheric shift in gravity. Just picking up one foot and another made her legs tremble.

Sheriff Rathburn flipped through the files of former employees, keying in on Kaiden.

"Recently fired?" he asked.

"Yes." She waved a dismissive hand. "It's not him."

"How do you know?" asked Rathburn. "He left on good terms?"

"Not initially. We had a falling out."

He waited and she explained.

"He threatened to go public with our arrangement, I paid him off."

"What arrangement?" asked Sheriff Rathburn.

"My followers think we're married."

The sheriff's brows lifted as if this was also news to him. He pushed back the brim of his cap. She inferred from his long stare that he did not approve.

"You made a statement regarding physical abuse but declined to press charges."

"I remember."

"Did he blackmail you?"

She never thought of it that way, but yes.

"Our fight was about money. He wanted more than I paid him. I wanted my followers to believe he left me. I'm not keeping a sullen, resentful guy here around my kids so I offered a healthy severance and reminded him I could still press charges."

"Seems like a suspect to me."

"And he knows how to drive the motorhome," she added.

Rathburn's radio crackled to life.

"Sheriff? You there?" The voice was female.

"Yeah? Over." He lifted his thumb from the side of the radio.

"We got a call from Albany PD. A Detective Choi. He's requesting a call back."

"What about?"

"He's with Ms. Watts' security person, Richard Garrow."

"Number?" he asked and then released the radio.

The woman rattled it off as he punched the number into his cellphone with his opposite hand.

Then he left Eliza to place the call. She watched him stand in the center of her walkway, speaking to an Albany detective on his phone. He glanced back at her twice, nodding as he listened. Had Richard told Rathburn who stabbed him?

Was it related to her children's abduction?

Eliza didn't remember leaving her seat. But she tugged on the sheriff's arm, no longer content to wait for answers. She needed to know what that detective was saying.

Rathburn thanked the Albany detective and ended the call. Then he turned to her, his expression grim.

"Your security guy identified his attacker as your assistant, Bailey Asher."

"What!" Every hair on her head stood up and a chill darted

down her spine. The buzz in her ears made her stagger, equilibrium lost.

Rathburn clasped her elbow.

"No! Why would she?"

"Richard told Detective Choi that Bailey Asher is not her birth name. She recently changed it."

Eliza's entire body tensed.

"What was her name before she changed it?"

"Naomi Bow."

SIXTY

Eliza gasped, hands at her throat.

"Do you know her?" The sheriff's expression told her that he knew exactly what her relationship was to Naomi Bow.

Of course Eliza knew the name.

She'd met her the night she'd scrambled up that hill from the wrecked hatchback, her heart pounding in her chest like the clapper of a church bell.

Did she know Naomi Bow?

Eliza had dropped to her knees beside the bleeding girl and felt for a pulse. Called for help.

Nothing had seemed real as she had knelt beside her body, praying to go back in time and miss the car.

When she had stood, she'd noticed the bloody water running down her legs. The pain broke past the shock.

She recalled knowing she would lose this baby and determining she was not going to jail. She had another child at home. And what kind of a mother would leave her daughter to be raised by a lousy drunk?

Neil had rolled onto his back in the road. It was a miracle no one had happened by yet.

Eliza had walked to the driver's side of the truck and hit preset number one. Neil's driving position. After that she'd inched around to the passenger's side and dragged herself into the truck.

Bending forward had been agony as she manually rolled the passenger seat forward, leaving her blood on the airbag, seat, and inner handle.

Finally, she adjusted the rearview mirror up and exited, waiting for the police.

When she'd left the truck, she found the girl on her side, staring at her.

Did she know Naomi Bow? She did.

But she had not known that her assistant and Naomi were one and the same.

Naomi Bow was not the only witness to contradict Eliza's version of events. Neil's brothers insisted they'd lifted him into the passenger seat. Unreliable witnesses, the prosecution had said. And clearly, the jury had not believed them or the low-income teen mom living in her car with her daughter. She was mistaken when she claimed to have seen Eliza leave the driver's seat and later return to both driver's and passenger's side. The evidence proved Eliza's husband had been driving *his* truck with a blood alcohol level far above the limit.

Eliza nearly believed it herself. But in her nightmares, she remembered finding the child beside the vehicle, a four-year-old girl, Claudia Bow.

"Do you know that name?" asked the sheriff again.

"Yes. She's the mother of the little girl that my husband struck and killed."

Bailey and Naomi Bow were the same person.

"Revenge is a good motive to take your children."

The panic that seized her escalated until her vision blurred. She gasped and choked.

Naomi.

Eliza had killed her child. They both knew it.

Now Naomi had taken her children. Eliza understood exactly what the woman intended.

Bailey hadn't come here for a job, or for work experience. She'd come for something more vital, and much, much darker.

She'd come for retribution.

"Didn't you recognize her?" asked the sheriff.

"No. She looks nothing like that..." Eliza checked herself before saying her first thoughts. Naomi Bow had been a skinny, homeless teen mother of a four-year-old. Eliza recalled the girl in the gallery at her husband's trial. She had ratty dishwater-blond hair, chipped black polish on her nails and could not have weighed more than a hundred pounds.

The woman wasn't watching the proceedings. Naomi was watching her. The defense had torn apart her testimony and her credibility. During a lunch recess, she had approached Eliza and whispered a word.

Murderer.

But then her voice changed, rising to the wail of a vengeful wrath. She'd howled until the court officers had escorted her out of the building.

She heard the teenager was not permitted back. Eliza had stayed away by choice. The verdict was predictable. The maximum sentence with the possibility of parole after decades behind bars.

Neil should have listened to her and bought the model with the automatic braking system. Then their truck would have stopped before the accident. Everything that had happened was his fault.

"Her hair was light, and her eyes were gray," said Eliza.

But her features were similar enough. She'd filled out. Become a woman. And with a wig or a bottle of hair dye. Contact lenses.

"Oh my God. She's going to kill my kids!"

SIXTY-ONE

AUBREE—THREE HOURS EARLIER

Aubree lingered in the living room as her siblings trailed their mother down the hall to the family's quarters and out of sight. She turned, needing Bailey to assure her that they could stop this.

"Tonight," said Bailey.

Her heart gave a little shudder, seeming to jump into her throat. Her skin prickled as the implications of what she was about to do scraped over her like a steel brush.

"Aubree. Do you understand? It has to be tonight. Leave your window unlocked."

"What do I tell Mason and Harper?" she whispered.

"We're taking them to see their dad."

"But it's lying. And he's dead!"

"We need them to come quietly. If you wake your mom, we'll never get away."

Her stomach tightened, bracing for some blow. "What about Charlotte?"

"We can't leave her."

Bailey was right, of course.

"No. We won't. Is it going to be okay?" she whispered.

"She bought you, Aubree. She bought you as if you were a goat or one of the chickens. We have to stop her."

"I know. But... I'm scared."

"I'll take all of you. I promise."

She nodded, feeling torn in two pieces. Earlier, she'd been so certain that this was right. That her mother needed to face the consequences of what she had done. And she and her brother and sisters deserved a normal home with school and friends.

But they were safe here. And it was all they knew. What if it was worse out there? What if going was a mistake?

SIXTY-TWO
BAILEY

Bailey paused in the foyer of the Watts' home to tear the gate alarm from the wall. Now the video screens recording their departure would not chime. After filming baby Charlotte's arrival, she had put Eliza's phone on *Do Not Disturb,* flipped on the mute button, and disabled alarm alerts. If she didn't notice, Bailey might get a head start. She didn't need much. Just enough to reach Albany, some forty-five minutes away.

She used the keys she had lifted from the office to check the Corvair Ultra Van, finding the tank full. Now she had nothing else to do but wait for the light in the downstairs windows to go out.

Two hours later, all was dark and all was quiet.

Bailey climbed into the motorhome with the key. Eliza had plugged an analog clock radio into the socket below the wooden plank that served as a dashboard. The numbers and clock hands glowed a pale green. The tiny cactuses seated in three little pots on the opposite end of the flat dash, that she had admired in Eliza's videos, were all plastic.

How appropriate.

Bailey flipped on her phone's flashlight to find the ignition, inserted the key, and gave a twist. The engine turned over but none of the odd collection of gauges and dials illuminated. In the beam of her phone's flashlight, she saw gauges for RPM, fuel, volts, oil, and a speedometer with an analog odometer built in.

The motorhome, that appeared so picturesque in the livestream, stunk of motor oil and gasoline. The fumes were already giving her a headache.

She pressed the accelerator. None of the gauge needles moved. A check under the dash showed a collection of unattached wires secured at the end with duct tape.

"So much for a gas reading."

No matter. She retrieved the gas can from the barn and dumped in the contents. It would be enough for a one-way trip.

Time to collect her precious cargo.

She drove the RV right up to their bedroom window, feeling a sense of anticipation that had left her years ago. It had gone with her reason to live.

But she'd regained both with her new purpose.

Aubree helped Mason out the window first. He climbed into the back like a trusting Labrador retriever, anxious for a road trip with no inkling it might end at the vet's office.

Harper was semiconscious and didn't fully rouse even when Bailey carried her inside the RV and laid her on the foam bench flanking the dinette.

Back at the window, Aubree passed out the sleeping baby. Bailey hardened her reserve as she cradled Charlotte. They walked together down the slope. Bailey waited at the open passenger door as Aubree settled in the bucket seat. Neither it nor bench seat had a safety belt, but both had been reupholstered with vintage fabric. So much the better. There would be nothing but the windshield between them and their final destination.

Once Aubree was seated, Bailey handed over baby Charlotte. Her big sister held the infant in her arms. It wasn't safe. Bailey knew what a huge vehicle could do to such a frail, fragile living thing because she'd seen it happen.

Once behind the wheel, she twisted the key, jerked the gear shift into position, and depressed the accelerator. In a few minutes they rolled out the front gate, leaving the farm behind. The Corvair chugged up the mountain and then glided down the highway toward the interstate. The wind whistled through the cracks in the weather stripping. Not far now.

A shame that she couldn't be there to see Eliza realize she'd lost them all.

"You're going too fast," said Aubree, holding baby Charlotte up to her shoulder and gently bouncing the infant.

"We need to get out of this county."

"Why?"

"Because your mom knows everyone here. They won't help us."

Behind them, Harper woke. A glance in the rattling rearview showed Harper and Mason perched on one bench.

"Where's Dad?" asked Mason, his voice relaying his fear.

That boy had very good instincts. She'd give him that.

SIXTY-THREE
AUBREE

Despite all these years of her family owning this vintage mobile home, Aubree had never actually ridden in it. Her mother never let them in any vehicles. Her dad used to drive it to the river, and they'd all just walk across the fields.

The elation of a grand adventure had begun to fade, and Aubree shifted in the darkness beside Bailey.

Before them, the concrete highway glowed gray in the head-lights while the rhythmic thump of the junctions in each concrete section of road lulled. The quiet from the back seat told her that Harper and Mason had nodded off on the padded benches. The silence allowed a gap for the doubts to creep in.

She'd lied to Mason. He wanted to wake up their mom, so she'd told him Bailey was bringing them to their dad.

The guilt nipped at her, eroding her confidence that she was doing the right thing.

What had she done?

She'd taken them out of their warm beds and into the night. Where were they going?

Aubree hoped this would be a better life for them, but once they told the police that their mom had probably killed their dad and *her* dad, it would all blow up online. Their followers would turn on their mom and the business would be ruined.

Was it too late to turn around?

"Maybe we should go back," said Aubree, her voice just a whisper, barely loud enough to hear over the motor's rumble and the wind blowing through the vents.

"What?" asked Bailey, raising her voice to be heard.

"Where are we going?" asked Aubree. She'd forgotten Charlotte's formula. When she woke up and started crying, she'd have nothing to feed the baby.

"Albany. I know a family court judge there. He'll help me get custody and find all your real mothers. Then we go to the police with a complaint against your mom."

Why hadn't Bailey told her any of this before?

"You think my real dad is dead, too?"

"The police will sort that out, after they see those graves."

That made sense.

"But he could still be alive."

"Yes. He might very well be."

"I don't want her to get into trouble."

"Aubree, she's locked you away like Rapunzel. And you can barely read and write."

"I can write."

"Your spelling is atrocious."

She didn't know that last word and it proved Bailey's point. Her mother hadn't given them the education the law required. At least that was what Bailey said.

Aubree summoned her courage and prepared to do the hardest thing in her life. She was going to have to tell what her mom had done.

"Is *your* mother still alive?" asked Aubree.

Bailey made a humming sound. "You know, I'm not sure. I left home when I was sixteen."

Aubree turned. But without dashboard lights, she could see

very little of the woman who promised to be their guardian, keep them together, and give them the life she dreamed of.

It was a lot, wasn't it? Maybe more than she could actually deliver. Her mom always said, "Under promise and over deliver." It kept customers happy.

"Why did you leave so young?"

"My dad hit me. I wanted out and there was this boy. I thought he was the answer. But he was stoned most of the time. When he wasn't, he was stealing cars. Catalytic converters, anyway. A few years later, he got arrested. My dad told me to lie in the bed I'd made."

Aubree wondered what that meant as Bailey continued.

"Anyway, then it was just the two of us."

"Us?"

"My daughter Claudia and me."

"I didn't know you had a daughter. Where is she?"

"She's waiting for me. We'll all see her soon."

SIXTY-FOUR

Aubree tried to imagine meeting her father. He'd have curly brown hair and dark eyes like she had. Did he think of her every day and miss her? Or was he buried in a grave by the river?

Once they got to the police, she'd tell them everything. And she'd be a hero for rescuing her brother and sisters. She swayed from side-to-side with baby Charlotte. Was the baby's real mother desperate to find the infant her mother had stolen?

Or had she bought this baby?

Either way, they'd probably give Aubree an award and then she could go to high school while Bailey stayed home with Charlotte. She would get a license and drive Mason and Harper to school every day.

"Aren't all these exits for Albany?" she asked, noticing another green road sign. This one read Everett Road.

"We have to get across the river. She's on the Rensselaer side."

Something felt wrong. The anxiety just got worse and worse. Aubree's chest felt achy.

Hadn't she said her judge friend was a man?

And, sure enough, the next sign said Rensselaer and an exit number. They were close!

But they didn't take the next exit. Just sailed past on the wide highway.

"Here comes the Hudson River," said Bailey. Her voice had a note of elation that frightened Aubree.

SIXTY-FIVE
BAILEY

This was it! Bailey reached the approach to the bridge spanning the Hudson. There was no fencing, no girders, no guardrail. Only a three-foot concrete barrier. From the far left, she'd have three full lanes to swing the RV at a right angle. Then they'd launch off the span and straight down a hundred and nine feet into the water. The fall should be enough to kill them all. But if not, the sinking vehicle would drag them to the bottom.

She pictured Eliza getting the news. Pictured her in court at her husband's trial, sitting there as they convicted *him* for *her* crime.

When she'd come to the Watts Farm, she'd planned to kill Aubree. Claudia and Aubree had been nearly the same age. It seemed fair. Let Eliza see what it was like to lose a child.

After discovering Eliza was expecting another baby, she couldn't wait any longer. She'd even stolen a truck to run Aubree down. Stolen wasn't the right word. Folks in Middleburgh were so darn trusting they often just tossed their keys on the dash when they left their vehicles. She'd borrowed a full-sized truck with intentions to run over Eliza's child, the same way Eliza had killed Claudia.

She was ready and willing to administer the justice Eliza had escaped.

Judgment would come for this woman, this killer, though long delayed. Let her suffer the loss of a child. Let her grieve and know that someone had finally held her to account.

Bailey had pictured her anguish, the inconsolable regret that came from such a loss coupled with the knowledge of who had done this to her and why.

And then she'd remembered Eliza's announcement, and the doubts crept in.

Losing a child was not equal to losing an only child.

And her miscarriage, infertility, and husband's incarceration had not stopped Eliza from growing her family.

Just before she ran Aubree down, Bailey recognized the flaw in her plan.

With three other young children at home to care for, would Eliza even have time to mourn Aubree? Or would she keep on building her empire and fortune and growing her family? That possibility caused her to swerve at the last moment and speed off.

The truck's real owner had not returned when Bailey parked the vehicle in the same spot. She hadn't noticed the owner watching. Too bad Richard had figured that out. Too bad he'd survived. If she'd had something more deadly than a three-inch blade, he wouldn't have lived to tell the tale.

But that night, as she swerved to avoid Aubree, frozen like a fawn in the headlights, she'd formed a new plan. Her first step: testing her theory with Kaiden, winding him up and letting him loose.

Eliza had fired him on the spot. Then she'd cried crocodile tears for her followers even as she'd monetized his leaving.

And the woman would do the same after her daughter's death. Likely have another baby to replace her.

She wasn't taking Eliza's eldest daughter. She was taking

what Eliza had taken—everything she loved. Then she'd leave her with what Bailey had had left—nothing. No children. No farm. No followers.

Right now, some of her own video footage, taken without her boss's approval, was uploading. In a few hours, it would be national news.

So many ethical questions for Eliza to answer. So many potential crimes. If Bailey wasn't taking her kids, the authorities certainly would. Her only regret was not seeing Eliza's epic fall.

The motorhome rumbled up the incline of the bridge. Just a few hundred yards to go. The apex and then the plunge. The epic fall would be hers.

She smiled, the calm and contentment wrapping her like a warm embrace.

There was something ahead of her on the road. Brake lights.

And then the siren sounded. First one and then two. She looked in the small rearview mirror, spotting the blue flashing lights of police vehicles.

A lot of police.

"Are we speeding?" asked Aubree.

"Aubree?" Mason stood behind her seat. "What's happening?"

"Go sit down," she told him. He didn't. Instead, he tugged insistently on his sister's arm until she joined him and Harper on the floor between the front seat and rear bench. Aubree drew Harper into her lap, held Charlotte with one arm and drew Mason close with the other.

A glance in the rearview showed the little girl clamping her hands over her ears as she wailed. Ahead, the bridge was alive with emergency vehicles.

Were they coming for her?

Just a quarter mile and she'd be at center span.

Now she saw them. A dump truck was parked on the right, blocking two lanes. Barring her access to the river.

"No," she wailed and pounded on the wheel. She had to change course; she knew she'd never reach the water. But they were already on the approach. How high were they now? Sixty feet? It would have to be enough. She spun the wheel, and the RV careened toward the cement barrier.

"What are you doing?" cried Aubree. "Mason, Harper, get down."

Something hit her from the right. A police vehicle, knocking the RV back into her lane. She turned, colliding with the squad car, grinding fiberglass against metal, but she could not move from the far-left lane. The police screeched to a halt, nearly hitting the truck, and she sailed through.

Ha-ha! She was clear. She needed more speed to breach the cement barrier.

An explosion caused the vehicle to shimmy and then swerve.

The tires. They'd blown all four tires and there were more police cars before her. An army of them.

She couldn't get through.

Bailey slammed on the brakes. The RV fishtailed and spun.

SIXTY-SIX
AUBREE

The RV rocked to a stop. Aubree huddled on the floor beside the dinette, Mason gripping her around the middle, Harper laying across her lap and baby Charlotte in her arms.

Bailey turned in her seat and glared, as if this all were somehow her fault.

What is happening?

"Bailey?"

"Now you'll never meet Claudia," she said.

"I'm sorry."

She said it again as the police yanked open Bailey's door and two officers dragged her from the vehicle.

The sliding door flew open next, and she faced a young officer, his gun aimed right at her face.

Aubree screamed and hunched around Harper. When she looked again, the officer had lowered her weapon. Charlotte howled as loudly as her tiny lungs allowed. Her face went from pink to scarlet under the overhead dome light. Mason and Harper huddled together like Ginger's kittens.

Then her brother, bless his heart, stood between her and the police and lifted his fists, offering a challenge.

"You're safe now, son. Don't worry," said the officer, casting one more look inside the motorhome. "Anyone else in here?" she asked Aubree.

"Just us."

Harper scrambled up on the dinette. Kneeling, she slapped her hands on the window.

"Bailey!" she cried.

Aubree turned to see them handcuff their rescuer.

"You don't understand," Aubree said. "She's saving us."

The officer gave her a mournful look and then pointed to the road. "Everybody out."

"Where are you taking us?" she asked.

"Somewhere safe. Somewhere warm."

"Please don't call our mother."

That stopped her. The officer turned and shouted to someone. A man peered in at them a moment later.

This man was big and dressed in nice clothes. No uniform. His coat flapped open, and Aubree saw a shiny badge clipped to his belt beside a small holster holding a handgun.

"Everybody okay?"

"Seem to be. But Ms. Watts here asked us not to call her mother."

"That so?" He looked at Aubree. "Afraid she'll be mad?"

"My mother kidnapped us as babies. She isn't our mother. Bailey was rescuing us."

At this announcement, both Mason and Harper wailed.

"You have to believe me. My mom's never been pregnant. She's been pretending and then she brings home a baby. This one." She lifted Charlotte for him to see, as if he could miss the shrieking infant in her arms.

"We're going to have the paramedics have a look at you. Then we're taking you to Albany Med. We can talk more there. I'm Detective Choi. This is my case."

"Where's Bailey?"

"We have her," he said. "She can't hurt you."

"Hurt us? She would never." What was he talking about?

Two men from the ambulance checked each of them, beginning with Charlotte who continued to cry, but without the same vigor. She needed feeding and a change and Aubree told them so. After their check, they let Aubree hold the baby until the lady from child welfare came and, just as Bailey predicted, she took Mason, Harper, and Charlotte, leaving Aubree with the police on the bridge.

She sat alone in the back of the police car as a tow truck arrived to remove the RV. If only they could have made it across the bridge, they'd all be together. And she'd finally have discovered the name of her real father.

But at the hospital, things changed again. Detective Choi arrived with a lady pushing Mr. Garrow in a wheelchair. The woman wore blue pants, a matching V-necked top and, around her neck, a cord with a plastic picture of herself attached. Aubree smiled at Mr. Garrow, despite his odd clothing. She'd never seen a man dressed in a gown and robe before. He even had little white half-slippers on his feet and a flannel blanket across his legs.

The lady pushing him, locked the wheels with little levers, and left them.

"Mr. Garrow!" She was so happy to see a familiar face she slipped off the exam table and gave him a hug.

He cradled her with one arm for a moment and then gave her a pat on the back.

"Aubree, we need to ask you some questions about Bailey Asher," he said.

"Okay."

Over the next hour or more, she told them everything. The nurses brought her food and milk that tasted funny, not at all like goats' milk. The apple sauce was too sweet, and the hash browns came cold, all stuck together in a paper sleeve. But she ate it all and drank ice water from a plastic pitcher.

She explained about the fake pregnancy and how Bailey said they were denied an education and were kidnapped. How her mother would never tell her anything about her real dad.

"And I'm afraid that she killed him and maybe she killed my dad, too."

She told them how she remembered another man and wanted to find him, and that she and Bailey found a grave on the property and some bones that might be her real father, and they had to get away from her mom so they could find their real mothers.

"She's trying to help us. We never leave the farm. We don't have any friends, except Morris."

"Morris?" asked the detective.

"He's the mule," explained Garrow.

"He's a donkey," corrected Aubree.

"Did you know about the schooling?" Detective Choi asked Mr. Garrow.

Her mother's security man shook his head. "She said she homeschooled them. That's not unusual, especially when you live so far outside of town."

Choi nodded and turned back to her. "Aubree, the nurse who examined you said you have severe tooth decay. When was the last time you saw a dentist?"

"A what?"

The men exchanged a look, and she knew she'd said something wrong.

"Have you ever received a vaccination?"

"A what?"

He blew out his breath. She didn't like being made to feel stupid.

"When can I see Bailey?"

"She's been arrested," said Mr. Garrow.

This news landed like a slap. "But why?"

"Aubree, she lied to you."

"No. Listen. It's my mom whose lying."

"One doesn't preclude the other," said the detective.

There was another word she didn't know. Aubree turned to Mr. Garrow.

"I need to see Bailey. Listen to her. She can tell you everything."

"Aubree," said Mr. Garrow, "Bailey is the one who stabbed me."

She backed away until she ran into the examination table. She tented her hands over her mouth and shook her head.

It wasn't true. They were lying to her, just like her mom.

SIXTY-SEVEN

BAILEY—FOUR AND A HALF MONTHS EARLIER.

"You use a raft?" Richard asked Bailey.

Eliza's personal security leaned on the fence, watching her through mirrored lenses. She got the feeling he wasn't just digging, but knew the truth, and that set her instantly on guard.

"What?" she asked, hoping confusion might buy her a few minutes to think how best to play this.

"To leave the farm. Marks at the river look like an inflatable boat. And the mud print on your step matches the one at the river."

"I walk to the river all the time."

He eyed her in silence as her heart slammed against her ribs.

"You're not Bailey Asher."

"What are you talking about?" she asked.

"I spoke to her—Ms. Asher. She's working on her master's at Cornell. Sent her your photo. She said your name is Naomi Bow. That you worked with her on a farm in Canton, NY after she finished her agriculture degree."

"I can show you my ID."

"Eliza already did. Changed your name—right? Then used

the new name and license number on the application, but you used *her* social security number. And that's fraud."

Bailey locked her teeth but said nothing.

"Why did you do that?"

There were a lot of reasons for a woman to change her name. She went with the most obvious.

"There's someone in my past that I can't have find me. He's in prison. When he gets out, he might kill me."

"Is that right?"

He didn't believe her. She saw that in the self-satisfied quirk of his mouth.

"That's a detail that Eliza needs to know. Especially if there is someone in your past who endangers her and her family."

"You're going to tell her?"

"Of course. My job is to protect them."

Eliza would recognize her real name instantly. This was so bad.

What should she do? It was all crumbling in her fingers. She had to stop this.

"You think the intruder is after me?"

"I don't."

"How do you know?" she asked.

"I tell you what. Let's you and I go tell Eliza that you changed your name and falsified your application."

"I did not."

"Your application and transcripts belong to the real Bailey Asher. That's not you. I know because you were serving time in the Jefferson County Correctional Facility when she graduated. Neglected to mention that in your application, didn't you?"

"This is a mistake."

"All right. That's enough. Let's go see Eliza."

Bailey wrapped her fingers around the cool metal object in her pocket.

She lifted her chin in the direction of the house.

"Here comes Eliza now."

Richard turned and Bailey drove a three-inch penknife into his kidney.

In rapid, staccato thrusts, she punctured more holes in his guts. Then she stabbed him twice in the opposite kidney. Richard staggered and dropped to one knee.

She stabbed him in the back, just below the shoulder blade on both sides more than once.

As he fell forward, she kept stabbing him in the soft muscle below his ribcage. The sharp knife sunk to the handle and then out in a flash. At last, he stopped crawling away, stopped moving all together.

Bailey stepped back. His shallow breathing and the amount of blood pouring from his many wounds assured her he would not live long.

Blood soaked the grass. Fast at first and then more slowly. If he was breathing now, she couldn't tell. Bailey resisted the urge to touch him, listen to his heart. She already had too much blood on her face and hair. Her hands were slick with the warm sticky fluid.

She closed the knife and walked to the river to the place where she'd beached the inflatable canoe on Tuesday night before shoving it under the cabin. There Bailey used her bandanna to thoroughly wipe down the blade, removing all fingerprints from the knife.

Eliza was right. These cloths were very handy.

Then she stooped, unlaced her boots and tied the laces together. With her footwear looped around her neck, she waded into the river and removed her clothing. The ice water made her shiver. But she stayed to finish the job, tying her shirt, sweatshirt, and jeans to a rock, then throwing them midstream where they sunk to the bottom.

She scrubbed her boots and then her body, using river sand

and mud in her hair, ears, and on her face. Then she scrubbed again.

Returning to the shore, she eradicated the marks Richard had spotted. Then she walked to her cabin naked, carrying her boots, enjoying the warm sunshine on her chilled skin.

Once back at her place, she headed inside, towel-dried her hair, pulled it into a bun, and tucked it under a hat.

Finally, she changed into jeans, a T-shirt, and a dark gray hoodie. Bailey exited her cabin in sodden boots. She walked back to the house, avoiding Richard's inert body.

In the front yard she spotted Aubree and waved. The girl looked miserable, so she stopped to comfort her and ended up helping her search the house. It was risky but the temptation was just too great.

And they found the pregnancy prosthetic in Eliza's room.

Aubree was right again.

And with the teen's help, she'd gotten out of the house without Eliza spotting her and before Aubree started screaming. Who could have imagined Richard would drag himself all the way to the backsteps?

With Eliza and Tory in the house, she'd easily made it to the office unobserved. Her hair and boots were still soaked, but everyone was too busy with Richard to notice.

Bailey tried to think. What would she be working on? She shook her mouse and opened Eliza's administration panel.

Her phone chimed with a text, and she glanced at the screen

Open the front gate for EMS

SIXTY-EIGHT

ELIZA—NOW

"We got them," said Sheriff Rathburn to Eliza.

"Are they all right?"

"No injuries."

Eliza collapsed onto the bench beside her empty dining room table. She folded her arms on the cool wood surface, lowered her head to her arms, and wept.

Her kids were safe.

Her kids were coming home to her.

All but one. That sweet little girl that was forced into the world too soon.

Someone took a seat beside her. She felt a small hand on her shoulder.

Eliza lifted her head. Deputy Sheriff Arias sat next to her and took off her cap, revealing a wide forehead, sleek black hair drawn back in a tight bun and an expression of sympathy.

"When will they be back?" asked Eliza. "I want to see them."

"The Albany police are taking them to the medical center for a health check."

Her head snapped around.

"No. They have to bring them home."

"Your daughter Aubree is speaking with detectives."

Eliza straightened as implications flooded in. "They can't question her without a parent present."

"Yes. They can," said Rathburn, "And no parental permission is required."

"That can't be legal."

"Your daughter is both a witness to and a victim of a crime," said Arias.

"*Multiple* crimes," added Rathburn.

The way he added and emphasized the word *multiple* made Eliza wonder exactly what Aubree was relaying to the police. She juggled running her business and keeping her kids safe. However, this might have caused her to neglect some important things. Aubree would tell the authorities everything that had happened to them. It would be all right. But the doubts poked at her with sharp sticks, causing her to shift in her seat.

After her accident, she didn't permit her kids in vehicles. They were huge killing machines. School buses were not even a possibility. When Aubree was young, she had homeschooled her.

But when was the last time she'd given her kids a lesson?

"Something wrong?" asked Rathburn. His intent gaze seemed accusatory.

Eliza lifted her chin in defiance. She was a good mother. Her millions of followers, sponsorship deals, and supporters proved that.

"I want them back here."

"We'll bring you to them."

"No. I don't leave the farm. I need you to get them and bring them home."

"Mrs. Watts, that is not going to happen," said Arias. "Your kids are at Albany Medical being checked out."

"I didn't approve that. You can't have them seen by a doctor without my permission."

"We can. And the detectives overseeing the case against Ms. Asher need you to come in for questioning."

"No."

"You are refusing to cooperate?"

"I am refusing. Yes."

The sheriff nodded at his deputy. The one Eliza thought was here for her protection until she saw her pull a pair of handcuffs from behind her back.

"What are you doing?" she screeched, leaping up from her seat so quickly her chair fell over, crashing to the floor.

"Eliza Watts," said Arias, "I'm placing you under arrest for child endangerment."

SIXTY-NINE
BAILEY

After waiting most of the night to be charged or questioned, Bailey was finally led into a drab, claustrophobic room that held a table, three chairs, and a video camera mounted to the wall in the corner.

She'd failed. Nothing they could do to her was worse than that.

Detective Choi waited in one of the chairs. She'd met him on the bridge along with her escort, a big, intimidating man whose shaved head showed numerous folds at the back of his neck, Detective Imani. Once she was settled, he sat beside Choi.

Bailey knew enough to keep her mouth shut under questioning. But it didn't seem to matter. They knew who she was. Knew she'd lured the Watts kids away from their mother with lies about their abduction from their real mothers.

And they knew about her daughter, Claudia, killed by the Watts' huge pickup truck. Knew about the trial. Her accusations. Eliza's husband's incarceration.

"I've spoken to Aubree. She told me about the bones you found. And I've spoken to Eliza Watts."

That murderous bitch.

"Ms. Watts claims the bone you showed Aubree was a long bone from a goat that died several years ago. And that she recently used the backhoe to bury a second deceased female goat."

She lifted her gaze from the table between her and Detective Choi.

"That makes it a grave. Doesn't it?"

Better than her daughter had gotten. She had no money for a grave or marker. The city had returned Claudia's ashes in a cardboard box. Bailey scattered them on her grandmother's grave and buried the rest beneath the pink perennials she had planted beside the marker.

She'd seen Eliza behind the wheel of that vehicle before the crash. And she'd seen her return to the vehicle and climb into the passenger side before calling EMS.

The help had arrived too late for her daughter.

"And every year you saw Eliza's following growing while you suffered from depression and were hospitalized right here in Albany for a while," said Choi.

Sixty days. The maximum allowed.

He checked his pad. "Multiple arrests. Petty theft, larceny, squatting. You joined the army. Trained as a logistics specialist. Assigned to Fort Drum, New York. After conviction by a civilian court on an assault charge, you served time in Jefferson County Correctional Facility, Watertown NY."

Fourteen months. And that gave a person a lot of time to think.

"You qualified for a prison work release program and worked on a farm in the Thousand Islands region, met Bailey Asher, stole her social security number, and used it on your application. A bottle of hair dye, contacts, and a name change, and you were now also Bailey Asher."

She blinked her brown eyes. Simple for them to see she wore contacts.

"You watched the Watts Farm flourish. Her kids grow. That must have been hard."

"You have kids?" she asked.

"No."

"Then you have no idea."

"Hmm..." He glanced down at the file before him. "Way I see it, you went to the Watts Farm to kill Aubree."

She peeked up at him.

"Even stole a truck to run her down. But the sheriff in Schoharie County found the truck. Said you left a nice print."

She glanced up. Had she? Police were not required to tell the truth. Bailey shook her head. He was lying. She'd wiped every surface of that truck.

"And their sheriff believes the boot print on the truck's floor mat will match the boots you are wearing."

The floor mats. She'd never thought about footprints. That one could be true. Should have tossed them in the river with the rest, she thought.

She had a sudden flashback of Richard Garrow telling her the boot print on her front step matched one by the river. He'd never seen the inflatable boat under the cabin. But they'd find it now.

"What changed your mind?"

Bailey said nothing.

"Just veered off and left her there. Was that the moment you had second thoughts about killing a teenager?"

She snorted. Had the Watts shown any regrets at killing her child?

No. They'd just lawyered up and denied everything. Tried to get the breathalyzer results thrown out. Tried to get the search of the vehicle declared illegal. Tried to invalidate the blood tests. Those two had done everything possible to avoid responsibility.

Now this guy wanted her to do differently?

"I did nothing wrong."

"Okay. No second thoughts. So maybe that was the moment you changed your mind about killing *only* Aubree. Decided to kill them all. That's what you were planning. Going to drive that motorhome off the Patroon Island Bridge with all her kids right there with you. Close to where your girl died out in Rensselaer. Just over that bridge."

He was right. She wanted justice. Wanted Eliza to be left with nothing.

She wondered how they knew where she was heading. How they got out in front of her. But asking would reveal he was right. Instead, she repeated the same thing she'd said since arriving.

"Charge me or let me go," said Bailey.

"Oh, we are charging you."

"I want a lawyer."

EPILOGUE
FOURTEEN MONTHS LATER

The letter was handwritten with green ink on white paper. At the top corner of each page was a little cartoon unicorn with a rainbow horn.

Dear Baily,

My case worker said that I can write if I use her address on the envelop. She helps me writing this too you.

They told me you never wanted to rescue us but were going to drive us all off that brige. I don't believe them because you were right about everything that happened.

Almost.

They took us from our mom. Mason, Harper, and Charlotte are in a foster home. All togather. But I'm in a group home. It's okay. I get to go to school now, like you said. I like the house mom & my roomate. She taught me how to use my new phone.

I don't have any social media accounts. They said there are to many haters out there & creeps like the guy in the milk shed. + it's bad for my mental health.

They took Mooris and the goats. They are in a petting zoo.

Morris has a live webcam in his pasture, so I can still see him sometimes. They even caught and adopted that old scabby tomcat. He's Morris frend and I see him online, to.

I don't miss Bonnet or the milking. I miss Thistle. Tory wrote. She said Thistle died of infection after bringing the twins. They put a white goat in the pastor so the kids would not be sad. She said she was sory. I new it!

They are calling me for dinner. I will write more later.

OK, I am back.

Mom is our reel mom. They showed me the birth certificates. I wish we had found them that night. She used surrogusty to have Mason, Harper & Charlotte because of an accident & she can't have babys without help. She told my caseworker to tell me she didn't want haters to say she wasn't a reel mom because of that. She said she did it to protect us from followers I guess.

So we were wrong on that. My brother and sisters all have the same sperm donor. Yuck. But we don't know who he is. It's all kept secret on account of privacy stuff.

Our dad isn't our dad. He was pretending I guess because mom paid him. He's not dead, but he's in jail for something he did. He took money from mom I think. At least that's what my roommate read to me. She gets news online.

Anyway, they said you know my reel dad because he is the one who killed your daughter. I didn't know she was dead when you told me about her. I'm _really_ sorry.

Mom lost cusstoady because she didn't teach us at home or let us leave the farm ever not even to see the dentist. Do you believe I have nine cavitys! One tooth was so bad they had to put a cap because there were too cavitys on one tooth. Maybe it was from all the candy I ate at your place. Ha Ha.

Anyways, it hurt but my teeths look good with the cavitys filled & all clean. They scrape them with a medel file!

It is lights out soon. So I'll write tomorrow.

I'm at school waiting for the bus. I can't tell you the school name but it's a huge school with two floors! 😄

My roommate showed me storys about my mom. They said she blew up the internet. Everyone is really, really mad at her. The sponsors want their money back.

She can't even see us anymore and I think that my brother & sisters will get adopted pretty soon.

I like school. It's fun to have so many subjects. I like science & math, but I'm pretty far behind. My worts subject is english.

Anyways you can write me.

The detective said your no friend or hero. He said you are a stalker, kidnapper and attemped murdur. I had to look up vigilante. I have a dictionary on my phone. But I don't think bad about you. Because I remember what you said and mostly it was right and you were nice to me. I miss movy nite!

You weren't really trying to kill us. Right?

Your Friend, Aubree 🩶

P.S. everyone quit & the farm is for sale to pay Mom's bills. She said on a talk show she gets nothing but hate mail & death threats. She lost the farm, her followers & she lost us kids to. My caseworker says her trial starts soon. Do you think they will put her in the same jail as you?

Bailey read that final part again as the laughter bubbled up from deep inside.

She hadn't taken Eliza's kids, but the State of New York had, along with everything else she loved.

A LETTER FROM JENNA

Dear Reader,

I'm so grateful you included *The Fake Mother* on your reading list. If you enjoyed Bailey's story and want to receive updates with all my latest releases, just sign up at the following link. Your email address won't be shared, and you can easily unsubscribe.

www.bookouture.com/jenna-kernan

I hope you enjoyed *The Fake Mother* and if you did, please consider leaving a review; your opinion helps other readers discover a book you appreciated.

The idea for *The Fake Mother* came from an article about "sharenting" (sharing + parenting)—a word I'd never seen before! Predictably, serious consequences can arise from posting a minor's information online. All parents today must deal with this complicated, controversial issue. And the topic inspired many story directions in my mind. What if bad actors exploit what a parent shares? What are the consequences of online fame for children? Do parents need their child's informed consent before posting? Will a post attract predators or lead to cyber-bullying? This story only scratches the surface of a heated topic, but I hope the subject gives readers much food for thought.

I love hearing from my readers – you can get in touch on my

Facebook page, through Bluesky, Goodreads or my website, if you are of an age to understand informed consent. 😊

Be well and happy reading!

Jenna Kernan

www.jennakernan.com

facebook.com/authorjennakernan

instagram.com/jenna_kernan

bookbub.com/authors/jenna-kernan

bsky.app/profile/jennakernan.bsky.social

ACKNOWLEDGMENTS

I couldn't have gotten this novel to you without the help of some vital people. Here are some of the individuals I count on.

After Hurricane Milton landed a direct hit on Sarasota in October 2024, my husband, Jim, often sent me off to a coffee shop while he managed some very noisy home repairs. His help allowed me to stay on track and make my deadlines which would have been impossible without him. He's always there to support me through story challenges, believing in my ability to write my way out of problems and celebrating each publication with me.

Thank you to my siblings for always buying my newest release and for bragging about me on occasion!

Special thanks to my agent, Ann Leslie Tuttle, of Dystel, Goderich & Bourret, for her advice and friendship on my publishing journey.

I am grateful for the invaluable feedback provided by my editors, especially Nina Winters. With this story, she cleverly suggested rearranging several key scenes and incorporating additional flashbacks to highlight crucial reveals and build tension. These changes have greatly improved the book. I'm so fortunate to have such a talented editor working with me.

Thank you, Bookouture team, for your dedication to books, authors, and readers, as shown by another amazing cover, excellent promotions, superb packaging, and strong marketing.

I appreciate all the early reviewers of *The Fake Mother* for their honest opinions and valuable feedback. These first readers are vital for improving books and helping new readers find this story.

My sincere thanks go to Sisters in Crime, Gulf Coast Sisters in Crime, Mystery Writers of America, Mystery Writers of Florida, International Thriller Writers, Authors Guild, and Novelist, Inc. for their invaluable guidance and support of writers.

Lastly, thank you to my readers. This story only comes alive in your hands.

Thank you!

PUBLISHING TEAM

Turning a manuscript into a book requires the efforts of many people. The publishing team at Bookouture would like to acknowledge everyone who contributed to this publication.

Audio
Alba Proko
Melissa Tran
Sinead O'Connor

Commercial
Lauren Morrissette
Hannah Richmond
Imogen Allport

Data and analysis
Mark Alder
Mohamed Bussuri

Editorial
Nina Winters
Imogen Allport

Proofreader
Jennifer Davies

Marketing
Alex Crow
Melanie Price
Occy Carr
Cíara Rosney
Martyna Młynarska

Operations and distribution
Marina Valles
Stephanie Straub
Joe Morris

Production
Hannah Snetsinger
Mandy Kullar
Jen Shannon
Ria Clare

Publicity
Kim Nash
Noelle Holten
Jess Readett
Sarah Hardy

Rights and contracts
Peta Nightingale
Richard King
Saidah Graham

www.ingramcontent.com/pod-product-compliance
Lightning Source LLC
LaVergne TN
LVHW040142010525
810128LV00005B/46

* 9 7 8 1 8 3 6 1 8 2 4 7 4 *